WATER
GRAVE

An Abbey Rhodes Mystery
Volume 1

WATER GRAVE

MITCHELL S. KARNES

WordCrafts Press

Scripture quotations taken from The Holy Bible, New International Version® NIV® Copyright © 1973, 1978, 1984, 2011 by Biblica, Inc. Used with permission. All rights reserved worldwide.

Water Grave
Copyright © 2025
Mitchell S. Karnes

Hardback ISBN: 978-1-962218-68-9
Paperback ISBN: 978-1-962218-69-6

Cover concept and design by Mike Parker.

Published by WordCrafts Press
Cody, Wyoming 82414
www.wordcrafts.net

To the men and women of the
Metro Nashville Police Department.
With a special Thank You to
Matthew, Candice, and Miranda
for your experience and insight.

Chapter One

Monday, October 23, 9:15 am—Living Water Church

Mark Ripley rushed into the baptistery changing room, slammed the door, and locked the handle. He scanned the room for his phone.

A loud thud reverberated through the tiny room as the entire doorframe shook. Mark searched under the towels. Another thud accompanied by the sound of cracking wood. He found the phone and glanced down at his lock screen, a picture of his wife and two children. He held the phone to his face to unlock it. Before he could dial 911, the frame splintered, and the door swung open. Realizing there was nowhere to run, Mark turned and tried to talk through the situation.

The wooden club struck the right side of his head with such violence that Mark spun sideways and toppled into the open clothes rack, dragging several white baptismal robes down with him. His phone flew from his limp hand and bounced off the wall, sliding into the opposite corner of the eight-by-eight changing room. It rested beneath the small bench.

His attacker nudged him with his foot. A few moments passed, and he nudged him again. Mark moaned. He touched his right cheek and temple, the source of his pain, and felt the warmth of his own blood. The man watched as Mark pushed up on all fours. The pastor's only thoughts were his phone and 911. Before he could move, the man swung the club again, landing a solid blow to Mark's back. The young pastor collapsed like a pile of soaking wet towels.

1

Chapter Two

Tuesday, October 24, 9:41 am—Living Water Church

Sergeant McNally's assignment of Detective Tidwell as my mentor frustrated me to no end. A detective who, like water, took the path of least resistance.

He snapped his fingers in front of my face. "Hey Rhodes, which way?"

"Sorry, Detective. It's just past Riverside at the bottom of the hill."

"What did I say about formalities? Save that for the brass. Just call me Tidwell or Sam."

"Yes, Detective." It came out before I could catch it.

"It's bad enough you look like a little girl; don't act like one."

I hate when they do that! Ironic. When I was twelve, everyone thought I was older and treated me as such. Now at twenty-four, I looked like an overdeveloped twelve-year-old.

Detective Tidwell loosened his tie and unbuttoned the top button of his shirt. He stroked the salt and pepper beard which gave him a distinguished look and glanced down the road. He had a deep sorrow that added ten years to his appearance. I suppose we were a chronological paradox. "Church murder…that's bad luck."

"What do you mean?" Maybe he had a bad experience too.

"Nothing good ever comes from it," he said.

I caught sight of the steeple and rubbed a sudden chill from my arms. I hated churches and church people.

It was a traditional small church building in the shape of an

2

L with a one-story sanctuary connected to the two-story educational wing at the base of the L, just like so many small churches I'd seen as a kid.

When we pulled into the driveway, Detective Tidwell said, "Remember, just follow my lead. You got something to say, say it; otherwise, just observe." As soon as he got out of the car, he straightened his tie and buttoned the first button of his suit coat. "If it's too much, Rhodes, get some air." He walked through the front doors and let them shut behind him.

I wanted to say, "This wasn't my first homicide, and I'm pretty sure it won't be my last," but nothing came out. I stood there staring at the closed wooden double doors.

As I entered the tiny four-foot-deep foyer of the small church, my partner made the introductions, saying, "Detectives Tidwell and Rhodes." I stared through the open double doors of the tiny foyer, fixated on the wooden cross on the far wall at the opposite end of the sanctuary. A Metro officer greeted us and printed our names and titles in the crime scene logbook.

He directed us to Officer Lee, the lead officer, who extended his hand to Detective Tidwell. Tidwell shook his hand then ducked under the crime scene tape dividing the foyer from the sanctuary. He glanced around the fifty-by-one-hundred-foot box of a room and walked down the center aisle. Officer Lee brought him up to speed.

I listened from the foyer as he recited the particulars of the crime scene from his memory and notes. He pointed to the baptistery which was situated behind a wall on the sanctuary stage and could be seen through an arched open space that began about chest high and ended two feet from the twenty-foot-high ceiling. Detective Tidwell walked across the hardwood-floored stage and stopped halfway between the pulpit and the baptistery window. He turned and listened to the rest of Officer Lee's report.

"Officers Hernandez and Smith are mapping out the crime scene and taking photos. Officer Grant has the church leaders spread out in the fellowship hall. CSI is on the way." He pointed to the baptistery. "Our vic's at the bottom."

I stood frozen at the entrance of the sanctuary. My eyes locked on the wooden cross hung at the back wall of the baptistery, powerless to turn away. I stood there like an idiot, holding the crime tape in my hands. The officer behind me asked, "Hey, Rhodes, How's the new gig?"

"Still learning where I fit in," I muttered. "For now, I'm just the shadow." I pointed to Detective Tidwell. "He's the lead."

The moment I said it, Detective Tidwell turned and said, "Hey, Rhodes, can we move on, or would you rather stay there and socialize?"

I rolled my eyes as I ducked under the tape. As I forced myself down the center aisle, I counted thirteen rows of pews. The décor was a mix of old and new. New ceiling, but old fixtures. Stained glass windows on the side walls, each depicting a scene from Jesus's life, with a can light pointed at each one. A modest stage with drums, keyboard, guitars, and a baby grand in the opposite corner. Classic baptistery in the center behind the pulpit…a clear, acrylic pulpit. Nice.

Detective Tidwell stepped up to the fourteen-inch-tall baptistery glass set in the bottom of the window. He looked down into the water. "That's something you don't see every day."

At five-six, I had to stand on my tiptoes to see over the glass window that allowed a view from the pews. I could hear the pump churning and noticed a slight movement in the water's surface. A man's body lay at the bottom, traces of a dark fluid seeping from the vic's mouth and nose. The body was already releasing liquids as it decomposed. "Do we know who he is?" I asked.

"The pastor, Mark Ripley. Thirty-three-year-old white male, married, father of two."

Detective Tidwell stared at the body. "Family been notified?"

"Not yet." Officer Lee flipped through his notes. "According to Faith Jones, the church secretary, the pastor's wife and kids are on their way back from St. Louis."

"Any witnesses?" Detective Tidwell asked.

"No, but the church leaders all have theories as to his death. He was discovered when they arrived for their Tuesday morning leadership meeting."

"How many leaders?" Detective Tidwell asked.

Officer Lee looked through his notes. "Twelve."

"That explains all the vehicles," I said. "Who called it in?"

"Owen Jenkins, the Men's Ministry leader." Lee led us out of the sanctuary to a small hallway at the side of the stage that led to the main hall of the educational building. From there we turned left to the doors of the changing rooms, one for men, and one for women. The door to the women's side was cracked, and the frame shattered.

I scanned the room before entering. Something didn't fit. "Why are the stairs and floor wet? The body's been there at least a day."

"According to Owen Jenkins, he saw the body and ran back to the church office to call 911. While he was doing that, the secretary and youth minister entered the church through the sanctuary doors. Noticing the baptistery light on, the secretary went up on the stage to turn it off. That's when she saw the body and screamed. The youth minister took it upon himself to check the body, believing the pastor was still alive. Owen Jenkins heard the commotion, came back to the sanctuary. As soon as he noticed the youth minister in the water, he yelled for him to get out." Officer Lee closed his notebook. "We taped it off the moment we arrived."

"What an idiot!" Detective Tidwell snapped.

The officer smiled faintly and read another note. "The youth minister's name is Jonathan Williams."

Detective Tidwell pinched the bridge of his nose. "You're telling me a well-intentioned staff member compromised our crime scene?" Tidwell didn't like complications. They took more time.

I recorded detailed notes in my book. "I'm sure prints won't help anyway. A church this size probably doesn't clean back here often." Turning to Officer Lee, I asked, "Did someone take pictures anyway?" Officer Lee nodded. "What about a sketched diagram with measurements?" He nodded again. Standard procedure. These were officers of East Precinct. They were trained well.

"Officers Hernandez and Smith will get those down to Homicide as soon as they're finished."

"Smell that? Bleach." I looked at the remains of the door and frame where someone had broken through. "Looks like someone tried to clean up." After donning sanitary booties and Nitrile gloves, we entered the crime scene, doing our best to preserve the integrity of the remaining evidence. I knelt by the stairs and pointed to a seam where the vinyl flooring met the rubber treads of the steps leading up to the baptistery. "There's blood here."

Detective Tidwell knelt beside me. "Here too. Look in the grooves of the stairs."

"Sloppy job. Must have been in a hurry."

Detective Tidwell turned to Officer Lee. "Could you see if there's a janitor's closet somewhere? If so, look for a looped-end string mop. If so, bag it. We'll have the lab check it for blood and prints on the handle."

"More here," I announced, holding out a white robe with spots of blood on the sleeve. "Do we have any Luminal so we can check the whole room?"

Detective Tidwell said, "CSI will." He called out for Officer Smith to take photos of the blood stains.

Detective Tidwell's phone rang. He answered it and listened. He lowered the phone from his ear and said, "CSI is pulling in now. If you don't mind, have them spray the room and light it up."

"Will do, Detective. Anything else?"

"If you have anyone to spare, I'd like to have them canvass the immediate neighborhood to see if anyone saw cars coming or going between their last church service and this morning."

Detective Tidwell sighed and asked, "Now, where are those witnesses?"

Chapter Three

Officer Lee directed us deeper into the belly of the whale. The fellowship hall was nothing more than a sixteen by ninety rectangular room filled with plastic-topped tables and black padded chairs. It ran parallel to the long hallway. The leaders were scattered throughout the room, monitored by an officer who had instructed them not to speak to one another until we arrived.

The moment we stepped into the room, a darkly-tanned, older man stood and asked, "How long is this going to take? I'm supposed to be on the construction site to meet with my client in forty-five minutes." He was large and obviously worked hard for a living. Even from across the room, I could tell his hands were dry and rough, and two fingers were missing their tips.

I recorded his comment in my notebook. I also noted the hand. It would make unique prints. No detail too small. I turned to Detective Tidwell. His jaw muscles pulsed again, revealing his displeasure. "You may have to postpone that meeting, Mr..."

"Jenkins. Owen Jenkins." The man who called 911.

Officer Grant handed a small clipboard to Detective Tidwell containing their names, church leadership titles, other day jobs (if any), and personal contact information. Tidwell slid his finger down the list of names until he found what he wanted. "Well, Mr. Jenkins. I understand you discovered the body?"

"Yes."

"You called 911 and chastised Mr. Williams for ruining our crime scene?"

"Yes." He puffed up his chest with each fact pointing to a job well done. I could tell he expected a compliment. He didn't get one. "Well, Mr. Jenkins, you might want to call your client and tell him your pastor has been killed, and you're going to be a little late. I'm sure he'll understand." Tidwell said it with such heavy disdain that Owen Jenkins sat down and shut his mouth. He looked around the room to the other leaders. Jenkins rubbed the sundried skin on the back of his neck.

Detective Tidwell focused on Owen. "We'll do our best to expedite our initial interviews and make this as painless as we can, but make no mistake, ladies and gentlemen, our priority here is to discover what happened to your pastor and find the person or persons responsible."

He looked across the room at a young man about my age with a chiseled body and a biking shirt that could have been painted on it was so thin and tight. "Don't I know you from somewhere?" Tidwell asked. "You look familiar."

"I seriously doubt it," the man said with a shrug. "I must have one of those faces."

"Oh, that's Jonathan Williams. He's our youth pastor," a large woman said with a big smile. I could tell she was trying to put on a good front. I made note of everyone's comments and the manner in which he or she made them. If she tried to hide her grief now, what else would she be willing to hide?

"And you are?"

"Faith Jones. I'm the church secretary. Need anything…anything at all, I'm your girl." Youth minister and secretary, the next two to arrive on the scene.

Detective Tidwell ignored the woman and kept his focus on the youth minister. He sat slightly taller than his peers, someone you might see in a Marvel movie. "I suppose you're right. Nothing is coming to mind." He turned to the woman and said, "Mrs. Jones."

"Miss Jones. I'm not married."

"Okay. Miss Jones. I understand you were the second person

to discover the body." She nodded. He glanced around the room and said, "We'll meet with each of you individually and ask a few questions."

Detective Tidwell turned to me. "You good taking a room and interviewing half of the group?" I nodded. Of course, I was. He acted as if I'd never worked a crime scene before. Tidwell tore the list in half and gave one part to me, keeping the other for himself. "We'll compare notes before we head back to Central and decide who needs to be questioned further." I nodded again. I made quick mental notes of their reactions to his last declaration and transcribed them into my book. He motioned for me to use the room marked, "Pastor's Study." *Great.* Deeper into the throat of the dragon I went.

He turned to Officer Grant and asked, "Is there another room I could use?"

"On this floor, there are two offices, a library, and a parlor. The rest of the rooms are connected to the fellowship hall."

"What's the other office?" he asked.

He pointed across the hall. "The secretary's."

"That'll be perfect."

Detective Tidwell took the main office, immediately across from the fellowship hall door. Officer Grant brought in the first person, Owen Jenkins. As the man entered the church office, the detective noticed a television screen mounted on the wall with a quad split screen. One of the views showed the main hallway which connected to the changing room. "Can we get the recordings for the past two days?" he asked.

"Recordings?"

"From the cameras," Detective Tidwell said as he pointed to the screen.

"That would be nice. Unfortunately, they're just live feeds. We don't record anything."

"That's unfortunate." He glanced at his notes. "You work construction?"

"Yes, sir. I'm a contractor."

"You must do a lot with your hands."

"God blessed me with big, strong hands. Work's good for the soul. This younger generation just doesn't get it. They've gotten so used to handouts; they think they're entitled. Work's a gift from God."

"I hear you," the detective said. "I admire hard workers." Owen nodded. Detective Tidwell asked a few other personal questions before finally directing them to the crime at hand. "So, I understand you discovered the body."

"Yes, sir. The baptistery light was on, and I saw the body just before I touched the switch to turn it off."

"I thought the light was still on when Faith and Jonathan came in."

"I guess in my hurry to call 911 I forgot to turn it off."

"Did you enter through the front doors of the church also?"

"No, sir. I came through the parking lot side of the educational building. I took the mail to the office and got a text. After I answered it, I set my phone down and looked through the mail to see if any of it was mine."

"How did you end up by the baptistery?"

"I always go through the pews to gather trash and straighten things up. Somebody's got to."

"Were you the first to arrive?" Detective Tidwell asked, staring down at his notes.

"No…well, yes." He had a look of confusion.

"Which is it?"

"Yes. It's just that…" He scratched his head and had a puzzled look. "The door was unlocked when I got here." Detective Tidwell looked up. "I didn't think anything of it at the time, because Mark's car was here."

"But no other cars?" Owen Jenkins shook his head. His brows

furrowed and his head tilted to the side. "Let me get this straight, Mr. Owens. You were the first to arrive, but the door was unlocked?"

"Mark's always early. I just came in, set the mail in Faith's office, and went straight to the sanctuary to pick up trash." His glance looked distant, as if he was trying to figure something out. "He left Sunday after the service, and the church is closed on Mondays, Mark's policy."

"Well, either your pastor came back after the service, or he broke his own policy and worked on Monday," Tidwell said. "There's no way he unlocked it today."

"Duke always locks up on Sundays."

"Duke?"

"Duke Stearns. He's the chairman of deacons." He paused for a moment. "Knowing Duke, I'm sure it was."

"It doesn't matter then. Obviously, the pastor unlocked it whenever he came back. Let's move on." Owen fiddled with his fingernail, which wasn't much of a nail at all. They'd been worn to a nub. He was missing the ends of two fingers, just past the last joint. "Work accident?" Tidwell asked, pointing to the fingers.

"Yes, sir. Never rush when you're cutting."

"You don't have Sunday night services?" Owen started to answer but kept quiet. He sat back in his chair and looked at Tidwell. "Something wrong?"

"That's a loaded question," Owen muttered. "Our worship, if you can call it that, is becoming more like a rock concert than a sacred time. Next thing you know, they'll have funny lights and fog machines." Owen's voice intensified as he described how the new pastor had replaced the traditional service and music with more modern practices and songs they didn't even know. "We used to have Sunday night worship too, just like clockwork."

"What happened?"

"Mark Ripley happened." Owen immediately looked up. His face showed regret for having voiced that aloud. "I mean no disrespect, but…" He stopped and seemed to plan his next few words

11

carefully. "He changed a lot of things, sometimes just for change's sake. I mean…we all know the saying, 'If it ain't broke, don't fix it.'" The detective nodded but remained silent. He wasn't going to stop the man if he wanted to dig his own grave. "Well, he got rid of our Sunday night service and replaced it with a bunch of little home groups. For goodness sake, why have a church if you aren't going to use it? Know what I mean?"

He looked to Detective Tidwell, who finally nodded. "Go on."

"Well, instead of coming to church, they break up into their own little cliques." He shook his head. "Who knows if they're even talking about the Bible. We can't be everywhere at once." He cleared his throat before adding, "God made us a body. You don't tear a body in little pieces and scatter it all over the city, do you?" Owen Jenkins rambled on about his frustrations with the church's new "vision."

"So, you didn't like Pastor Mark's changes?"

"No. Not much. Too much talk about grace and love, and too little about discipline and obedience."

"The changes obviously frustrated you."

"Yes, sir."

"Enough to kill him?"

Owen perked up. "No, sir. Murder is a sin. That's number six."

"Number six? I don't follow."

"The sixth commandment, 'Thou shalt not kill.'"

"So…" Tidwell paused.

"I make no bones about it. I didn't like his ideas. Things were just fine before he came. I spoke my mind to his face, man to man. I'd never kill a guy…especially a pastor."

Owen Jenkins was definitely a prime suspect. Too convenient that he arrived first.

When Duke Stearns entered the room, even the untrained eye could detect that he had a chip on his shoulder, much like Owen Jenkins. Duke was in his early eighties; his gray hair was cut moderately short and combed straight back. He had it all fixed

in place with some sort of hair cream. His face was taut and his posture rigid. Detective Tidwell noticed the neatly polished black cowboy boots. Duke Stearns looked through the window in the door separating the two offices and said, "What is this, bring your daughter to work day? What is she…fourteen?"

"I assure you Detective Rhodes is more than qualified to handle this case." He wasn't going to have anyone bash his partner. "And just so you know, she's twenty-four with six years of experience."

"She looks soft," Duke said.

"Take a seat."

"I prefer to stand," Duke said, folding his arms across his chest.

"Suit yourself. State your name please."

"Morris Stearns, but everyone calls me Duke."

"Mr. Stearns, do you still work?"

"Sometimes," he said. "I'll drive if the job suits me." Even when he talked, his lips barely moved. Everything about the man showed immense internal tension.

"So, you're a truck driver, cab driver, Uber driver?"

"Trucker, sixty-two years and counting," he said. It was the first time a hint of a smile broke the statuesque features of his face. He sat in the chair opposite the detective.

"Impressive. I see here that you're the chairman of the deacons?" the detective asked, now looking at his notes.

"Yes, sir."

"What exactly does a deacon do in a church that has Elders?"

Duke bristled. He was wound tight. "I've been a deacon in this church for forty-three years, Mr. Tidwell."

"Detective Tidwell, if you please."

"Well, I don't please. I know what you're trying to do, Mister, and I ain't stupid. No two-bit cop is gonna make me say something I didn't intend to say. I don't want nobody puttin' false words in my mouth."

"I have no intentions of…"

"And furthermore, Mr. Tidwell, I do as I've always done as a deacon. I serve God and this church."

"I didn't mean anything by my question, Mr. Stearns. I sincerely want to know. You see, I grew up in a church where the deacons were in charge of everything, including the pastor. If Living Water Church…" Duke cringed. Detective Tidwell picked up on the flinch immediately. "Do you have a problem with the church's name?"

"You can call a skunk a horse, but it still stinks."

"You think the church stinks?" Tidwell asked.

"There you go twisting my words."

"I was just following your analogy."

"I know what you're doing, Mister." He folded his arms over his chest again, which he puffed out like a banty rooster. "The church is, was, and will always be East Nashville Baptist Church to me. That's the name in our original Constitution and Bylaws, and it should stay that way."

"The sign says, Living Water Church."

"Of course, it does. Brother Mark waited until he had enough new members to swing a vote, and then he changed it. He had a plan from the get-go. He dropped *Baptist* altogether. Says it drove off more folks than it attracted."

"I can see that really upsets you."

"Ya think?" Duke pointed his finger at Tidwell. "You better watch what you say next, Mister."

The open threat shocked him. "I didn't realize deacons were in the business of threatening others with violence, Mr. Stearns."

"I ain't perfect. Nobody is. But I love God and this church. I'll do whatever it takes to protect it."

"Including murder?" Tidwell asked.

"I knew you'd try to throw that one on me. Well, I wouldn't do such a thing."

They bantered back and forth for a while. Detective Tidwell ran his fingers through his curly hair and turned the conversation back to the details of the crime. Duke confirmed Owen's earlier statement. The church was locked Sunday at noon. He made a

point to say the real work of the church was still done by the original members. "I bet those new people don't even tithe. All he preached about was love, grace, and forgiveness."

"Isn't that what Jesus preached?" Detective Tidwell asked.

"Sure, but the last thing He said was, 'Teach them to obey all My commands.' He taught obedience…discipleship. Brother Mark didn't preach those things. A Christian needs both sides."

It was obvious Duke was loyal to a fault. He loved the church but resented change. Tidwell let Duke ramble on while he wrote a note in his book, "Why would Pastor Mark be here on his day off?" He added Duke to his list of suspects. *So far two for two. These guys resented their pastor. Both had motives to kill him. Both have strong hands.*

As he interviewed one of the elders, Tidwell noted another interesting fact. The leaders were split two to four. Owen and Duke were members prior to the new pastor's arrival, and the other four came as a result of Mark Ripley and his "vision." The latter couldn't say enough good things about him. Tidwell made a note to ask Detective Rhodes if she spotted this trend in her interviews.

✝✝✝

I completed my fourth interview and dismissed the man, another new elder of the church. I called for the officer to bring in the next person, my fifth interview. Jonathan Williams, the youth minister. "So, Mr. Williams…"

"Call me Jonathan. Mr. Williams is my dad."

"So, Jonathan, I understand you compromised our crime scene this morning." I intended to gauge his reaction to my blunt statement.

He lowered his glance to the floor like a little kid who'd just gotten caught stealing. "I wasn't thinking. I saw a body under the water and next thing I know, I'm trying to pull him out."

I glanced across the desk. Why were Jonathan's clothes dry? They'd still be soaking wet if he went in the baptistery this morning.

15

"How is it that your clothes and shoes are dry? Have you changed since this morning?"

"Yes. Everything was wet. I had a spare change of clothes upstairs."

"You just happen to have a change of clothes here with you?"

"Always. When you work with youth, you never know what's going to happen. I keep spares of everything here."

"That's convenient." I put my pen to my lips and studied him for any physical signs of deceit. His story threw up all kinds of red flags. Why would he barge haphazardly into a crime scene and then just happen to have a change of clothes on the premises? I could tell at first glance that the pastor was beyond saving. If he's the murderer, could this have been premeditated? I'd had my fill of these "angelic" church people. They act all innocent and honest, but I know better. They're just people like the rest of us.

"Learned it the hard way," he said. He leaned back and put his hands behind his head, flexing his biceps.

I looked back at my notes. "How did you see the body?" I asked.

"Faith, our church secretary, screamed, and I went to see what was wrong." He leaned forward and spoke with nervous angst, wringing his hands. "That's what anyone else would do, right?"

I intentionally left his pleading gesture unanswered. Instead, I pressed him, asking, "How did Faith discover the body?"

"The baptistery light was still on, and you know, Faith's always worried that we're not going to have enough money to pay all the bills, so she reached over the window to turn them off. The switch is on the inside. Anyway, that's when she screamed." His rambling betrayed his anxiety.

"Were you in the room with her?"

"Yes, ma'am." *Ma'am? I'm his age.* He sat there and presented himself as a true southern gentleman, complete with a million-dollar smile.

Unfortunately for him, his attempts were the antithesis of what worked on me. Sincerity and humility will go a long way to

16

sway me to sympathy. Arrogance and narcissism fall flat. "Detective will do fine. Please, continue."

"Well, my car's still in the shop, and Faith didn't want me to ride my bike since I've been sick, so she picked me up on the way here. Normally, I come in through the fellowship hall door so I can head on up to the youth room, but Faith always comes in that way, you know, because her sister, God rest her soul, needed wheelchair access. She died of a stroke." He paused and swallowed. "I guess old habits die hard. I mean they're hard to break."

He didn't seem to know what to do with my distant professionalism and emotional apathy. "Are you always this chatty?" I asked with a condescending smile.

"You make me nervous." He smiled and tugged on the lobe of his right ear.

I leaned back in the pastor's chair. "Just relax. These are standard questions, Jonathan."

"Yes, ma'am…I'm sorry. Yes, detective." He continued to stare at me…study me.

I still don't like it when men look me over like that. I sat up sharply. "If you have something to say, spit it out."

"You're really pretty and have, like, Disney Princess eyes."

Disney Princess eyes? Are you serious? "You do realize we're investigating the murder of your pastor, don't you?" I didn't know how to take him. He was certainly handsome and had that boyish, country charm, maybe a little too boyish. I could tell he didn't like subjecting himself to a woman. I could use that to my advantage. I pressed forward.

He rambled on about the history and recent changes of the church, his relationship with the deceased pastor, and about being sick the past three days. I set my pen on the desk. There was no point in trying to write notes. A summary of this conversation would suffice. I made a note to check on his alibi.

Jonathan reached into his back pocket, grabbed his phone, and asked, "May I?"

"No phones. Not until we're through here."

"But it's important. I think I know who killed him."

I leaned forward. "You think you know who killed him?" He nodded. "Why didn't you lead with that?"

"It just hit me. If you'll let me turn my phone on, I can show you." Jonathan powered up his phone. "It was posted as a live feed to our church's website, but we had to pull it. You'll see why." He uploaded the video and fast-forwarded to the place of interest. "Watch this." He turned the phone so I could watch. The band finished playing and a young man in a white robe descended into the baptistery. "That's Pastor Mark."

The pastor spoke with grace and power. He spoke of the many blessings God poured upon their church over the past two months. He spoke of God's vision coming to life at Living Water Church. I quickly noticed a lack of self-praise. He turned it all to God. A sharp contrast to my father. I rubbed goosebumps from my arm. Even with my hatred toward the church, Mark Ripley made it sound appealing and genuine.

I continued to watch as Pastor Mark gave credit to God for the seven people who'd chosen to follow Jesus Christ as their personal savior in the past three weeks. Then he turned and extended his hand to a young boy in his teens. Pastor Mark introduced him to the church and asked a series of questions, all to which the young boy answered quietly, "Yes." Then he baptized the boy.

"What does this have to do with his death?" I asked. Was this his attempt to redirect my attention elsewhere? To show me the pastor's character?

"Keep watching."

The pastor turned in the other direction and extended his hand. A woman and her daughter stepped into the water. He introduced them, gave a brief synopsis of their testimonies, and baptized them. Then another woman, a petite Latina, entered the water and took his hand. The moment the pastor began questioning her, a shout echoed through the sanctuary. "Como te atreves!"

A huge man came rushing down the aisle, pointing his finger at the baptistery, shouting in Spanish. Jonathan continued, "Owen said he's threatening Pastor Mark, saying that he undermined his authority and placed a curse upon his family."

"Who said that?"

"Owen Jenkins. He's our Men's Ministry leader."

"Is he the man that was so eager to get to his meeting this morning?" I asked, trying to connect a face with the name. I only had half of the list. The curse of being a visual learner.

"Yes. That's Owen." Jonathan resumed the video.

So, Owen Jenkins speaks Spanish. I listened attentively as Pastor Mark replied calmly to the man's threats. I was shocked by the pastor's reply. "Your pastor spoke Spanish too?" I was sensing a pattern here.

"Yeah. That's one reason we've had so many Latinos joining our congregation. He was about to start a whole new service just for them."

"Really?" I made note of that in my book. "How did the church react?" I knew how territorial church members could be about their buildings and ministries.

"Mixed, I guess. But conflict never stopped Pastor Mark from doing what he thought was right, no matter the consequences."

"What did you think of the idea of a Spanish service?" I asked, trying to keep Jonathan focused on the case.

"It was a bold move, but a good one. It's not something the previous pastor would have risked." Jonathan stopped talking when the man in the video slapped his hands on the glass of the baptistery and pointed for the woman to go back up to the stairs from which she had descended earlier in the video.

I noted the location of the handprint on the baptistery glass. We better go back and lift those prints.

"Here it comes. This is where he told Pastor Mark if he interfered in his family matters again, he'd kill him."

"What's his name?" I asked.

"Alvaro Garcia. He and his wife, Sophia, live with his brother's family somewhere off Shelby Avenue. I'm sure Faith has their address."

"That video is on the church's website?" I asked, making another note in my book.

"It was. I marked it as private so no one else can see it."

"How'd you do that?" I asked. I hate technology. It could be wonderful at times, but it's just taken over the world, and if you're like me and barely know how to use it, you're out of luck.

"It's simple really. I oversee the church's social media platforms. I just changed the video from public to private."

"How do I access that video?"

"Give me your phone number, and I'll send it to you."

I gave him my card and asked if he remembered anything else, give me a call. I concluded the interview with Jonathan and said we may call him later for more details. He was still a suspect. Too friendly and too cooperative.

The final leader to interview was Maeve Kennedy, the Women's Ministry coordinator. She was a large woman whose oversized clothes only served to accentuate her weight. I noticed rather quickly she had difficulty sitting between the arms of the chairs opposite the pastor's desk. She looked very uncomfortable but boasted a beautiful smile.

"Mrs. Kennedy."

"Ms. Kennedy. I'm not married." She pulled at the end of her shirt and folded her arms over her stomach.

I tried not to stare, but my eyes betrayed me. "I apologize. The officer's notes say, 'Mrs. Maeve Kennedy.'"

"That's incorrect. Just call me Maeve. Everyone else does."

"Okay, Maeve. Tell me about yourself, your role here at the church, and your relationship with the pastor."

Maeve gave a limited background of herself. I quickly got the sense she was self-conscious. Maeve preferred giving details of her ministry with the women of Living Water Church. She spoke of the many community projects they had; such as a single mother's program, a mother's night out quarterly event, and the new group for the Latino women in the congregation. Her eyes sparkled at the mention of women's ministry.

She was relatively new at the church, coming on just eighteen months ago as a part of the pastor's vision to reach the women of the immediate community. She spoke well of Pastor Mark and seemed to be on board with his ministry and vision for the church.

Finally, I mentioned the video of the past Sunday's service. Although Maeve didn't say anything about the incident or the supposed threats given by Alvaro Garcia, she did mention her new friendship with his wife, Sophia, who had struggled with the decision to get baptized. "Alvaro was not keen on her choice." Maeve also said, "I can't imagine anyone wishing harm on the pastor. Everyone loved him."

I thanked Maeve for her time and let her go. As I was walking out of the pastor's office, a small, framed poster caught my eye. It displayed a verse that read, *'For I know the plans I have for you,' declares the LORD, 'plans to prosper you and not to harm you, plans to give you hope and a future' ~Jeremiah 29:11.*

Yeah, right. Tell that to your dead pastor.

Chapter Four

The CSI team left the medical examiner's cart outside the second changing room. Mark Ripley's body lay inside a long black bag. A young woman stood at its side. Although she had tucked her hair beneath the protective cap, a purple lock escaped beside her left ear. I extended my hand. "Detective Rhodes." She shook my hand and nodded. I looked at her badge. "Any initial findings, April?"

She unzipped the bag, exposing Mark's head. She pointed as she talked. Her voice was soft and airy. "He has a blunt force trauma to the right side of his head. There's also bruising around the neck. We'll know more when we get him back to the lab."

"Can you tell if he was facing his attacker or looking away?" I asked.

"By the angle of the damage on his cheek and temple, I'd say he was staring at his killer."

Detective Tidwell signed the forms releasing the body and asked, "When will we know the time and cause of death?"

The M.E.'s assistant cleared her throat and said, "Everyone's backlogged right now. We'll contact you the moment we have something." She immediately pushed the cart past us and rolled it down the church's wheelchair ramp. She wasted no time loading Pastor Mark's body and driving away.

Well, that didn't inspire confidence. A member of the CSI team called us into the room. We donned more sanitary booties and Nitrile gloves and reentered the room. Someone turned off the overhead light, and we watched in silence as a member of the CSI

22

switched on the UV light, revealing the results of the Luminol spray. We studied the scene, assessing the blood splatter, trying to determine exactly what happened.

"Okay, Rhodes. Impress me," Detective Tidwell said as he took a step back.

No pressure. I scanned the room. Blood splatter on the back wall. White robes stained with blood. A small circle of blood in the back left corner, with traces of blood reaching out in lines between the grooves of the gray vinyl flooring. Obvious trail leading up the narrow stairway to the water above. "He must have been hit here first," I said, indicating the central point from which the splatter traveled in all directions.

"Or cut. That's a decent amount of blood." He stopped himself. "Sorry. Go on."

"In my humble opinion," I resumed, trying not to correct him in front of the CSI team, "this has the classic splatter pattern of a headshot with some kind of heavy blunt instrument."

He nodded. "Keep going."

I analyzed the room, everything was covered with blood, including the robes. The door was cracked, and the frame splintered. "He hid in here." I checked the handle. "The handle is still locked. Whoever killed him kicked in the door." I took a couple of steps back, to the edge of the changing room, for a better perspective. "I'd say, in that moment of terror, the pastor froze like a deer in the headlights, and the murderer hit him." I swung a pretend club while everyone watched. *That's not right.* "No, if he was hit with a right-handed swing, the blood splatter would be to the left and the left side of his head would be damaged."

I stepped back to the entrance and pretended to swing again, this time from the left. *Yes. That's it.* "He swung from the left. Just enough to stun the pastor and open a wound to his head. Our vic stumbled into the rack of robes, clutching a few in a vain attempt to steady himself before falling to the floor."

"Go on," Detective Tidwell said.

23

"Then he fell right there." I pointed to the circle of blood. Kneeling beside the spot, I asked, "See here?" He nodded. I noted parallel handprints in the blood. "He tried to get up." I stood and pretended to bring the club straight down. "He fell to his stomach here. No additional blood splatter, so he was probably hit in the back." I moved next to the place, careful not to step on the bright white spots indicating blood. "This is where the murderer scooped him up and dragged his limp body to the top of the stairs."

"I agree with you in theory. So, where is the murder weapon?" he asked. "And why toss him in the water?"

"The weapon was either taken or disposed of nearby. As far as the water." I paused for a moment. I knew why I would have done it. "Either forensic countermeasures—or this was personal. Detective Tidwell narrowed his eyes at me, tilting his head slightly like he didn't get it. "What better way to punish a pastor than dump his body in the church baptistery?" I remembered something my father said. Maybe symbolism was the key. "Did you know when they baptize someone, Protestants call it, 'the death of the old self'?" He shook his head. "Kind of like a water grave." I looked at the robes and said, "What a symbol of hate and irony."

"I'd cast my vote on the personal vendetta. As sloppy as this scene is, I don't think the killer was worried about forensic counter-measures." I nodded in agreement. "So," he continued, "we're looking for someone who either hated the pastor specifically or someone who just hates Christians generally."

They both triggered something deep within me. I'd struggled with thoughts of revenge in the past. In a way, I could understand the killer's motive. In my dark fantasies as a young girl, the pain I would have inflicted was always fitting and very, very, personal. Revenge often is. I, too, would have sent a powerful message or an image that would let others know, without a doubt, why he was killed. I, too, secretly shared a deep hatred for the church and its hypocritical people...especially my father. Unfortunately, no matter what I tried, the past didn't disappear easily. And now, of all places and times, I had to deal with a murder and a setting that brought it all home. A shudder coursed through my body. I looked around, but everyone was staring at the images of blood. Thankfully, no one noticed.

"I said, anything else, Rhodes?" Detective Tidwell asked. "Where's your head today?"

If he only knew. Then I remembered seeing something at the near end of the fellowship hall. I stepped out of the tiny changing room and walked across the hall. There it was; a piano bench with only three legs. Resting upon a nearby table, a C-clamp, a Phillips head screwdriver, a box of two-inch wood screws, and a bottle of wood glue—everything needed to fix the bench but the fourth leg. Someone was in the process of fixing it. The fourth leg should be nearby. Unless— I leaned back into the hallway and asked the officer, "Any sign of a piano bench leg?"

"No, but we did find a cell phone. We bagged it as evidence."

"Did any of your officers find a strange wooden club?"

"No. They did a twenty-foot perimeter search of the grounds, looking in all of the shrubbery, but came up with nothing. We didn't have time for a thorough search of the extended woods."

"Odd that it's not right here with the bench. Someone had every intention of reattaching it." I thought for a moment before adding, "I bet it's covered in his blood. It might even have a nice set of fingerprints." I made a few notes in my book. "Anyone check the trash outside?" He nodded. "So much for an easy solution." I knew that would kill Detective Tidwell. He liked in and out, clean investigations that didn't take a lot of effort or time.

Once in the hallway, Detective Tidwell removed his booties and gloves. "Good assessment, Rhodes. You have a nice eye for detail."

"Thank you, Detective." That's going to be a hard habit to break. I wasn't so sure I wanted to. Discipline, respect, and vigilance. That mantra will be with me forever.

Chapter Five

Detective Tidwell and I exchanged notes from the morning's interviews. We also shared copies with Detectives Baxter, Hawley, and Spence, other day-team members of our Homicide squad. Metro Nashville centralized its homicide efforts years ago. Instead of each precinct having its own Homicide unit, Nashville decided to station all homicide detectives in a centralized location and organized them in teams of four to five individuals. These teams usually put all eyes on the initial parts of the investigation to determine suicide, accident, or homicide. Once established as a homicide, the team on duty made preliminary investigations.

Then, once the crime scene was thoroughly searched, photographed, diagrammed, and the evidence tagged and bagged, that information was set before the team. Tidwell and I were part of a five-detective weekday team that gathered to examine the Ripley case. We carefully spread the diagrams, crime scene log, descriptions, notes, and freshly printed pictures of the crime scene across the conference room table built for twelve for our team to go through. Detective Tidwell snuck a glance at me. "Give us what time you can spare. Rhodes and I can take this one."

"Absolutely!" I couldn't hide my smile. Even though I knew deep down Tidwell didn't trust me or respect me yet, I preferred it being just the two of us. I was the only female on the day shift and the newest detective in the group. In fact, other than Detective Leslie Ware on the night shift, I was the only woman in Homicide.

Nashville's push for thirty percent of their officers to be female by the year 2030 hadn't reached homicide, which remained a predominantly male unit. Their loss.

Although they were focused on cases of their own, each examined the evidence and gave a few helpful tips. As they left, Tidwell sighed and said, "I've got a dead pastor, and my best leads are other church leaders."

"I'm not so sure," I interjected. "We may have a better suspect than the leadership." I immediately took out my phone and played the video of the baptismal service from Sunday. He liked solid evidence. "As you can tell, this man, Alvaro Garcia, was angry with his wife and Pastor Mark." I pointed to the large Latino entering from the back of the sanctuary. "He's yelling at her for undermining his leadership as a man and husband."

"You speak Spanish?" Tidwell asked, his eyes wide.

"Yes." I'd kept that information to myself as long as I could. I knew with this case, it was time to show what I could do, that I was more than just a "pretty girl."

"Where'd you learn it?" he asked.

"I picked it up from the other kids in Central America." I fidgeted in my seat. Suddenly, the attention was stifling. I inadvertently pulled at my shirt, straightening out the wrinkles, a nervous habit I picked up as a child of critical parents.

"When were you in Central America?"

"Does it really matter?" I didn't want the conversation to go any further in that direction. My past was mine. I spent years burying it, avoiding it, and denying it, even to the point of changing my name. With that momentary slip, I nearly blew it. Desperately wishing to redirect the conversation, I snapped, "Pay attention to the video!"

"Easy, kid. Just curious is all."

Kid? A major pet peeve.

"Let's just take a breath and remember we're on the same team. Now, back that video up and run it again. Tell me everything that's said in Spanish. I really don't care when and where you learned it, as long as you interpret it correctly."

"Yes, sir." I slid my finger back on the bottom of the screen and restarted the video where Sophia Garcia descended the baptistery steps. "Now, according to Jonathan Williams, the youth minister, Owen Jenkins thought Alvaro was threatening the pastor, but I disagree. I believe Alvaro is saying that to his wife. Knowing they're from Honduras, it makes more sense. I know that culture well. By going through with the baptism after he specifically forbade her to do so, Sophia undermined his authority and embarrassed his manhood."

I turned back to the video. "He and the pastor engage in a conversation here, but it isn't as heated as his words to his wife. Look!" I pointed where he slapped his hands on the baptistery glass and pointed up the stairs. "He's looking directly at Sophia, telling her to get dressed and come home." I stopped the video. "All he says directly to the pastor is, 'I told you not to interfere!' He doesn't say anything about killing him or even causing him harm. The warning justifies Alvaro's interruption of the service."

"Okay, he definitely has motive," Detective Tidwell said. "I get it; pride is a huge deal to his culture. I think the youth minister may have something here."

I sighed. I knew he'd jump at the first obvious suspect. *He'll probably close the case today.* I had to at least slow him down. "I know he really looks angry, and easily capable of such a thing, but my gut tells me he didn't do it."

"He's still on top of the suspect list," Tidwell said.

List? That's encouraging.

"We have motive. What about opportunity? Fast forward the video and see if he hangs around or leaves." I played the end of the video. We listened intently as Alvaro's voice faded in the distance. "Sounds like they left."

I glanced at my notebook and flipped a couple of pages. "According to Maeve Kennedy, the woman's ministry leader, the

Garcias grabbed Sophia's clothes and bolted out without changing. She left wearing the church's baptismal robe. Maeve claimed she was in the changing room, assisting the women being baptized that morning."

"Do we have any other viable suspects at this time?"

Detective Tidwell and I flipped through our notes and agreed that we should check the alibis for Alvaro Garcia, Owen Jenkins, Duke Stearns, and Jonathan Williams. "Neither Jenkins nor Stearns seemed the slightest bit upset the pastor was dead," Tidwell said, describing each man's mannerisms and irritability.

"I interviewed Jonathan," I said.

"The youth minister?"

I nodded. "He was a little too helpful and…" I paused, looking for the right words. "He flirted with me during the interview."

"You have to admit the video is important, and that was his lead," Detective Tidwell said, "but he might just be trying to throw the dogs off of his scent." He moved on, saying the leaders fell into two varying camps, a group that seemingly resented Pastor Mark and the many changes he made to the church, and a group that appreciated his dynamic leadership. I nodded in agreement. "For now, anyone falling into the first group makes the list of suspects."

There he goes again…a list. I thought he'd jump right on Alvaro Garcia and turn everything over to the DA's office.

"What did the Jonathan think about the pastor?"

I thought for a moment. Maybe my gut was off. Maybe I was just bristled by his arrogance. "He praised Pastor Mark and his vision," I admitted. "He said they were getting ready to start a Spanish service."

"Put him at the bottom of the list but check his alibi." His phone rang. "Detective Tidwell. Yes. Hang on a sec." He searched both his coat pockets for a pen and the table for a sheet of paper but couldn't find either. He repeated the pertinent information aloud so I could hear. "This was Monday morning? The pastor arrived at nine. Another vehicle arrived at ten. Did you happen to run the plates?" He frowned and looked at me, gesturing for me to write this down. "An old brown Ford 150 pickup with a rusted back left fender." He nodded and said, "A big Latino…uh-huh… he only stayed ten minutes and then peeled out of the parking lot. Got it. Thanks."

When he hung up, Detective Tidwell looked over at me and said, "Find out if Alvaro Garcia drives that truck."

So much for that list of suspects. "That sounds like Alvaro," I admitted. With a heavy sigh, I added, "So, he has motive, means and opportunity."

Tidwell added, "Yes, and according to the neighbor, he only stayed ten minutes and left in a real hurry."

"That definitely fits our window of time," I said. It didn't make sense. It was too obvious. "Nobody is that stupid. He'd have to know we'd suspect him."

Detective Tidwell and I put all the Ripley murder evidence back in the box and took it to our cubicle. The Homicide room consisted of a wide grid of cubicles set up in pairs. I set the evidence box between our desks on the floor where each of us could have quick access.

My transfer from East Precinct to Homicide was quick and the training a whirlwind. The caseload was high and our numbers too thin. I really had no time to enjoy the transition from patrol officer to homicide detective. All in due time.

At the back right of the room, the Cold Case detectives worked tediously and meticulously, searching for any signs of new evidence. Immediately across the aisle from our cubicle, the Homicide Sergeants flipped through the month's caseloads and made notes to check up on each case and report their findings to the Lieutenant. He, in turn, reported to the Captain. I loved to observe and speculate…a game I played as a kid.

I wheeled my chair to Detective Tidwell's side of the cubicle and listened to him read the M.E.'s preliminary findings. "'Due to the elevated temperature of the water, which continually circulated

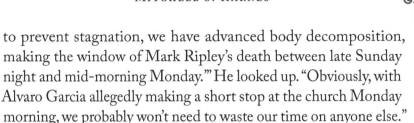

to prevent stagnation, we have advanced body decomposition, making the window of Mark Ripley's death between late Sunday night and mid-morning Monday.'" He looked up. "Obviously, with Alvaro Garcia allegedly making a short stop at the church Monday morning, we probably won't need to waste our time on anyone else."

And there you have it. *No…no…no.* "Are you sure about that? We don't need to have tunnel vision."

"First things, first. Let's find out if he owns that truck."

"Okay. I'll run a search," I said.

"If it's his truck, we've got the smoking gun."

Still, I knew we needed to keep our minds open. We hadn't even had second interviews yet.

Detective Tidwell was ready to close the case and move on. "If the eyewitness testimony is true, the pastor was alive Monday morning at nine. Hopefully, the M.E.'s office will move quickly, and we'll have an official cause of death. In the meantime, we should go back and look for that weapon." He glanced down at a note he made in the meeting. "Let's ask the neighbor who saw the truck if the man had anything in his hands when he left. Admit it, Rhodes. This is probably going to be a slam dunk on Mr. Garcia."

"What about Stearns, Jenkins, and Johnson?" I asked.

"Go ahead and verify their alibis to rule them out. I doubt we'll need to." He searched through his notes. "I want to know more about Stearns' and Jenkins' whereabouts on Monday morning. Neither of them seemed heartbroken about their pastor's death."

"I agree. Owen Jenkins was in a hurry to get out of there. Anyone else?" I pushed the case of interviewing other suspects, not putting all our eggs in one basket.

"Other than those two, everyone else on my list seemed truly shocked and saddened. Even though Jonathan liked Pastor Mark, you did say he seemed eager to point us to Garcia." Detective Tidwell paused for a moment, then added, "Strange that no one else mentioned the incident Sunday?"

"He was a little too eager for my taste," I said. "When I

mentioned the baptismal incident to Maeve Kennedy, she said Sophia Garcia was torn between the decision to get baptized and her husband's instructions forbidding her to do so."

"I wonder why he didn't want her baptized?" Tidwell asked.

"She didn't say, but my guess is they're Catholic, and he took offense to a second baptism. Ms. Kennedy said she prayed with Sophia and told her to read…" I looked for the reference in my notes. "Acts chapter five."

"What's it say?" he asked.

"How am I supposed to know?" Why does everyone in Nashville think I should know Bible references at the drop of a hat?

"I thought you were a church kid or something. Sarge did say this was up your alley."

"I was a church kid long, long ago. That doesn't mean I'm a walking biblical reference book."

"Look it up in your Bible," he insisted. "It could be critical to the case."

"I don't own a Bible," I argued.

"Find one or buy one of those apps. Go to the church and borrow one if you have to. Meanwhile, get the Garcias in here."

"Of course, Detective." I'd Google it later, but I wasn't going put my hands on a Bible. He looked at his watch. "Let's go talk with the pastor's wife and kids, make sure they know. They should be back from St. Louis by now. He let out a heavy sigh. "Worst part of the job," he said. "We also need to get that Women's Ministry lady in to see if we can get more on this rift between the pastor and the Garcias. That should give us time to get the cause of death. I want all my i's dotted and t's crossed when we talk to Alvaro. Then we can go ahead and lock him up."

I knew it. Going the easy route…just like everyone said he would. "I'm still not sure…"

The phone rang, and he answered, "Detective Sam Tidwell. Yes, sir, Lieutenant. I'll be right there."

Was that about me? He glanced my way the moment he hung

up. Maybe it was about my quick transition into the Homicide squad…questions about my ability to work a crime scene. If so, what would Detective Tidwell say about me? I chewed on my right thumbnail. Nasty habit. There wasn't much to chew on. I'd worked it down to the nub again. I watched in silence as my partner left the main room and entered the Lieutenant's office. I needed a distraction. My mind was running scenarios again. I turned to my computer and searched for Acts chapter five.

Chapter Six

W e were on our way to the Ripley home when my phone rang. "Detective Rhodes. Yes. Do you have the results? Uh-huh. Thank you." My shoulders slumped as I admitted, "They just confirmed it. Alvaro Garcia owns a 1992 Ford F-150."

"Don't sound so disappointed, Rhodes. We're just following the evidence, which happens to lead to Alvaro Garcia."

"I know, but it doesn't feel right to me. My instincts are usually spot on," I said. My gut was telling I wasn't wrong, but maybe it was just my pride.

"I understand, Rhodes. You don't think he did it, but the facts are stacking up against him. You'd have a tougher time proving his innocence than his guilt." He looked at the address on the mailbox and said, "This is it."

"How much does she know?" I asked looking at the house. Typical ranch-style house for East Nashville.

"I'm not sure, but in a church that size, people talk. I'm sure by now she knows he's dead."

He parked the car, and we walked to the front door. "I hate this part of the job," he said. "Too many bad memories." His hand began to shake as he rang the doorbell. It was one of those camera doorbells. He pushed the button again.

A voice asked, "May I help you?" Detective Tidwell stared at the door in silence. His body stiffened. "May I help you?" the voice repeated.

I leaned in front of the camera and held up my shield. "Detectives Tidwell and Rhodes."

The door opened and a red-haired woman in her mid-thirties wearing a floral print ruffled-sleeved dress said, "Come in. I've been expecting you." She wiped the tears from her puffy, bloodshot eyes. Obviously, she'd been crying. She knew. Although she tried to perk up and welcome "her guests" properly, her smudged mascara and streaked makeup betrayed the depth of her sorrow. She forced a smile. "I'm sorry, but I must look quite the mess right now." She motioned for us to enter and go into the den. I walked in first. Detective Tidwell followed silently. Susan Ripley disappeared.

I did what I was always in the habit of doing; I took in my surroundings. Simple and quaint. Well-kept and clean. Small ranch probably built in the seventies or eighties. Updated. Freshly painted. *Nice.*

She returned after making a quick attempt to look more presentable by removing her eye makeup all together. "I'm Susan." She had bright blue eyes that tried to project a sense of welcome and joy, but the fact they were bloodshot and swollen told another story.

"We're very sorry for your loss, Mrs. Ripley," I said, shaking her hand.

"Susan. It's just Susan. No need for formalities." She wiped her eyes again and took a seat in a chair. She was five-two, maybe five-three, and petite. Susan Ripley was a beautiful woman. Not exactly what I pictured for a pastor's wife. My expectation was someone like my mother, an older, square woman with little to no makeup. "Won't you sit down?" Detective Tidwell and I sat on opposite sides of the couch. "Faith called me earlier today and gave me the bad news. She's such a sweetheart. I could tell she was so worried about us…that I might not be able to drive the rest of the way home." Susan took a tissue and wiped her nose. "Never in my worst nightmares could I imagine this."

"I understand." I decided to take charge of the conversation. Something strange was going on with Tidwell; he kept oddly silent.

Unlike him to let me lead. "Tell us what you know, and I'll do my best to fill in the rest."

Susan shared the details Faith had given her of finding him at the bottom of the baptistery this morning as they arrived for the Tuesday morning leadership meeting…more details than I expected her to know at this point. As far as she knew, it happened between Sunday morning's service and Tuesday when they arrived. "Do you have any idea what happened? When it happened?" Susan asked. "Was it an accident? Did he stumble and hit his head? Or was it…" She was rambling but suddenly stopped, probably searching for a nicer word than murder. "Was it on purpose?" Such a dainty way of saying, "murder."

Two small children peeked around the corner of the hallway partition. The younger one whispered, "Mom?"

"It's okay." She waved them forward. "You can come meet our new friends."

New friends? Don't lie to your kids, lady. We're here to report your husband's murder. That's not what friends do. She was too nice…too perfect…like a Stepford wife.

The boy raced into the room and plopped down on the couch between Tidwell and me. "Hi. I'm Danny. I'm six." He held his hand out. "You're pretty."

I smiled and shook his hand. That kind of comment coming from a kid didn't seem to bother me. "Thank you. You're handsome yourself." I rubbed the top of his head.

"Is this your husband?"

I couldn't help but laugh. Detective Tidwell was as old as my father. "No. He's my partner…a fellow detective."

"You're a detective? Really? No kidding?"

I unclipped my badge and handed it to Danny. "It's the real deal."

He handed the badge back and said, "Got a gun too?"

"Yes, but I'll just hang on to it if you don't mind." That's always the first thing kids want to know. *Too many video games available. Guns far too familiar…way too early in a kid's life.*

36

Danny pointed to Susan. "I call her Mom, but my sister says she's not our real mom." He showed me his arm. "I guess you knew since we're black."

"Danny! Where are your manners?" Susan blushed. "I'm so embarrassed."

"She don't like the word *black*. Says color shouldn't matter."

I leaned in close and pretended to study his arms. "To tell you the truth, I didn't even notice. I couldn't tear myself away from that gorgeous smile of yours." His smile widened, revealing two missing front teeth. He took my hand and gave it a gentle tug. "Wanna play?"

I looked him in the eyes. "I can't today, Danny, but maybe we can do that another day. Right now, I need to talk to your mom for a bit."

He smiled again and ran back down the hall, yelling, "She's coming back! She's coming back to play with me."

Susan apologized again. I waved her off, more intrigued with the girl who stared and stood as still as a statue. I said, "Hi." The girl still didn't say anything. She didn't move a muscle, didn't even blink. "What's your name?" She remained motionless and only continued to stare.

"Her name is Hannah, and as you can guess, she's shy." Susan gave the girl a disarming smile. "It's okay, Hannah, you can go back to your room or play with Danny." The girl stepped backward slowly but didn't break eye contact. Instead, she gave an inkling of a smile, almost imperceptible, but I have a gift of noticing such small details. Lieutenant Daniels said it was my greatest strength.

"Did you know that my name is Hannah too?" The girl shook her head, and I thought Susan Ripley was going to start crying again. "I'm named after a lady in the Bible." The girl pointed to her chest. "You too?" She nodded. "Well, I guess that makes us twins." Hannah smiled and ran down the hall to Danny's room.

Susan put her hands over her heart. "That was amazing! She hasn't responded to anyone outside the family since we adopted her. You have such a way with kids."

"It's not a big deal," I said dismissively.

"You're wrong. It's a very big deal." Susan pressed out the wrinkles in her dress. It was the same nervous habit I had. "After this is all over, I seriously want you to come back. The kids love you."

Love me? They don't even know me.

"Ma'am," Detective Tidwell said, finally breaking his long, awkward silence. "If you're okay with it, I'd like to ask you a few questions."

"Certainly." She wiped her eyes and stood abruptly. "Where are my manners? Do either of you want something to drink? I have water, sweet tea, diet soft drinks."

"No thank you, Ma'am."

"You must call me Susan." Even though we said no to her offer, Susan slipped away into the kitchen and poured three glasses of sweet tea.

Tidwell looked across the couch and asked, "Why did you lie to that kid?"

"I didn't." I don't know why I revealed my secret to the girl. Kids get to me…bring my walls down…incite pity. My lost innocence, I guess.

"You told her your name was Hannah."

"That's not a lie, exactly. My birth name was Hannah Leah Abelard." He stared at me, searching my face for any signs of deceit in my face. "I legally changed my name to Abbey Rhodes when I turned eighteen, right before I left for the Army."

"Why?"

"Long story for another time. I just thought, seeing her like she was, maybe it could help. She seems so lost." I accepted the glass of tea and took a sip. "I can relate."

"I just love southern sweet tea," Susan said. "In the north, we just don't know how to make it right. For some reason my mother always tried to sweeten it after it cooled. To make it right, you have to…"

"Mrs. Ripley," Detective Tidwell interjected, "we need to stay

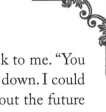

on task." She nodded but turned her attention back to me. "You really do have a way with kids." She finally sat back down. I could tell her mind was racing…probably wondering about the future without her husband. "We've had them almost two years now. We adopted them shortly after moving to Nashville. Mark was so good with them. Me…not so much. I'm feeling a little lost right now."

I wondered if Susan Ripley was lonely or just avoiding the imminent discussion of her husband's death. "You're fine," I said, doing my best to assure Susan. "You have a lot going on right now. From what I've heard, your husband was a good man," I said to comfort her. Truth is everyone speaks nicely about the dead. Why would this guy be any different? I didn't trust pastors…or churches. There was a reason someone killed him…some skeleton in his closet. We just hadn't discovered it yet.

"If you don't mind my asking, how did he die?" Susan said. She put her hands together as in prayer and put them to her lips. I could tell she was preparing herself for a difficult truth.

Detective Tidwell said, "Honestly, we're not sure yet. We're waiting on the results…" He quickly redirected her from the inevitable images of an autopsy. "Do you know anyone who might want to kill your husband?" Not very smooth.

Susan thought for a moment. "Wow. That's right to the point. It's one thing to know Mark's gone." She paused and wiped her eyes with a tissue. "It's another to…"

"Take your time," I said. "Can you think of anyone whose feathers he may have ruffled?"

Susan laughed despite her grief. "Now that's a long list. I don't know whose feathers Mark didn't ruffle, including mine from time to time." Her head tilted up and her bright blue eyes widened. "Wait! Mark made a list of names and issues. Excuse me." Susan rose from her chair and hurried down the hall. She was gone for a few minutes and then came back with a folder. "It's all in here. When the church first called us, Mark contacted the local association and talked with the Director of Missions. They'd met on a mission trip to Matamoros, Mexico. Mark was recruited as a translator. Anyway, when Mark remembered his friend Ernest was the Director of Missions in Nashville, he asked Ernest for any issues facing the church."

She held the folder out for me to take; the folder shook with the trembling of her hands. I grabbed the folder with my right hand and instinctively took Susan's shaky hand with my left. She was a wreck. I don't know what I else expected her to be. I went into trauma training mode. "It's okay. Take a deep breath. Everything is going to trigger the pain for a while. You'll manage them better each day that passes."

"Sounds as though you've lost someone." Susan stared at her own trembling hand.

"You could say that," I said. *Not going there...not in a million years.* I handed the folder to Detective Tidwell.

"You weren't kidding," he said. "This is quite a list."

"Mark confronted each issue head-on, grabbing it by the horns, so to speak." Susan paused to take a sip of her tea.

"Over the two-plus years of his tenure at the church, Mark addressed each challenge—each complication—aggressively and saw the signs of growth and progress he'd hoped for. He baptized more people over the past two months than he did in total at our previous church. He was happy his efforts were bearing fruit." Susan paused reflectively before adding, "With a new name, Living Water Church, and new enthusiastic leaders, his...*our* sacrifices seemed to be worth the effort and pain. The future looked bright."

I let go of Susan's hand and leaned over to see the list. "If you knew there were this many problems with the church, why did you still come?" It looked more like a church to avoid than one to come to, especially when it meant subjecting one's wife and kids to a myriad of conflicts.

Susan took a deep breath and let it out slowly. "Mark is...was always called to troubled churches. He said it was his Nehemiah calling."

"Just *his* calling?" I spit out the question the moment I detected a little resentment in Susan's voice. It was selfish of me, but I wondered if she in some way felt like I did.

"Well, the man is the head of the household. He's the minister. I'm just the support," she said.

Nope. Not even close to what I was thinking. "Are those his words or yours?" I asked callously. It triggered a bad memory, something my father would always say anytime my mother or sister voiced an opinion of any sort about his ministry. Again, I had to fight a shudder that coursed down my spine.

"Mark never said those things to me. My father taught me to follow those words of God. Women should know our place," Susan said. *Cop out.* "I was raised to believe that way."

"Did your husband believe that?" I asked, pushing for his stance on the issue of women.

"No. Mark always treated me as an equal. My father and Mark didn't exactly see eye to eye on the issue. Mark believed we were equal in God's eyes and gifted to serve as God would have us serve. Mark hired the best staff there was, women or men." She continued, "But back to your earlier question, Mark felt strongly about this church for some reason, especially because it had a world of trouble. It's as Jesus said, 'It is not the healthy who need a doctor, but the sick,' Matthew nine-twelve." She stood, brushed the wrinkles from her dress again, and made her way to the couch. Another Stepford wife move. Susan pointed to the place between the two of us. "May I?"

"Certainly," I said, scooting over to make more room.

Susan pointed to several parts of the list that had the initials "MR" written next to them. "See those?" I nodded, following her drift. "These are issues that have been resolved since we came. The church is making progress. God's blessed us."

Blessed you? God called her to a place she didn't want to go, her husband just got murdered, and she'd been left to raise two kids on your own. How was that a blessing? I had to take a deep

41

breath and let it out slowly before I said something I knew I'd regret later. *Inquisitive, not inquisition, Abbey.* "Resolved how?" I asked, trying to conceal the anger in my heart.

Susan explained point by point as she went through the list, giving us details about each problem and the specifics of its solution. "When the issue was finally resolved, Mark initialed it." She elaborated on the people in the original congregation who welcomed his forthright attention to conflict and his ability to move the church forward. She also spoke of the church's history of stagnation and decline. Two details both Owen's and Duke's testimonies denied. "When we came, the people were desperate for a sign of hope, anything to show God had not abandoned them. They were working themselves to death, but they had no direction." Susan also described how God brought new vibrant leadership to the church, leaders who shared Mark's God-given vision for growth and love.

"Of course," she admitted, "there were those who resented the change, who didn't like the new pastor's blunt ways." People like Owen and Duke. Susan didn't shy away from this discussion at all. Mark convinced the elders to let some leaders go and replace them with new ones who shared the vision of the church. He led the church through a name change as well as a structural change. The deacons who were used to making all the decisions were now relegated to a servant's role, a role Mark insisted was biblical. He added the role of elder and filled those positions with his new leaders. It took Susan half an hour to share the details of the past two years at Living Water Church. By the time she finished, my list of suspects expanded exponentially.

As he was closing the folder, Detective Tidwell noticed a hand-written note on the back of the last page. "What's this?" he said.

"Alvaro Garcia?" Susan asked. "Why would Mark put him on the list?"

Detective Tidwell looked at me and said, "Uh-huh." He put the folder under his arm. We thanked Susan for her time and the

wealth of information on Living Water Church. As we rose to leave, Susan hugged me and said, "I sincerely hope you will come back and visit with us." *Awkward.* I inwardly grimaced. I don't like hugs, especially from people I barely know. Susan was too friendly for my taste. What is with Southern people? I patted her on the back and pulled away, signaling the time for embracing was over.

Detective Tidwell gave Susan his card and said she could call if she needed anything or thought of anything new. "Oh, there are two more questions I have to ask. What's in St. Louis? And do you know why someone would choose the weekend you're out of town to do this?"

Was he implying what I thought he was implying? I couldn't help but wonder where he was going with that question.

"I grew up in St. Louis. My parents still live there. The kids and I were just visiting, but Mark couldn't break away this weekend because of all the new Christians wanting to be baptized."

"Is there anything about this weekend that would make it significant to…"

No," Susan said before Detective Tidwell could ask it again. "I don't know why anyone would do this in the first place, especially on such a joyous weekend." She wiped the water from her eyes.

"Sorry if I offended you, Mrs. Ripley, but I had to ask." He turned to go. "Please call if anything comes to mind."

As we were backing out of the drive, I noticed Hannah pulling the curtain aside and staring. I waved and detected a trace of a smile on her lips.

We rode in silence all the way back to Central. I wanted desperately to ask him what happened when he rang the doorbell, why he froze and seemed to disappear mentally, but I let it go for the time being. I also wanted to know if he thought Susan was somehow involved in her husband's death. Tomorrow we would interview Maeve Kennedy and the Garcias. There would be plenty of time for such questions after the interviews.

Chapter Seven

9:25 pm—Harmony Apartments, Nashville

I drove home and entered the lobby of the Harmony Apartments building and walked past a small gathering of twenty to thirty-somethings. Another singles mixer. No, thank you. I hurried past the group, made my way to the elevator, and pushed the up arrow.

"I don't think we've officially met." *Not now.* I was too tired to even turn and acknowledge him. Undeterred, he stepped beside me and extended his hand.

"Aaron Richards."

I looked at his hand but didn't reciprocate the gesture. I was wiped out from a long day, but I tried to be kind. "Listen, Aaron, I don't mean to be rude, but it's been a really long day, and I'm exhausted."

"I understand," he said with a smile. It was a perfect smile... too perfect. No one has teeth like that without help. "I was just trying to be neighborly."

Neighborly? Who says that? The elevator door opened, and I stepped inside. He followed. This guy was presumptuous. I pushed the number twelve. Again, trying to be kind and yet giving him a little stronger hint, I turned and asked, "What floor?"

"The same. I guess you don't recognize me," he said.

I was worn out from the full day of investigations, and he was stepping on my last nerve. I was in no mood for *neighborly* banter. "Should I?" I asked with a sigh. This guy wasn't taking a hint.

44

He smiled again. "I live two doors down. We've ridden the elevator together before."

Really? "I'm sorry. I just don't remember you," I said. "My mind is usually on work."

"What's your name?" he asked. "If we're neighbors, it might be nice to call each other by name."

Give it a break, Aaron. I thought about saying Hannah just to get rid of him but decided to be nice…at least try to. "Abbey."

"That's a pretty name," he said. "Almost as beautiful as your eyes." *You've got to be kidding me.* "I haven't seen you at any of the socials here."

I turned and said, "I appreciate your efforts to be a good neighbor and all, Aaron. Unfortunately, it's been a really long day, and I'm not in the mood tonight for anything other than supper and sleep." The elevator chimed and the door opened. "Have a nice night, Aaron." I walked to the right and straight to my apartment. I wasted no time in unlocking the door and closing it behind me. I turned and looked through the peephole.

Aaron stood quietly in the hallway, staring at my door as if I'd suddenly change my mind and come running to him. After standing there a few minutes, he went to the right and entered his apartment. *Finally.*

I lived in a small, one-bedroom apartment with a living room, kitchen, bedroom, and bath. I liked the simplicity and convenience. Besides, it was all I could afford on my budget if I wanted to live in the city. I selected Harmony, which opened a year ago, for its convenience. I could easily walk to any event this side of the river in downtown Nashville. Although living in the center of Nashville's entertainment district was expensive, I'd worked since I was fourteen and saved every penny I could to have this opportunity. I even chose to live in the army barracks to save money. All those sacrifices enabled me to be down on Lower Broad at a moment's notice, experiencing any one of Nashville's endless entertainment offerings. It was rough living so prudishly at the time, but I was blessed with the ability to survive on delayed gratification. I could put up with almost anything as long as I knew the future would be different.

I'd grown quite fond of my solitary life, not answering to anyone else outside of work. Even though I knew my neighbor was just being nice, tonight was one of those times I did what I wanted to do and felt not even a sliver of guilt for choosing to be alone. I microwaved my meal and plopped down on the couch. I positioned the couch to face the window instead of the television. I rarely turned it on anyway, preferring the view of Nashville's skyline to the news or entertainment of television. I took a deep breath and let it out slowly. I did it again and again until I felt my muscles relax. Then I stared out the window in silence. From my apartment's vantage point, looking toward the convention center, I counted at least ten cranes. The city was still exploding with growth. And, of course, I could see the famous Batman building as it was so affectionately called, with its two side towers as ears of the superhero's mask. A fitting symbol. We all wear masks.

After eating and opening my mail, which consisted mostly of junk, I showered, changed into my pajamas, and opened the closet doors. I needed something to distract my mind from the church and bad memories. Reaching on the top shelf, I grabbed a photo album. When I pulled it off the shelf, a present fell to the ground.

I tossed the album to my bed and knelt beside the present. It was a wrapped box the size of a small book, with a card attached to the top. I read the words written on the outside of the envelope. "Hannah, have a blessed birthday. Miriam."

Why do I still have this? My sister, Miriam, gave it for my eighteenth birthday. I never opened it, but for some reason I couldn't bring myself to throw it away. Miriam was my final tie to the family, and that birthday was the last time I spoke with her. As I held the present in my hand, memories began to flood over me… bad memories. I had to dam them up…now…protect myself. I tossed it back to the top shelf in the far-right corner of the closet, far out of reach.

Needing some positive thoughts, I flopped down on my bed and opened the album. I smiled when I saw the first picture, my first day in Germany. Six fellow soldiers and I knelt arm in arm in front of a banner that read, "18th Military Police Brigade—*Ever Vigilant.*" I learned to love those words, "Ever Vigilant." I flipped through pages of pictures: boot camp, MP training exercises, battle gear, dress uniforms, and various buildings on the base. Rough times but days that chiseled my previously questionable character into the person I am now. I truly became a new person. Looking back to the album, I flipped to a much different section, a more personal side.

Pages upon pages of recreational trips throughout Germany: sports venues, historical sites, wooded areas, lakes, and rivers. I sighed and gently ran my hand over the images. *Good times.* I'd never before traveled outside of any town, city, or village where my parents lived. I had broken free, and it was appropriate that I had a new name and a new outlook on life. The Army gave me new life; it gave me discipline. I eventually put the album back on the shelf of the closet. Before turning in for the night, I pulled one of my army uniforms off the rack and held it in front of me. Looking in the mirror, I must admit, I proudly admired the patches, badges, insignias, and medals I had earned. Promoted to Sergeant in just three years. Not bad for a high school graduate. Bet he still wouldn't be proud of me. I'd never be enough for him.

I hung the uniform back on the rack and turned out the light. Exhausted, I fell fast asleep within minutes.

Chapter Eight

Our interview with Maeve Kennedy confirmed an ongoing struggle between the Garcias and Living Water Church. As I suspected, the Garcias were Catholic and had been baptized as infants. I remembered my father facing that issue often in his Central American missionary efforts. Many Central American Catholics did not understand the difference between a Christening (what my father called a baby dedication) and a believer's baptism. In his many attempts to explain the matter, my father would always stress the significance of an individual's choice to follow Jesus. It made sense.

According to Maeve, Mr. Garcia was initially ambivalent about his family's decision to attend the church and its small groups. But he gave in as he realized going to the church made his wife and children happy, which in turn made him happy. Maeve said the peaceful arrangement stopped abruptly the day Sophia came home from Living Water Church one morning and announced she had prayed to receive Jesus as her personal savior and was going to follow up with believer's baptism. That upset her husband Alvaro, to put it mildly. He didn't understand. She'd already been baptized. There was no need to do it again. If she did, he felt Sophia was telling God her first baptism meant nothing, that it didn't count. And if she believed hers didn't count, that meant she thought his didn't either. Even if his wife had been convinced to believe this lie, he knew better.

Sophia told Maeve, no matter how she tried to explain it, Alvaro never understood her desire or need to be baptized a second time. Sophia was convinced it was the right thing to do, so she continued to push the matter. After two weeks of pressing her husband to come with her and see for himself, Alvaro Garcia gave her a mandate. No Garcia was ever allowed to attend the church or any of its functions again. He absolutely forbade them.

When Sophia and her children stopped attending church functions, Pastor Mark and Maeve visited the home and tried to mediate on behalf of Sophia and the children. Alvaro was adamant. His family could not return to Living Water under any circumstances, and the pastor was warned not to interfere in the matter again. Pastor Mark said he would honor Alvaro's wishes.

Maeve continued, explaining that she met with Sophia for coffee shortly after that encounter. She scheduled the meeting intending just to pray with Sophia, but the woman cried and begged for advice. Maeve directed her to read Acts chapter five, which says, "We must obey God rather than men." Sophia took that as a direct word from God to be baptized, so she slipped away secretly to Living Water and its women's groups.

She told Pastor Mark everything was okay, that Alvaro changed his mind and had given his blessing for his wife to be baptized the following Sunday. According to Maeve, Pastor Mark trusted Sophia and assumed everything had been worked out. Apparently not. Maeve described the terrifying and awkward incident at the worship service where Alvaro stopped the baptism and whisked Sophia away.

Detective Tidwell and I thanked Maeve for her time and information, then sent her on her way. Next, we would divide and conquer the Garcias, separating them for the interviews and checking the story of each against the other. Since a wife could not be forced to testify against her husband, we would interview them separately and see what each had to say. Technically, Sophia would neither be confirming or denying her husband's testimony.

And, if Detective Tidwell did it right, she would not be incriminating him either.

Mr. and Mrs. Garcia sat in two different interrogation rooms, waiting for us to come. Detective Tidwell said, "I'll take the lead. For now, I just want you in there as an interpreter. If you have a question or want to make a comment, slip me a note."

I nodded but inwardly grimaced at the coddling. *I can handle an interview!* I took a deep, calming breath. Inward discipline. "Who do *you* want to interview first?" I asked as pleasantly as I could while managing to stress the "you." I despised having to feign ignorance and submission like the classic dumb blonde of days gone by, but I learned in Guatemala as well as the army it was rewarding to do so. I learned to excel in subterfuge. It was a perfect skill for the interview. It was a shame the men wouldn't let me use it.

"Let's speak with her first," he said. "I want to confirm Maeve's statement. Then we'll know where we stand with her husband." Detective Tidwell glanced once more over his notes. "Let's let Alvaro sweat it out in room B."

He opened the door to interrogation room A and stepped aside to let me slip by. It was nothing more than a brightly lit ten-by-ten box of a room with a small table, one chair on the back side and two chairs in the front. A small black microphone rested in the middle of the table, mounted on a tiny tripod. A camera for a video feed was mounted in the top corner. We took our seats. A large two-way mirror was positioned strategically to our backs so observers could study the suspect's face. "Do you speak English?" he asked.

"Yes," she answered with a heavy accent.

"Good. My name is Detective Tidwell. This is Detective Rhodes." She nodded and forced a weak smile. Her eyes darted back and forth between us. She held her hands together to limit the nervous shaking. "We just have a few questions for you today." Detective Tidwell took his time, deliberately letting the silence add to her stress. "I need to make sure you understand that we will be recording the conversation." Sophia Garcia glanced nervously down at the microphone and to the mirror behind us. She nodded. "Say, 'Yes,' if you understood what I just said."

"Yes."

"Do you know Maeve Kennedy?" he asked. She nodded again. "Mrs. Garcia, would you mind speaking your answers into the microphone?"

She leaned forward and spoke directly into the mic. "Yes. I know Maeve." She leaned back and folded her arms over her chest.

"What's the nature of your relationship with Maeve Kennedy?" he asked.

"I don't understand?"

"How do you know Maeve? What is your connection to her?" Detective Tidwell asked, trying to clarify his question.

"She is a friend and my Christian leader." Sophia thought for a moment and added, "She teaches me the Bible." She unfolded her arms and put them on the table. She glanced back and forth between us again.

"To your knowledge, was Maeve aware of your husband's command that you have no contact with anyone from Living Water Church?" Sophia scratched the back of her left hand but kept silent. "Mrs. Garcia, did Maeve know your husband was upset with you and the church?" She nodded. "For the recorder, please," he said, pointing once again to the small microphone.

"Si. Yes, my husband knew she was upset." She stopped. "Sorry. Maeve knew Alvaro was upset."

I leaned forward and asked, "Why did you go back?" Both Sophia and Detective Tidwell glanced over at me curiously. It was the first time I'd spoken upon entering the room. I looked directly at Sophia, knowing full well Detective Tidwell was staring a hole through me. I could sense his pulsing jaw muscles without even looking his way. "If you knew your husband was upset, why did you return?"

Sophia remained silent, looking back at Detective Tidwell

as if she needed his permission to answer. "Answer the question, Mrs. Garcia," he said.

"Because I had to."

"Did the pastor pressure you to return?" I asked. I truly didn't understand why the woman felt the need to return and risk punishment from her husband. "Why did you *have* to go back?"

"God wanted…wants…me to follow His word and His will…" She paused for a moment, searching for the right words. "How do you say in English…"

Sensing her struggle with the language, I repeated the question in Spanish. Sophia's face brightened as she poured out her feelings in Spanish. "What did she say?" Detective Tidwell asked.

After Sophia finished speaking, I turned and interpreted it for him, saying, "Acts chapter five. She had to obey God even if it meant disobeying her husband. She had to learn more. She had to be baptized. God told her so."

"That's all she said? Seems like she said a whole lot more than that."

I smiled and said, "That's it." He wasn't the first person to wonder that.

"Ask her if God spoke audibly to her."

"What is audibly?" Sophia asked.

"Out loud."

"No…no. It was His word…La Biblia." We pursued this conversation until we realized it was going in circles. "Pastor Mark can tell you," Sophia added.

"Pastor Mark?" he asked curiously.

"Yes. He and Maeve can explain it better. They are so good with the Bible."

Detective Tidwell made a note. "Did Pastor Mark tell you to disobey your husband?" he asked.

She thought for a moment. "No…he thinks Alvaro told me it was okay." She spoke in Spanish, so Detective Tidwell waited impatiently for me to interpret.

"She's having a difficult time putting the right words in English." I explained. "Pastor Mark and Maeve came out to the house to explain everything to Alvaro, but Alvaro still refused to let Sophia and the children go back to Living Water. Then she met Maeve for coffee. When Sophia read her Bible after the meeting, she remembered Pastor Mark's sermon on that same chapter and him saying, 'Even if you're the only one in the world to obey God, you must choose to do so.'"

"God spoke through them both," Sophia said. "I must follow God." She smiled.

"So, the pastor didn't tell her directly to disobey her husband?" Tidwell asked.

"Not exactly," I said. Sophia nodded, agreeing with my interpretation.

"Did Pastor Mark believe you had permission to be baptized?" he asked.

"Si…Yes." She looked at her fingernails. "I told him my husband was okay."

"But he wasn't okay?" I asked.

"No. I lied. I must tell him I am sorry," she said.

"Your husband?" Tidwell asked, making notes as he asked.

"Pastor Mark. I must apologize for lying to him," Sophia said. Her eyes began to water. "God does not like us to lie." She looked up through teary eyes. "I made such a trouble for him. All because of lie. I must apologize for ruining the service."

"I don't think she knows," I said, looking at Tidwell.

"Knows? Knows what?" Sophia asked.

Detective Tidwell turned to her and said, "Pastor Mark is dead. We're investigating his murder."

Sophia screamed. It caught us all by surprise. After crying hysterically for several minutes, Sophia began to calm down. She stared at Detective Tidwell through tear-filled eyes. Her face and hands trembling, she asked, "Who would kill such a man? He cared for everyone." We didn't answer. How did you tell a woman that her husband was our prime suspect? Sophia repeated the question. Suddenly her face sagged, and her eyes teared up again as she realized why she and Alvaro were there. "Alvaro? No, no, no, no. Alvaro never." She kept insisting that he may have a temper, but he would never harm anyone…that he has a big mouth but does not harm anyone.

"Mrs. Garcia," Detective Tidwell began. "Where were you Monday morning between the hours of nine and twelve?" She looked confused. "Monday between nine and noon."

"Work." She began shaking her head vehemently. She turned to me and began spouting off in Spanish. Even against Detective Tidwell's commands to speak in English, she continued.

I spoke Spanish in a soothing tone, doing my best to calm Sophia Garcia. Finally, after several tense moments, Sophia stopped talking.

"What in the world did she say? And what did you say to her?"

I could tell he was angry. At least he was passionate about something. "She cannot believe you think he killed Pastor Mark. She swears she was with Alvaro from the moment they left the church together on Sunday until they both left for work on Monday."

"Your husband was seen at the church Monday morning, the day of the murder," Detective Tidwell said.

"No. You lie."

"Afraid not," he said. "We'll be checking with your work as well." Turning to me, he said, "Get contact information for her work." He rose from his chair and gave me a menacing scowl. "I'll see you outside." He was ticked.

Chapter Nine

Detective Tidwell paced back and forth in the tiny hallway outside of interrogation room A. His jaw muscles pulsed, and he spoke through clenched teeth the moment the door shut behind me. He ripped me for stepping beyond the parameters of the interview. "When I say you interpret only and slip me a note when you have a question, you do it!"

I bit my lip and paused, but only for a moment. I was like an old-fashioned pressure cooker, and Tidwell just took the cap off the top. I exploded. "She needed to speak freely, and Spanish is the only way she can," I stomped my foot. I was angry but trying desperately to control my temper and my mouth. *Discipline!* I screamed inwardly. I was far more successful with "Ever Vigilant" than I was with discipline. Vigilance came naturally. Discipline was against my nature. It took commitment and practice...lots of practice. I closed my eyes and took a deep breath. I did it again. After counting to ten, I opened them and said as calmly as I could, "The only way Sophia could say exactly what she wanted was to speak in Spanish."

"Yes, but…"

"Let me finish, Detective Tidwell." I stood my ground. I knew I was a rookie, but I added value to this team. It was time they knew it. "She's terrified. She doesn't know if we're sending her or her husband to jail, or both." I consciously tensed and then relaxed my muscles from the top of my head to the tips of my feet. He waited impatiently. I made him wait anyway. "If you want me to sit in there and be a mindless puppet, I won't do it." He started to object, but I put my hand up and continued. "I know you think I'm just a little girl, but I'm not. I'm a grown woman. I'm a good cop. I'm your partner, a co-equal detective of Homicide." He started to speak again, but I stopped him once more. If I didn't get it all out that moment, I knew I wouldn't ever get it out. "I know you're supposed to be my mentor, but I'm not as green as you think. I saw my share of action in the Army and at East." I turned and walked to the other interrogation room.

He stood in the hall for a moment. "About time you showed a little backbone," he said, just as I was walking through the door to interrogation room B. A few moments later, he joined me and Alvaro Garcia. "What have I missed?" he asked.

"Nothing. I waited for you." I sat rigidly in my chair. I still had a lot of anger boiling beneath the surface. I vented just a fraction of what I held inside.

He sat next to me, smiled, and turned to Alvaro. "Do you speak English?"

"Si. I speak little English." His accent was heavier than his wife's. I knew immediately, his English was limited to basic conversation, and even that would be a stretch.

"I need to inform you that we will be recording our conversation," Detective Tidwell said, looking at his notes.

"Si, I speak little English," Alvaro said with a forced smile.

Detective Tidwell rolled his eyes and looked to me. "Go ahead."

I translated and pointed to the microphone. Alvaro nodded. "Alvaro Garcia nodded in affirmation of recordings."

We ran through a series of basic questions, setting him up for the important ones. "Ask if he knows Pastor Mark Ripley." I did. Alvaro nodded. We asked about the tension between his family and the church. He admitted to the conflict. "Ask about the baptism service."

Alvaro explained that Sophia completely disobeyed his instructions. He said he was angry because she humiliated him. He also admitted to telling the pastor to leave his family alone.

We both took notes. "Before we move on," Detective Tidwell said, "ask him how he knew she was being baptized that morning."

It was a great question. I hadn't even thought of that. I translated. "He says a man from the church called him and told him."

"What man?"

I translated. Alvaro was quick to respond, saying, "A man saying he was the leader of deacons."

"Duke Stearns?"

"Si."

Detective Tidwell made another note. "We'll pursue that later. Ask him where he works."

He spoke in Spanish. This time I smiled like the Cheshire Cat. *He's going to love this.* "He says he worked for Jenkins Construction, but he was let go Monday because he took off without permission."

"Jenkins? Not Owen Jenkins?"

"Si. Owen Jenkins."

"This is beginning to get complicated," I whispered. "We have ourselves the makings of a conspiracy." Now, Detective Tidwell would have to slow down, look at all the evidence, and consider multiple suspects.

"You might be right," he said. "Wait a minute. Did you say Monday?" Detective Tidwell flipped through his notes. "Ask where he was Monday morning at ten o'clock." I knew where he was going with this and translated the question. Alvaro's eyes widened with fear. He didn't answer.

I pointed to the microphone. Alvaro began wringing his hands. I watched as sweat beaded all over his face. He began to rattle off his story. The moment he stopped, I translated. "He says the church lady called and asked him to meet with Pastor Mark at the church."

"The church lady?" I asked. "Maeve?"

"No. The other one."

"Tell him to show me the call log on his phone," Tidwell demanded.

I translated and Alvaro complied, scrolling back to Sunday

night before the murder, showing the call log for that night. "That's the church number all right," I said. It was an easy number to remember that ended in seven thousand.

"Let's not beat around the bush then," Detective Tidwell said. "Ask if he knows what happened to Pastor Mark."

The moment I asked him that question, he jumped to his feet, knocking his chair to the ground. He paced like a caged animal. His eyes wild with fear, a sense of panic filled his face. He looked for another way out. We held out our hands, a visible sign for him to settle down and then pointed back to his chair. Alvaro rattled nervously on in Spanish, pacing back and forth. I knew he was a big man by the video, but seeing him in person, pacing nervously, Alvaro looked like a mountain with legs. Detective Tidwell tapped on the window.

Two uniformed officers came in through the door and grabbed Alvaro by the arms. For a moment, it looked as though Alvaro was going to toss them both aside and make a run for it. One of the officers put the chair back in place, while the second held Alvaro. Not wanting this to end violently, I spoke soothingly and coaxed Alvaro back to his seat. He complied but continued to eye the door. The officers let go of his arms, and one positioned himself against the wall, immediately behind the chair. The other left the room after whispering something to Detective Tidwell.

I asked the question again. Alvaro nodded. I asked how he knew. Alvaro answered. I filled Tidwell in. "I asked if he knew what happened to Pastor Mark. You saw him nod, so I asked how he knew about Pastor Mark." Obviously, he hadn't told his wife. I wrote in my notes and said, "He says he saw the blood."

"What blood? Ask him."

I translated and listened as Alvaro described entering the church through the parking lot side entrance. Walking down the hall, he noticed the broken door and looked inside. The changing room was covered in blood.

"What did he do?"

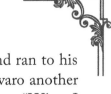

I asked the question. "He says he panicked and ran to his truck. He drove straight back to work." I asked Alvaro another question. He looked at both men before answering me. "When I asked why, he says he knew we'd think he did it."

"He's right. We do."

Of course, you do. "Wait," I let that sink in. "He said there was blood everywhere. According to our timeline, he didn't have time to clean it."

"That's why it was such a sloppy job, Rhodes. He rushed." Still jumping to the easy solution. Tidwell said, "Tell him CSI is checking his truck for evidence of blood." I did, but Alvaro had no reaction to the news. Detective Tidwell gave instructions for the officers to put Alvaro Garcia in holding, despite my objections.

"Come on! This doesn't make sense, Detective Tidwell."

"Because you don't want it to, Rhodes. I need to make a phone call." He rose and left the room.

I asked Alvaro one more question before the officers took him away. He nodded his head and made the sign of the cross over his chest. Then, he left with the officer. I sat in the chair, my arms resting on the table, and waited for Detective Tidwell to return. A few moments later, he popped his head in the room and said, "Come on, the M.E.'s office is ready for us."

"I don't think he did it," I said as I got up to leave. "He swears by the Lady of Suyapa, the Patron Saint of Honduras." Tidwell said nothing. "Come on, Detective, you've got to know this is too easy."

"Don't sound so disappointed. Sometimes we get lucky and find the smoking gun. In this case, Alvaro Garcia is still holding it."

All I could do was shake my head.

Chapter Ten

5:20 pm—Forensic Lab

Ten minutes later, at the Middle Tennessee Regional Forensic Center, a facility used by the Davidson County Medical Examiner's Office, Detective Tidwell and I met with Dr. Mandy Coleman, the attending pathologist. She'd pulled her hair into a bun and tucked it into her cap, but I could still see the traces of gray. "We appreciate your office expediting the autopsy, Doctor Coleman," he said.

"Now, Sam, how long have we known each other? Don't put on airs for your new partner."

"Okay, Mandy."

"Thankfully, Sam, we're having a slow month," Dr. Coleman said. She walked through the double glass doors. "Put on the gear before you come in."

"First name basis?" I whispered, sensing a little history here.

"We've both been around a while," he said.

"Uh-huh," I couldn't help but smile.

We each donned a green smock, gloves, and a plexiglass face shield and met the pathologist at the stainless-steel gurney holding Mark Ripley's body. I stared at the open chest cavity exposing his internal organs. "This always creeps me out," I admitted, "no matter how many times I see it."

Detective Tidwell smiled. "You flinched like that when we first arrived at the church."

"I don't like churches. Here, it's the combination of things," I said. "The sterile environment, the dead bodies laid out like field-dressed animals, and that horrid mix of smells."

Dr. Coleman said, "You get used to it."

"I don't think so, and I don't want to," I said. "It's like going into a butcher's shop selling human remains that threw bleach on the floor to cover the smell."

"Nice image, Rhodes."

"I always have that creepy feeling they're going to pop up any moment. Too many horror movies."

"Can we get on with it, Mandy?" Detective Tidwell asked.

"Of course." She handed him the printed results. "This poor guy really had a rough go of it."

He read the cause of death aloud. "'Multiple modality trauma to include manual strangulation, blunt force trauma injuries and drowning?' Well, which is it, Mandy?"

"All of the above," she said. Dr. Coleman pointed to the throat. "Whoever strangled Mr. Ripley had very strong hands. There are multiple contusions, not just to the trachea but also to the muscles surrounding the trachea and outward." She pushed a flap of skin from the throat. "Look here." We each leaned in to get a better look. "The hyoid bone is fractured. That takes a lot of power, especially with one's hands alone. There are no ligature marks showing otherwise." She placed both hands on Mark Ripley's head and tilted it to his left, exposing the opposite side of his skull. "He was struck here first. Then once in the back."

"So why strangle him?" I asked.

"Because those injuries didn't kill him. Someone grabbed him around the neck and squeezed hard enough to bruise the tissue on every side." She moved his head back in the upright position and pointed to evidence of bruising on each side of the neck. "See?"

"What am I looking for?" I asked, not afraid to admit I was still ignorant of this part of the job. I'm an avid learner.

"Thumb marks on either side of the neck just above the Larynx," Dr. Coleman said.

"So, he was choked to death?" I asked. I was totally confused. What actually killed him?

"Inconclusive," Dr. Coleman said. "He also had water in his lungs and bruising on his chest where he was held down. Thus, we have a multiple modality diagnosis." She removed her gloves and looked at Detective Tidwell. "Sam, whoever did this was strong but very, very sloppy. I don't think it was premeditated…at least his initial plans didn't pan out." She looked back at Mark Ripley's body. "Mr. Ripley suffered greatly."

"So," he began, looking back and forth between the report and the pathologist. "Mandy, let me make sure I hear what you're saying. He was hit twice with a blunt object, once in the head and once in the back." She nodded. "We know at that point someone picked him up, carried him to the baptistery, and threw him in the water, which, to me, means that person must have gotten in the water with him and choked him. That still didn't finish the job, so he held the man under the water until he was dead?"

"That is consistent with our findings," Dr. Coleman said.

If there was a God, then He either lied about loving His children, or He was powerless to intervene on Mark's behalf. Or, Mark Ripley wasn't who he claimed to be.

"How much did Mr. Ripley weigh?" Sam asked.

"Sixty-seven point twelve kilograms, which is approximately one hundred forty-eight pounds."

Sam said, "He's not that heavy, but that's quite a feat, especially with a narrow, steep stairway. According to the crime scene, the only part of Mark Ripley that left marks in the blood were his legs and shoes, which means our murderer carried the bulk of his weight."

I looked at the M.E.'s report. "That's a lot of anger and a lot of trouble. If he just wanted Mark Ripley dead, he could have hit him a few more times and left the body in the changing room." I thought for a moment, then asked, "How long would it take a person to do everything you described?"

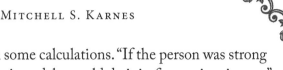

Dr. Coleman ran some calculations. "If the person was strong enough and highly motivated, he could do it in five to six minutes."

Tidwell popped me in the shoulder. I knew what he was doing. I smiled. "Could a person kill him, clean up the scene, and leave the building in ten minutes?"

"Ten minutes?" Dr. Colman put a finger to her chin and tilted her head in thought. "Possibly, but that would really be pushing it. The person would have to know the church and where the cleaning equipment is to do it in ten. No time for second-guessing. No time to rest. On the other hand, if a person wanted to pause and savor any part of the kill or take time to clean thoroughly, it probably took forty."

I punched Tidwell's arm. "But it is possible?" he asked.

Dr. Coleman shrugged her shoulders. "It would be a stretch, but yes, it is possible." She walked to a small table and grabbed a bag. "Before I forget, we found his wallet, his keys, and his comb in his pockets. Wallet had three hundred dollars cash in it." She handed it to Detective Tidwell and said, "Sign here."

With my gloves still in place, I glanced through the wallet and flipped through the bills. "Rules out robbery as a motive."

"Take those back to Homicide, Rhodes. Let's see if the IT department got anything off his phone while we're at it." He took his smock and face protection off on his way to the door and said, "I nearly forgot. What was the official time of death?"

"Best I can do is give you a two-hour window; as my assistant told you earlier, the circulated and heated water makes it difficult to be more precise than that."

"That's great," I said. "What's the window?"

"Eight-fifteen to ten-fifteen, Monday, November 23." Well, that was consistent with the neighbor's testimony.

"Thanks, Mandy," he said with a wave.

"Don't be a stranger, Sam." She winked, but he didn't see it.

We exited the room and quietly made our way through the building on the way back to the parking lot. "I know what you're going to say, but my gut still says he didn't do it," I said the moment we stepped out of the building.

"Oh, come on, Rhodes," Tidwell said. "What else do you want? A video of him killing the pastor?"

"That would make me feel better, but I'll settle for the bloody weapon with his prints."

"We have all we need for the D.A. Ten minutes is tight, but possible. Get a good night's sleep, and we'll wrap this up tomorrow morning."

"Tomorrow?" I asked. "But we don't have the results from his truck yet."

"I didn't have it checked," Sam admitted. "It was a ruse so I could gauge his reaction."

"I don't understand," I said.

"It would just be a waste of time and money. We have all we need."

"But…"

"I have one errand to run first thing, Rhodes, and then I'll be back at Central to sign the papers. Make sure all the evidence is in the box."

Tidwell had a reputation for rushing to a verdict, but it felt so much worse being a part of an expedited case without thoroughly ruling out all other options. And no matter how long I stood there and argued for taking our time, his decision was made.

Chapter Eleven

I decided last night to investigate on my own. Tidwell made up his mind. He took the first viable suspect and ran with it. To my credit, he did tell me to get a good night's sleep. And the only way I could do that was to call in some suspects myself.

"I appreciate your willingness to meet with me so early this morning." I looked across the table. "Do you mind stating your name for the record? And please, speak into the microphone."

"My name is Morris Stearns, but I prefer to be called Duke." He was rigid and kept an angry look on his face. When I called him last night and asked if he could come in and clarify a few things about the case, he didn't answer right away. It was easy to see Duke was a skeptical man and had a general distrust of the government, which obviously included the police. "You sure you're old enough to be a detective?"

I ignored the question. "I want to confirm a few things I have from Detective Tidwell's notes of your conversation on Tuesday, October twenty-fourth." I paused to look through the notes. "I understand you're a truck driver." He nodded. "If you could, please answer into the microphone."

"Yes."

"And I understand that you are a deacon of the church?" I asked.

"That's right." He tightened his lip and sat completely erect in his chair. I could tell he was expecting me to pursue the tension between the deacons and elders, but that really didn't interest me at the moment.

"I see from Owen Jenkins' interview that you lock up the church after the services?" He nodded. I pointed once again to the microphone.

"Yes."

"That's awfully nice of you to do," I said trying to fan his ego a bit.

"East Nashville thinks it changed. People move in by the wagon full, but it's still East Nashville. Can't be too safe." He rested his arms on the cool metal table. He was beginning to relax.

"I agree," I said. "I worked the East Nashville Precinct for three years." His eyes narrowed…his body tensed. I could tell he was expecting a trap. "You really don't trust people do you?"

"I didn't say that." If it was possible for his posture to get any more rigid, it did at that moment.

I had him on the defensive now and decided to keep him there for a while. Keep him confused, so he wasn't sure what to expect next. "In fact, I gather by your comments about elders and the church's name change, you didn't trust Mark Ripley."

"I never said that," he said. "I disagreed with him. Big difference."

"He came in and started changing things right off the bat, brought in his own people, and they became a voting majority. It wasn't the same church after that. Surely, that bothers you. I mean you probably asked yourself, 'What's this guy going to do next?'"

"Doesn't mean I didn't trust him," Duke said through clenched teeth. "I thought I came down here to explain something. Now you're accusing me…"

"I'm not accusing you of anything, Mister Stearns. I'm just trying to assess your relationship with the pastor."

"I'm the chairman of the deacons," he said as he pointed in my face.

"I'm not sure what that means," I said, hoping to get something

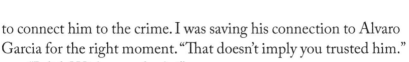
to connect him to the crime. I was saving his connection to Alvaro Garcia for the right moment. "That doesn't imply you trusted him."

"I did. Without a doubt!"

"But you didn't like him?"

"No." He'd said it too quickly.

"What didn't you like about him?" I asked. "It seems to me that Mark Ripley did exactly what the church called him to do." Duke remained tight-lipped. I could tell he was wary of making another mistake. "According to my research, the church has grown from an average attendance of forty-one to just over two hundred in his tenure. That's five hundred percent growth in two years, if my math is right. Your church's involvement in the community is well-known and admired. You're preparing for a Spanish worship service. Should I go on?" Duke didn't move. Even though he remained stoic, I could tell I'd struck a nerve. "I know you disagreed with the church's name change. Why is that?"

His eyes narrowed again. "I know what you're trying to do, Missy, and it won't work."

"What am I trying to do?" I asked. "And it's Detective Rhodes."

"You're trying to pin his death on me."

"Should I?" I asked as I leaned back in my chair.

"No, ma'am. I didn't like him," Duke said. "I think we pretty much disagreed on everything, but I didn't kill the man."

"Really?" I asked, making notes in my notebook. "You don't even care to hide your animosity?'

His jaw muscles pulsed as he clenched his hands into fists. "Don't throw your ten-dollar words at me, girl."

"Animosity? It means your dislike, hatred, hostility." I sat motionless, hiding the pleasure I felt inside for getting a rise out of the man so easily.

"I knew it!" Duke said, pointing his finger in my face. He wasn't a huge man, but it was obvious he was strong and worked with his hands. They were large and rough. He stared a hole right through me. I could tell he was gauging his next move and the consequences for each. I looked him over. He did the same to me, looking over my modest one-hundred nineteen-pound frame. Duke sat there tapping his three-hundred-dollar cowboy boots on the floor. Was he contemplating a physical confrontation? I noted the dark tan on his arms ended abruptly at the end of his short sleeves. I had to admit it would be easy to let this man intimidate me. Fortunately, I'd seen worse in the Army.

Just as I thought I pushed too hard, too fast, and blown the interview, Duke sat up straight and said, "Now, now, officer…"

"Detective Rhodes."

"Okay, Detective. I'm sorry." He smiled. Obviously forced. "We got off to a bad start. I didn't like Brother Mark, but I didn't hate him either. Sure, we disagreed…a lot, but I respected the man." I laughed. I didn't mean to do that aloud, but it caught him by surprise. "I did."

"You're sitting there telling me you respected Mark Ripley, after all the changes he made?"

"Yes." Duke's visage loosened a bit. "Brother Mark always met me face to face…man to man. He let me speak my mind." Duke glanced at his hands and rubbed the palms as if he had a stain that wouldn't come out. "Didn't change his mind, but he never went behind my back."

That was it. The opportunity I was waiting for. "Then why did you go behind his?"

He truly looked shocked. "I…I never…"

"You told Alvaro Garcia about the baptism so he could spoil the service."

"That's not true!" His entire body snapped to attention again. His face reddened and his jaw muscles clenched. Everything about the man hardened. "I never said a word to that Mexican!"

"He's not Mexican."

"Who cares! I'm glad he rattled Brother Mark's cage and made the church think twice about lettin' the Mexicans have their run of things."

"You know the Garcias are from Honduras," I said, correcting his prejudicial statement.

"Same difference," he snapped back. That statement made no sense to me. How can something be the same and different? "They're all invading our southern border. Before you know it, they'll take over."

"So, you hate all Latinos?" I asked.

"I don't hate 'em, but they got their place, and we got ours. We were better off when everything was separate. Know what I mean?" I didn't answer. I knew exactly what he meant, but I also knew whatever I said in response would be recorded too. "I mean Alvaro's a good guy and all, but a lot of people are afraid of him. He's big and angry all the time."

"Do you think he killed Mark Ripley?" This was the moment. If he said, "no," I could use that to get Tidwell to take his foot off the accelerator.

He didn't hesitate. "No." He looked directly into my eyes. "I think he was angry, and he had a right to be. He warned Brother Mark and the church to stay away from his family." He paused before continuing. "But I really don't think he did it."

"You don't think he did it, but what I want to know is how sure are you? The evidence is pretty thick against him."

"Yeah, they got that video of him, but I still don't think he did it." He paused again. Then he snapped his fingers. "I know who could tell you for sure…Owen Jenkins. He'll tell you the guy is all talk, a bag of hot air. He mouths off, but he never does anything about it."

"If he felt that way, why did Owen fire him?"

"He what?" Obviously, Duke didn't know. "Well, you really need to talk with Owen about that."

"If you don't think Alvaro killed Mark Ripley, then who do you think did?"

"I've given a lot of thought to that. You know who might have a good reason for doing it?"

I leaned in. "Who?"

"That Green guy who wanted to buy our lot."

"The green guy?" I didn't follow.

"Yeah. He owns some development company. They'd given us an offer for the church, and we told him we would do it, but it'd take a church vote to make it official."

"You mean Quentin Green of Green and Associates Development?" I knew of the company. They would buy a house, raze it to the ground, and build two skinny two-story boxes they called homes in its place.

"Quentin Green. Yeah, that's him. I bet he had a *million* reasons to be angry with Brother Mark. Our new pastor tabled the offer until he had enough people in place, new members that believed in his vision, to outvote the rest of us."

I caught his distinction. "Who's us?" I asked casually, keeping my eyes on the paper where I was taking notes.

"Original members," he said matter-of-factly. "We were going to relocate the church to a safer place. Brother Bill got the motion started but didn't stick around to see it through."

"Brother Bill? Who's that?"

"The former pastor. Bill Heithcock."

Now that's another solid lead. Even though he was sadly misguided, I could tell Duke loved the church. In his mind, he was doing the right thing.

Detective Tidwell burst through the door. "What are you doing, Rhodes?"

Chapter Twelve

After Detective Tidwell dismissed Duke Stearns, he walked back to his desk and demanded I sign the paperwork he had prepared for the judge showing probable cause to officially arrest Alvaro Garcia for the murder of Mark Ripley.

"Duke just gave me two more suspects. I've got a gut feeling Alvaro's innocent."

He shook his head and held out his pen. "We don't arrest on our gut. We arrest on facts."

"And we arrest the first chance…" I caught myself and shut up. I sat in my chair, opposite his, and explained that I reached out to Duke Stearns last night and asked if he could meet with me early this morning. "I wanted to see if he had anything new… anything that might lead us away from Alvaro Garcia."

"Would you just give it up, Rhodes?" Tidwell said. "Alvaro's our man. The evidence and witnesses have gift-wrapped him for us, and we've done the same for the D.A."

"But we haven't even looked at the other suspects. Everything we have is circumstantial."

"Rhodes! Sign the paperwork. We've got other cases. This one's over."

I slumped in the chair. "But what if he's innocent?"

"He's not!" His harsh tone had heads popped up from several other cubicles to see what was happening.

"You wouldn't care if he was!"

He shoved the paper in my face and said, "Sign it."

"Don't you want to at least follow up on Jenkins, Johnson, or my two new leads?" I was pleading with my eyes. "Give me a day."

"No! You came here thinking you know everything. You don't."
He turned away from my gaze. "Fine. If you won't sign it, I'll get
Sarge to." He waited a few moments in silence. I knew what that
meant. Without another word, I took the pen and scribbled my
name on the paper. Detective Tidwell walked the form over to
the administrative assistant of homicide and asked her to scan
the document and send it to the judge. As soon as she took it, he
left in a huff.

I sat in the cubicle alone, half wanting to cry, half wanting to scream. I'd failed. I anticipated his response the moment I
decided to go behind his back and interview Duke Stearns. *Idiot!*
Going rogue and ignoring protocol again. I glanced at my notes
with Duke Stearns. Then my curiosity got the best of me. *What's
a phone call or two going to hurt?* Couldn't be any worse than it is.
He hates me already.

I looked through our original contact list and found Owen
Jenkins. I took a deep breath and dialed his cell. "Jenkins."

"Yes. Mr. Jenkins this is Detective Rhodes from Homicide.
Do you have a moment?"

I could tell he covered the phone's mouthpiece and barked
some orders. "Sure, but only a moment."

"Thank you. I just met with Duke Stearns, and he said I should
ask you," I began. Always use connections when you have them.

"Ask me what exactly?"

"Two things. First, do you think Alvaro Garcia is capable of
murder?"

"You don't beat around the bush, do you?" he asked. Owen
Jenkins took a deep breath. "I think he's physically capable of killing
someone, but I don't think he'd ever really do it."

That's what I was hoping to hear. I jotted down his reply.
"Then why did you fire him?"

"Who told you that?" he asked.

"Alvaro."

He took a deep breath and let it out. "I fired him because he left the job site without permission. Now, before you ask me, yes; it was Monday. But I fired him because it was his third strike." He paused, but I didn't say anything. "I know what it looks like, Detective. I've run it through my mind a hundred times since Tuesday. I even went over to their house and asked him directly that morning."

I didn't know what to ask him now. So many questions raced through my mind. "And you still don't think he did it?"

"No. Not a chance."

"What makes you so sure?" I was losing hope. I wanted some-one else to affirm my initial thoughts.

"It's like I've told Duke a dozen times or so. The guy's all bark and no bite."

I wondered something. "Why would you discuss him with Duke Stearns? You have to admit, that's strange."

He laughed. "Not if you know Duke."

"I don't follow."

"Duke's the same. A big talker, always walking around like he's got a giant cob up his butt." He paused. "You probably don't understand the…"

"Oh, no. I follow. My dad used that expression too," I admitted.

"Okay then. Well, I was comparing him to Alvaro."

"Uh-huh." I still wasn't following him. "What's that have to do with the murder?"

"They both talk a big game, but their threats are just that… threats. Get me?" Owen asked.

"I think so."

"Can I ask you something?"

I said, "Sure. I'll answer if I can."

"Are you going to arrest him for it?" I told him we were. He deserved the truth. "Then I take it you don't believe he did it either? Is that why you called?"

"I suppose," I admitted. "I'm just not as certain as my partner, but he's been doing this a lot longer than I have." Had to keep a somewhat united front.

"Got to run, but I'll tell you what I tell all the people in my company. If you think something's wrong, fight to prove it. Don't wait for the mistake to show itself and hurt us all."

"That's good advice," I said. "Thank you." I let him go.

I Googled "Quentin Green and Associates." I sat there a minute and debated the foolishness of it all. If Tidwell was right, I'd really find myself on the outside looking in. That's all Sergeant McNally would need to cut me loose. But, if I just rolled over, I'd never forgive myself. Better to be out of work and able to live with myself than to hate myself for compromising my principles.

Back and forth I went, talking myself into and out of the decision to call Quentin Green and get a feel for his role in the murder, if any. There had to be a reason both Duke and Owen believed Alvaro was innocent. Didn't there? I'd only been in the Homicide unit for two months…far too short of a time to cause waves. Waves? If I did this and was wrong, this would be a bloody tsunami. However, if I was right but said nothing, an innocent man got convicted. I'd lose a job. He'd lose his freedom. Not really a choice.

I dialed before I lost my nerve for the tenth time. The phone rang, and the receptionist answered. I explained who I was and that I would like to speak with Mr. Green about the case. The receptionist transferred my call, and within minutes, Quentin Green agreed to see me in an hour. I copied his business address and made a list of questions I wanted to ask. I hoped Tidwell would be busy the rest of the day following up on the warrant and booking Alvaro officially. By then, I was hoping to be able to present a solid lead on someone else. Oh well…all or nothing.

But what if I'm wrong?

Trust your gut, Abbey.

Chapter Thirteen

The Green and Associates office was just off Briley Parkway, near the Opryland Hotel. It wasn't fancy. Just a four-office suite with a conference room and a reception area. I walked to the receptionist's desk and waited for her to hang up the phone. She had a caramel-colored pixie haircut and large dangling earrings. I noticed her acrylic nails and wondered how she was able to press the digits on the phone. "May I help you?" she asked.

I showed my badge and identified myself. "Is Mr. Green available?"

"Please, take a seat. I'll let him know you're here."

Furniture was sparse and spread far apart. I sat in the nearest chair and glanced over at the LCD television hung on the far wall. What's the point of having news playing with no sound? I scanned the reception area. Mr. Green displayed former development projects from left to right on the far wall, all containing before and after shots. To me, the new houses all looked the same.

"Detective Rhodes, he'll see you now. Right through the doors on your right."

I followed her directions and reached for the door, but it opened for me. A black man in his late thirties, wearing a charcoal grey suit, smiled and said, "Please come in."

When I entered his office, I quickly took note of his diplomas, certificates, and awards. He displayed them so clients would notice as they walked in. Obvious, but inspiring. Blueprints covered the top of a nearby table, as well as one by the window. "Impressive."

"Thanks. Now what can I do for you?" he asked.

I pointed to a leather chair across from his desk. He nodded. "I just heard you lost a sizable bid you placed on Living Water Church's land."

He thought for a moment. "Living Water Church? No. I'm afraid you're mistaken."

"Maybe the name East Nashville Baptist Church is more familiar to you?" I watched for a reaction. "On Eastland Avenue."

"Oh, yes, I remember that church." His lack of a reaction disappointed me. No animosity in his voice.

"How?"

"Well, Detective, if you're here, I can only guess you know how I became reacquainted with the church?"

"Did their decision to back out of the deal make you angry?" I asked. "I mean that surely cost you a nice chunk of change."

He laughed. "Only time and paper," he said. "Not the first time a deal fell through, and it won't be the last. Nature of the beast." He turned around in his chair and grabbed a pitcher of water. Filling his own glass, he asked, "Would you like one?"

"Please." I waited until he poured the glass with his right hand and handed it to me with his left. It wasn't enough to indicate whether he was left-handed or not. "Are you saying you weren't the least bit upset?"

"Of course, I was upset, but the next day I didn't give it another thought."

"Really?" I sipped my water and took a moment to read his accolades. "I have a hard time letting things go, myself."

"It's much easier than one thinks. Look forward rather than backward."

"Sounds simple enough." I made a few of those forward moves myself, but I also managed to keep an eye over my shoulder. Ever Vigilant, I suppose. If it's so easy, why can't I stop looking back? *Focus, Abbey.* This wasn't about me. "When you lost the deal, you just looked forward?"

"Absolutely. You know, I owe a lot to that church. They reached

out to my apartment complex when I was a kid, even picked us up with a bus and brought us to VBS." His glance grew distant and reflective. "I guess I was seven, maybe eight. Anyway, they fed us lunch." He leaned forward, placing his elbows on his desk. I noticed his hands were normal size. He wasn't a big man to speak of either. "That may not seem like much to you, but to a hungry kid without a school lunch, it was everything."

"Sounds nice."

"It was more than nice. They fed us, loved on us, and kept inviting us to all their activities, just like we were one of them." He sighed for a moment. "For an all-white church to welcome black kids and let us play and sit with their own kids, it was huge for me." He rose and walked over to a picture of an old house. "This was my first project. That church gave me hope, told me I could be anything I wanted to be. They even offered a tutoring program for a while, and I really needed it back then."

"So, you really weren't mad when they chose to keep the place a church?" I asked.

"Heavens, no." He turned to face me. "Truth be told, I'm glad to see that old place thriving again. I hope they make it."

"And you have no ill will towards Pastor Mark Ripley?"

"Not an ounce. I hope he makes a go of the place, and they end up buying more land." He laughed and sat back down. "You came out here to ask about that deal? That was over a year ago. Why now?"

"Because the pastor is dead," I said flatly. "He's been murdered."

Quentin Green put his hand over his mouth and looked out the window. "Any idea who did it?" I kept silent. "Aww no. You think I did…over a busted deal? A deal that terminated a year ago?"

"The thought crossed one church member's mind. Without the pastor, you could renew your bid for the property."

"They rejected my offer, and I moved on." He rose and opened the door for me. I could tell I offended him. He didn't seem nervous at all. "If that's why you're here, you wasted a trip."

"I'll see myself out, thanks," I said. Wasted trip? Not really. One more person off my list. Back to the drawing board. *Can't give up yet. Alvaro's innocent.*

Chapter Fourteen

Thirty minutes later, I tried to slip into the Homicide room unnoticed. It didn't work. "Rhodes, conference room. Now!"

"Yes, Sergeant." *Crap!* I put my things on my desk and made a one-eighty.

Sergeant McNally stood, holding the door to the interrogation for me. His face said everything I needed to know. I was in hot water or up that creek without a paddle. He closed the door and sat across from me. "Let me tell you, Rhodes. I'm as old school as it gets." I knew that. "Not a fan of this thirty-by-thirty initiative to boost the number of women in uniform, no more than I was of affirmative action."

That explains a lot. Doesn't think women can do the job.

"And it's not why you think. I believe a person should be hired and advanced on merit alone. You get what you deserve, and you earn your consequences…good and bad." He paused to let that last part sink it. "Do you know why Metro centralized homicide years ago?"

I thought it was rhetorical, but when he sat there staring at me, I realized he expected an answer. "Because it was more cost-effective to do so, Sergeant?"

"True, Rhodes, but that's not the only reason." Sergeant McNally aged quite a bit since the picture in his office was taken. He'd lost the last of his curly hair, and his thick mustache had turned completely gray. He was barely six feet tall, but his arms and legs were thick. His stomach bulged out, but not in a flabby, jelly-like way; it was firm, probably from the many nights drinking.

Sergeant McNally was a big man, which is why some called him Fort McNally. Even though they didn't look it, his muscles were still rock hard. He wasn't someone I'd choose to fight.

Sergeant McNally's dogged tenacity was widely known throughout Metro Police. His no-nonsense demeanor and forthright manner served as a double-edged sword his entire career. On the positive side, it helped him to drive his people to close many crimes destined for the Cold Case unit. On the negative, it knocked him down in rank a few times when he "pissed off his superiors"…his words, not mine. If it weren't for his lack of verbal filters, he would be at least a lieutenant by now…probably captain. But he didn't play the political game, which is why he remained a sergeant. McNally was a great detective, and he expected the detectives under his command to follow suit.

"Homicide was centralized," he began, "so that detectives could help one another solve difficult cases…impossible cases. We could have more eyes looking at the evidence and more voices sharing possible scenarios that led to more convictions. We could help each other…depend on each other."

Thinking the Sergeant was speaking of my case, I said, "Exactly! I'm so glad you agree."

He shook his head. "I think you've mistaken my history lesson, Rhodes."

"You're not encouraging me to stick to my convictions?" I asked.

"Far from it, Rhodes. There is no Ripley case. We've turned it over to the D.A.'s office, which means it's out of our hands." I sank into the chair. "Let go and move on."

"But, sir…"

"Let go and move on." He set a folder on the table and opened it. "This is your file, Rhodes." I swallowed at the lump in my throat. Here it comes. "I'm making a note *in pencil* here, stating you disregarded orders to cut that case loose. If I catch wind of anything remotely resembling an investigation into Mark Ripley's murder, I'll put it in ink, and make it official."

"Yes, sir." Warning, but not permanent yet. Thin ice, but I was still above water.

"Let me give you a little advice, not as your sergeant, but as a fellow detective." I perked up. This was the first sign of compassion he'd given me in the two months I'd been at Homicide. Maybe my doggedness reminded him in some small way of his. Maybe, in his eyes, I was earning my place in Homicide, but just needed a push back into my boundary lines. "Don't alienate your partner. Believe it or not, Detective Tidwell is trying to help you." He made sure the camera was off. "You could learn a few things from him. But get out of your own head long enough to realize he needs you as much as you need him. *That's* why I put the two of you together."

I worked so hard to prove myself worthy—superior—that I'd already managed to drive a wedge between myself and my partner. "Yes, sir." Was I too self-absorbed to realize Detective Tidwell may still have something to teach me, so arrogant that I didn't think I had anything to learn? "He needs you." What did that mean?

"Susan Ripley called to check on you last night and to say the funeral was scheduled for Saturday at noon. I want you to pay your respects at Mark Ripley's funeral tomorrow, but don't get sucked back into thinking the case is still open." I stared blankly at the wall. Not back to the church…anything but that. "If I've learned anything from my wife, it's that women need closure more than men. Not trying to be sexist, just real. Rhodes, do this so you can have closure and move on. Understand what I'm saying, Rhodes?"

"Yes, sir." Close the case…close the contacts.

"Okay, find Detective Tidwell and make things right. That's all." He stood and grabbed the folder off the table.

I left in silence. *You got a second chance, girl. Don't blow it this time.* I set out to find Detective Tidwell and apologize.

Chapter Fifteen

Saturday, October 28, 11:00 am—Living Water Church

I obeyed orders even though it bothered me to go to Living Water Church a second time and face my demons. Besides, Susan Ripley had asked me to come to Mark's funeral, and there was something about her that made me feel safe. I followed the direction of a young man pointing out an open parking spot on the lawn of the church. If parking was any indication, Pastor Mark Ripley was a very popular man. I steeled my nerves, walked through the church doors, and shook the hand of the greeter. He offered me a small program that gave a snippet of information on Mark's personal and professional life. I took a deep breath and let it out slowly before entering the sanctuary for the second time.

I'd hoped to beat the crowd by coming an hour before the service, but I failed. I glanced around at the variety of people attending, people of various ages and races. I stood in line and waited to pay respects to Susan and the kids. As I did, I continued to scan the crowd, spotting many of the leaders Detective Tidwell and I interviewed just four days prior. I was greatly surprised the family was able to have a funeral so quickly; the Medical Examiner's office released his body just yesterday.

The youth minister, Jonathan Williams, was easy to spot because he was surrounded by teenagers. He saw me and waved. I nodded but looked elsewhere. Maeve Kennedy noticed me and made a beeline through the crowd. "Is it true that Alvaro killed Pastor Mark?"

I thought for a moment before I responded. How could I answer her honestly, tell her I thought he was innocent, without throwing Detective Tidwell under the bus? He said we're just following the evidence…right? "Unfortunately, that's what the evidence tells us," I said. It was a good compromise. That's not exactly a lie.

"I can't believe it," Maeve said. I could sense the disappointment in her demeanor and voice. "I knew he was angry. Poor Sophia."

"I'm sure she's confused and hurt," I said. I was certainly confused.

"It's my fault," Maeve said. "I mean, if I hadn't reached out for that meeting and given her the Bible verse, she'd probably have stayed home."

True. Couldn't say that…it would be rude. I tried to encourage her with something. "Well, you can't blame yourself," I said. "Sophia made her own decision; so did Alvaro." The line moved forward, and I counted the number of people still in front of me. I was exposed, vulnerable, open for dialogue. I had to find a seat quickly. "I didn't realize your pastor was this popular."

Maeve looked around the room and smiled. "He truly was a Godly man, heavily involved in the community. He will be missed." Maeve spotted a group of women from her Bible study and said, "I'm glad you came, Detective. Would you please excuse me? I need to talk with my girls over there." She pointed to the group of young women entering the church. I nodded, thrilled to be free.

Finally, I made my way to the front. I felt the muscles in my neck and back relax at the sight of the closed casket. Still, that last image of Mark Ripley's chest opened for the autopsy flashed before my eyes. I was so focused on the memory, I didn't notice Susan, who rushed up and hugged me. I stiffened and patted Susan's shoulder. When the children spotted me, Danny waved, and Hannah smiled. "Thank you so much for coming," Susan said. "I know this goes way beyond your duty, Detective Rhodes."

"Just call me Abbey. I'm not on duty today."

"Abbey? I thought you said your name was Hannah?" Susan asked, pausing to wave at someone to the side.

"It was once," I said. "I changed it when I turned eighteen. I needed a fresh start."

"Oh, but Hannah is such a pretty name." Susan smiled back at another friend who passed by. "I can't believe how many friends have come to support us this morning."

I looked around once more. "I know. Listen, I didn't mean to confuse you about the name. It was a long time ago, and I was full of spite and anger then. Like I said, I needed a fresh start."

"Don't we all." Susan patted my hand like a mother would her child. "You'll have to tell me all about it sometime."

I looked at Susan and then turned around to see the line behind me. *Idiot!* She was signaling you to move on, that others needed her attention too. "Oh, right. I am sorry for your family's loss." Embarrassed for missing the social cues, I turned to her left and made my way to the narrow side aisle and to the back of the church, where there were still a few open seats.

"We need to get together for coffee sometime," Susan said as I walked off. I feigned a smile and continued toward the back.

Before I got halfway down the side aisle, I noticed Faith Jones, the church secretary waving frantically to me. She pointed to an open seat beside her. *Oh, these spunky church people drive me nuts.* I looked to the back and then to Faith, whose smile lit up the room. *What the heck?* It was only for an hour. Surely I could stand her bubbling optimism that long. I slipped past a few people in that row and sat next to Faith. Besides, maybe she could give me the dirt on some people.

"I'm pleasantly surprised to see you today," Faith said. "I see you've gotten to know Susan."

"Is she always that…friendly?" I asked. I immediately regretted it. Faith was as friendly as they come. I'm sure she took offense. "That sounded awful."

"No, no. Susan is most definitely friendly. She's a physical touch person, a hugger." Faith placed her hand on my arm. "But she's only that way to people she likes."

"She did that the first time we met," I said. "She doesn't know me enough to like me." It was an awkward show of affection. I never was much of a touchy-feely person, and I was very protective of my personal space.

"Oh," Faith began, squeezing my arm. "You sure caught the attention of our Jonathan." I glanced across the aisle. As soon as Jonathan noticed I was looking, he smiled and waved. "Don't you think he's handsome?" Faith beamed. "He needs a confident young woman like you to keep him in check."

Seriously? That boy needed a leash. "Sorry, but I'm really not interested. Besides it wouldn't be appropriate." That was as nice as I could be. I turned away and stared at the baptistery. How could they carry on as if nothing happened here? He died this week…right there. Surely, a funeral home would have been more appropriate.

"The nerve!" Faith said under her breath. I followed her stare and locked in on a middle-aged couple in line to see Susan.

Unable to assess the disposition of the couple, I asked, "What did they do?"

"Oh," Faith said, putting her hand over her mouth as soon as she realized how loud she said it. Faith glanced around, but no one was paying any attention to her. She whispered to me, "Pastor Mark was doing marriage counseling one night while I was still in the office, and Mr. Cook threw a fit. He screamed all kinds of obscene things at Pastor Mark and said he ought to kick his…well, you know."

"Really?" It piqued my interest. "How long ago?" I continued to observe the couple, especially the man, hoping to see something unusual when he met up with Susan.

"About two weeks ago, I think." Faith scratched her head. "No, come to think of it, that was a week ago Monday."

My eyes widened, and I turned my head. "A week before he was killed?"

The couple in front of us turned. The woman put a finger over her lips and said, "Shhh."

"Sorry," I whispered.

Faith whispered in my ear. "If we didn't know it was Alvaro, I'd say look into Mr. Cook's alibi. But who am I to tell you? You're the detectives."

Some detectives! We jumped at the first possible suspect and threw the book at him. "It seems a lot of people were frustrated or angry with your pastor."

"Yes," she said with a sigh. "He did have a tendency to rub people the wrong way." Faith motioned to the packed room. "But I guarantee you, there's not a person in this room that didn't believe Pastor Mark was genuine in his faith and passionate about the truth. He may not have tempered his words with political correctness, but he worked his tail off to fight for the right things."

"I'll admit," I whispered. "I don't like religious people very much…too much pain in my past…but I'm beginning to warm up to *him*."

At first, Faith looked disappointed, but when I explained my statement, she softened and seemed to understand. "Pastor Mark always spoke about people the church has hurt over the years, even with good intentions." Faith gently patted my leg. "He would have loved you."

I've heard that before. Besides, I had enough "love" from ministers. I turned abruptly when I heard a gravelly voice behind me.

It was Duke Stearns. "Surprised you're here, Detective."

He called me "Detective." Sweet!

"Surprised to be here," I admitted. "It's strange being here after this Tuesday, but I feel for his family." It was the truth. From the first moment I met Susan Ripley, I felt something was amiss… something different. No one who's suffering her kind of loss tries this hard to comfort everyone else. I wasn't sure if Susan was some kind of Stepford wife, or if she was the real deal. "I hope they can carry on."

"I do too," he said. It was strange to hear this man whisper. He seemed too hard to be capable of any kind of softness. "It's going to be really hard on her. Thankfully, she has her own job and works out of the home." Duke looked at Susan and then the kids. "I imagine she'll head back to St. Louis before long."

So, he does have a heart. Maybe I misjudged him. "Who will take over in Mark's...?" Absence wasn't the right word. Thankfully, before I thought of the right one, Duke answered the incomplete question.

"The elders will until we put a pastor search committee together. Things like this either bring us together or drive us apart."

"Well said." In his own strange way, Duke cared for the people of the church. As the music stopped, Duke patted my shoulder softly and leaned back into his pew.

An older gentleman walked up to the podium and adjusted the microphone lower. "On behalf of the family," he began, "I want to welcome you and thank you so much for your calls, your prayers, and your presence today." He was short and feeble in appearance, but the more he spoke, the stronger he seemed to be. He smiled. "I know you all smelled that wonderful Baptist cooking," he said. "We want to invite you to stay and fellowship with the family and each other as soon as the service is over. The family will have a private graveside service later this afternoon."

I listened as he spoke of his friendship with Mark Ripley, of that mission trip they shared, of Mark's passion to make sure everyone had an opportunity to know Jesus. That part struck a nerve, and my body instinctively quivered. He went on to describe Mark's passion for the church and the community, gesturing to the crowd as he did. He laughed and said, "Mark once told me of his family's hardheaded nature, saying his hometown people would say, 'You can tell a Ripley coming a mile away, but you can't tell him much.'" Everyone laughed. Susan laughed and then wiped her eyes with a tissue. She was putting up a good front, but I could tell she was barely holding herself together.

The preacher shared so many positive things about Mark Ripley; I began to believe he was a saint. The minister got me thinking...of the past. He said, "One thing Mark once told me that I will never forget. 'Own the truth, or the truth will own you.'"

The truth? Whose truth? On that thought, I went into autopilot and instinctively pulled myself into emotional check, in defense mode, letting the words bounce off harmlessly. Without realizing it, my old walls flashed into place, and my heart hardened like Pharoah's. I looked at the wispy gray hair on the top of his head and slowed my breathing.

When the man sat down and the music played, I stared straight at the baptistery window, focusing on the area Alvaro Garcia had slammed his hands. Of course, the windows had been cleaned, but I knew the exact spot from the video. I'd mastered the art of redirection at the age of fourteen. It served me well over the years.

Faith leaned in and whispered a few things, but my mind didn't allow them to register. I nodded politely and stared at the baptistery. After a few more testimonies of the young pastor's dedication and a song called "It is Well," the older man approached the pulpit again. "I would be remiss if I didn't share the Gospel story with you right now. Mark would want it that way." So, as he had promised, the man told the story of Jesus and ended with a plea that everyone there invite Him into their hearts. I rolled my eyes. I knew that emotional trick from my father.

The funeral ended with another invitation for everyone to stay and eat lunch at the church. They rolled the casket down the aisle; Susan, Hannah, and Danny followed it out. I waded through the crowd like a salmon swimming upstream. I pushed against the flow, trying desperately to reach the exit.

Right before I made it, someone grabbed my elbow and held it firmly. I turned, expecting it to be Duke Stearns, but instead, I was met with a grand, boyish smile. "Going somewhere?" he asked.

"Mr. Williams."

"What did I tell you, Detective? It's just Jonathan."

"In that case," I said, "it's just Abbey." I in no way intended that to be taken as an encouragement to further the conversation. Unfortunately, he took it that way.

His eyebrows lifted, and his smile widened. He pushed through the crowd and helped me reach the exit. "Well, Abbey." He paused. "Do you ever have time for social activities?" *Are you kidding me? Are you pushing for a date?* I had to cut this off right now.

"Not since I joined Homicide. We're on call twenty-four, seven." It wasn't exactly true, but it sounded nicer than, "I'm not interested," or "This really isn't appropriate."

He brandished a wide smile. "If you have an occasional moment and would like some company," he began, "give me a call. I believe you have my number."

I said nothing. The crowd thinned out, and I noticed a teenage girl staring our way. I looked away and then looked back. The girl was still staring. She was young, probably in her early teens. She had a woman's figure for such a young girl, but the look on her face betrayed the pain she held inside. Her eyes were dark and distant. I recognized the look all too well. "Who's that?" I asked.

Jonathan turned. His smile disappeared. "That's Skylar. She's one of our youth." He waved. Skylar put the sleeve of her blouse in her mouth and chewed on it. Her eyes never left mine. I couldn't tell if she was studying me or sizing me up. "She's had a rough go of things," Jonathan said. "Her mom left her last year, and her dad's really tough on her."

"Tough on her? How? Does he abuse her?" I asked, suddenly jumping into my detective's role.

"I…uh…I'm not sure." Skylar appeared to be studying us, then walked quickly through the doors leading to the fellowship hall. "She's a sad case."

"Where does she live?" I asked.

"Right across the creek from the church. Why?"

"I'd like to talk to her," I said.

89

"It would be better if you spoke to her here with me. Skylar is extremely shy and doesn't trust people she doesn't know." *That sounds familiar.* "She's at church every time the doors are open, so you could join me Wednesday night," he said. "I think she's more comfortable here than her own house."

"We'll see."

"Don't forget to call if you have time."

He wouldn't stop hitting on me. I looked at my watch. "I'm afraid I need to run."

"Another time perhaps?" Jonathan turned and engaged in a conversation with a young couple exiting the service.

I made mental notes to follow up on two things: Mr. Cook's comment to Pastor Mark and the young girl named Skylar. Personally, the girl was of primary interest to me. If she was being neglected or abused, I'd have to do something. Too much about her reminded me of my younger self.

Chapter Sixteen

4:37 pm—Home of Lieutenant Matthew Daniels

Matthew Daniels had been my Lieutenant at East Precinct. I rented a room from him and his wife for the past three years, prior to moving into Harmony Apartments on the first of July. They were the closest thing to family I had. "Lieutenant, I appreciate you and Sherry letting me come over and let off some steam."

"I keep saying you don't have to call me Lieutenant anymore. You're not at my precinct. You can call me Matt."

"I heard you, but it just wouldn't seem right," I said. I could never call him Matt. I respected him way too much to act as if I were his equal. He would always be Lieutenant Daniels to me.

He watched silently as I put everything I had into each punch. The heavy bag jerked and clattered on its chains. I battered it with an incessant string of punches, occasionally spinning and striking the bag with my forearm or heel. I would always pretend it was the man who violated me when I was fourteen. I only wished I was this strong and knowledgeable back then. I could have stopped him. I felt the sweat running down my back. I had to wipe my forehead several times with my wristbands to keep it out of my eyes.

"I haven't seen you this worked up in months," Lieutenant Daniels said.

I ignored him. I didn't want to begin this discussion. Instead of responding, I continued my barrage of punches. I was striking so hard, my knuckles bled through the white tape on each hand.

Finally, fully exhausted and sore, I stopped, rested my hands on my knees, and breathed heavily. "Too many things…hitting me all at once. My old methods just aren't working."

"You know what I'm going to tell you. Don't you, Abbey?"

"Yes, sir. See the shrink."

He laughed. "She's not a shrink," he said. "You make it sound like a person has to be crazy to talk with a counselor."

"Isn't that what you think? I'm crazy?" I waited for a response. "That I'm going to have another breakdown? Well, I can handle it," I snapped. "I always have." I hit the bag two more times. We'd been down this road a hundred times over the past three years. I knew he meant well, but my inner thoughts were *my* inner thoughts. I wasn't about to reveal my weaknesses and quirks to some stranger.

In his typical wise way, Lieutenant Daniels waited a few moments before he said, "Abbey, Metro has counselors for a reason. We've all seen them from time to time. It's the nature of our profession." He always had a way of making things sound nice, better than they really were. He called it "normalizing."

"Yeah, like you've ever gone." I grabbed a towel and wiped the sweat from my face and neck.

"Of course, I have," he said. "Anyone worth his salt…her salt… will take advantage of the opportunity to vent frustrations, share pain, and get advice from a professional counselor. God knows everyone else is eager to give advice without solicitation."

I laughed. "When in the world did you need someone's advice?"

He transitioned into a pensive mood. His features changed… darkened. His eyes glazed over. "Did I ever tell you about the first time I responded to a fatal car accident?"

"I don't think so," I said. I walked over to the basement steps and sat down.

"I was working in North Carolina. The call went out and I responded. When I got there the car had flipped, the metal twisted and contorted. A woman and her two sons…I think they were middle schoolers. Anyway, they stood there and stared at the

car. She was in tears. They were in shock. I came up to them and realized someone was still in the car…the driver."

He paused to take a deep breath. It was obvious this incident still caused him emotional grief. "You don't have to tell me, Lieutenant, if you don't want to."

He took another deep breath and wiped the water gathering in his eyes. "It's okay. You need to hear this. Twenty-one years ago, and it still chokes me up." He looked over at me. "I knelt beside the car and looked in. I immediately wished I hadn't. He was a mess. I had no doubt he was dead." Lieutenant Daniels looked down as if he was there on site, staring at the deceased driver of the vehicle. "So, I told myself, this family needs to be comforted. I need to say something positive to them. I walked back where they were standing and said…if you can believe it…I said, 'Everything's going to be okay.'"

He wiped tears that were now flowing down his cheek. "Immediately, the older boy said, 'No, Mister, it's not going to be okay. That's my dad in that car.' It hit me like a ton of bricks. I wanted to get out of there as fast as I could. Well, the other first-responders arrived and were hustling to get the body out of the car. One guy said to the family, 'Get out of the way.' I grabbed him by the arm and jerked him around. I can't tell you what I said, but he got my message and gave them a little more respect and compassion."

Lieutenant Daniels stood. "It took me a couple of months, and a lot of prodding from my partner, to admit I needed help in processing that moment. I took advantage of the counseling services for six months. It still gets me, but I stopped having the nightmares and trying to take back what I said." He put his hand on my shoulder. "The second reason I saw a counselor was for my failing marriage. This job demands a lot, and it can destroy a marriage if you're not careful. It did mine. Thank God, I met Sherry. She understands the nature of the profession, and I've learned a little more balance along the way."

"She's a good woman, and you're a really good man. You make a great couple."

"Nice deflection. My point is that you don't have to carry the world on your back, Abbey. And you certainly don't have to carry all the pain by yourself."

"Sh…oot, you're good, Lieutenant."

"Nice catch. You know how I feel about vulgar language."

I smiled and started to walk back to the heavy bag. "Why see a counselor when I have you?" I turned and winked, putting my walls right back in place.

"Come on, Abbey. You didn't come here just to hit the bag. Spit it out."

I stepped to the bag and put my arms around it. I leaned the bulk of my weight on the bag, not because I was physically tired, but I was wiped emotionally, and that was not comfortable. "I don't even know how to start."

"As I always say, the beginning is the best place." He tapped the step where he still sat and waited for me to rejoin him.

I shared my frustration with the changeover to homicide, how, unlike the East Precinct, I could be in a room full of people and still feel alone. Yes, even though I contributed and felt appreciated for some of my insights, at the end of the day, the detectives all went their separate ways. I shared everything about the Ripley case that haunted my dreams and waking hours. I included new evidence about the Cooks. I confessed my anger and humiliation, having to apologize to Detective Tidwell and agree to no longer pursue anything about Mark Ripley's murder. "He's so apathetic it kills me. I mean why continue to work when you don't care? He's old enough to retire with full pension and benefits, especially with twenty-five years on the force."

Lieutenant Daniels smiled. To him, fifty-four wasn't old. It's funny how one's perspective changes over time. He knew me well enough to understand my incessant drive for excellence, and he understood that I expected the same of everyone. That's what I

learned in the army. No weak links…perfection from all. Lieutenant Daniels also knew that no officer or detective worked in a vacuum. He told me so. "You need to give him some grace, Abbey."

I scoffed. "Grace? He's a quitter. No, he isn't. I can respect a quitter. At least someone who quits makes a choice. Working without trying is…inexcusable. I hate apathy!"

"Listen. I don't know him personally, but I do recognize the name. Before you write him off, do your due diligence and research his past. We all have our tragedies, and we all carry that weight around our necks. You of all people should know that, Abbey."

I nodded. He was the only person that knew my past outside of the participants. Then it sunk in. Research Tidwell? "What happened to him? What do you know?"

"Look it up. Maybe you'll have a little compassion towards Detective Tidwell. Just as you put up your emotional walls, he uses apathy as his means of self-preservation." Lieutenant Daniels put his arm around my shoulder. "You're good at what you do, but you get so driven you forget we protect and serve people, not just solve crimes. You need to remember, treat people as people not just as clues that get you closer to the answer. If we can't appreciate the people we serve, we're no better than those who use and abuse them."

He'd pushed too far. "I'm nothing like the…" *Abuse!* Wait. I shifted gears immediately. "Hey, there's this girl named Skylar at Living Water. She lives right behind the church. The youth minister thinks her father may abuse her, but he has no proof."

"Want me to look into it?" he asked.

"Would you?" I gave him a pleading puppy dog face.

"Hey, stop that. I already offered." I hugged him. He feigned disgust. "You're nasty. Go take a shower before supper. I'm not letting you sit at our table without one." He wiped my sweat off his face. "I know Sherry would never say anything to you about your stench, but I'm brutally honest, remember?" He looked at his watch. "She'll have supper ready at six."

Chapter Seventeen

8:56 pm—Harmony Apartments

Finally home, I lay at one end of the couch with my head propped up on a throw pillow. I glanced at the night sky. A storm was brewing. After all these years, I'd finally returned to the city of my birth. That's about the only claim I had to Nashville. My family left for Central America when I was seven months old, only to return occasionally a week or two at a time to raise money for my father's mission efforts.

After three tough years in Nicaragua, our first mission field, my father moved the family to Honduras, where we stayed seven years. My father started several churches across the small country and returned to each regularly to train the young leaders. When I was ten and a half, we moved to Guatemala, where they remain. Shortly after my eighteenth birthday, I left for Grafenwöhr, Germany and my three-year stint in the Army as a part of the 709th Battalion, a unit of the 18th Military Police Brigade. Ever Vigilant!

I joined the Army as an escape from Central America and my family. It was the furthest location from home. The decision was one of convenience. In the Army, I would have free room and board, and I could continue to build my savings until I eventually moved out on my own. I loved the Army. It was really the first time boundaries made sense to me. Everything had structure, and the rules were consistent. The people with power over me were fair and stable. My need for structure and my drive for justice both found a home in the Army. It was there that I worked diligently

on my reading and writing abilities, doing my best to become a new person and put the past completely behind me. Having a new name made it even easier.

After serving my three-year contract, I opted to return to the States and continue in the only legitimate career I'd really ever known…law enforcement. I still felt so young, only twenty-one years old. With the help of my post commander and his connection to the Chief of Police, I got a job with Nashville's East Precinct.

The phone rang jerking me out of my daydream. Thunder boomed outside my window. I answered the phone.

"Hello?"

"Is this Abbey?" It was a woman's soft voice.

"Yes. And this is?"

"Susan Ripley."

Why was she calling me at this time of the night?

"Is something wrong?"

"No." She paused. "I…I just wanted to thank you for coming to Mark's…"

"You're welcome. It's the least I could do."

There was a long silence. I expected to hear children's voices in the background, but it was strangely silent. "I wondered if we could meet for coffee tomorrow."

"Coffee? Maybe sometime, Susan, but tomorrow is out of the question. We have a few cases to work on, and I'll…"

"I understand." There was disappointment in her voice, a sense of loneliness. Just what I didn't need right now.

"I'm sorry, but we keep pretty busy from the time we wake to the time we go to sleep."

"I know this may sound invasive, but why did you change your name? You said your name used to be Hannah."

I wondered why I'd opened that door. I searched for a way of answering without revealing too much. "I was eighteen, upset with my father, and desperately needed a fresh start. It made perfect sense at the time."

"Why Abbey Rhodes?" she asked.

Surprised by the direction of her questions, I answered, "Because my dad hated the Beatles."

She laughed. "I wondered if your name had anything to do with them."

"I didn't really like them, but I knew of that album. It seemed like a cool name."

"It is. What did you say your given name was?"

"Hannah Leah Abelard."

"Biblical names. Is he in the ministry?"

Not going there. I felt the heat rise to my face. Instinctively, I balled my hand into a fist. *Take a breath, Abbey.*

"You don't have to answer if it makes you uncomfortable."

She could sense my mood over the phone. Before I could catch myself, I said, "Yeah, he named me after a woman who gave up her child and a woman her husband didn't want."

"There's more to their stories than that, Abbey."

I'm sure there was, but I wasn't in the mood to listen. "Listen, Susan, I'm exhausted and have to catch some shuteye." Before she could respond, I added, "We'll talk more soon," and hung up. I hoped she'd forget about me and move on.

I took a deep breath, settled my nerves, and opened my laptop. I could tell my window of sleep was gone for the night. I googled Detective Sam Tidwell, Nashville Police Department. I perused the various listings that popped up with the search. I found everything from his LinkedIn account to his interviews, to even his own Facebook page, which by the look of it, hadn't been updated in years. After fifteen minutes of searching and reading, I found the article to which Lieutenant Daniels alluded.

"Decorated Detective Suffers Personal Tragedy." I looked at the date. Three years ago. I read and gasped. I scrolled down to the images and the caption that read, "Detective Sam Tidwell discovers the bodies of his wife and daughter." Next to that picture, they had a family photo. *Oh, God. She looks like me!* I

studied the picture. Darken his daughter's hair and we could be twins. Creepy!

According to the article, Detective Tidwell had an exemplary record of solving cases and compiling evidence for the D.A. With a conviction rate in the high nineties, he was the talk of Nashville. It also mentioned that he and his wife separated due to his long absences from home and his obsession with the job. Feeling neglected, his wife and daughter moved out of the home and into a small apartment, the very apartment where someone broke in just three weeks later, brutally raping and murdering the two women. Detective Tidwell discovered the bodies. Feeling personally responsible for their demise, he vowed not to stop until he found their killers.

I searched and searched for the results of his efforts, but I never found anything stating what finally came of the case. *I'll ask Sarge tomorrow. Surely, he'll know.* I closed the laptop. Is that what he was trying to tell me?

I called Lieutenant Daniels to see what happened, but his phone went straight to voicemail. He was asleep already. I grabbed a quart of Haagen-Dazs Double Belgian Chocolate Chip ice cream and a large spoon…my favorite comfort food. I would just run harder tomorrow morning. I stared out the window of the twelfth-floor apartment and ate several bites, savoring each one. Flashes of lightning filled the skies over Nashville.

Lieutenant Daniels' advice ran like a broken record through my mind. Was I guilty of using people? The prospect of it haunted me all night. I tossed and turned until about four o'clock in the morning before falling asleep. One and a half hours later, the alarm buzzed. *Great.* I reluctantly rolled out of bed and forced myself into the shower. I'd run later.

Chapter Eighteen

Monday, October 30, 10:15 am—Homicide

Back at Homicide, I absentmindedly flipped through the case folder. My mind was obviously elsewhere. All this time I had worked with Detective Tidwell, I never even asked if he had family. When I was a part of East Precinct, my day shift group knew each other and socialized with each other. They were family, an environment Lieutenant Daniels worked hard to foster. Since I moved over to homicide, I worried so much about earning the right to be a detective that I missed the most important evidence placed before me. My partner was depressed and alone...as alone as I was, but he probably didn't have anyone like the Daniels. Every day he came to work, he was faced with the fact that he had failed his family.

Not only had he neglected them, but he had also failed to solve their case. A man who solved nearly every case he had ever taken couldn't solve the one that mattered the most. His desk put him fifteen feet from the Cold Case unit, knowing they couldn't solve it either. His wife and daughter died horrible deaths, and he was powerless to avenge them. Top that off with the fact his new partner looked exactly like his daughter.

I stared blankly at the page before me, less interested in my newest case than I was in a three-year-old cold case. I wanted so desperately to reach out to him, to offer him comfort. How do you start a conversation like that? You can't just say, "Hey Tidwell, I hear you lost your family," or "Tidwell, I'm so sorry about your family. I didn't know." If he wanted to talk about it, he would have

broached the subject himself. I wondered why there were no pictures on his side of the cubicle. Now I knew. Who would want to face that tragedy every day? I understood. My half of the cubicle was void of pictures as well.

"Are you deaf or just ignoring me?"

"What?" I turned in my chair. "How long have you been standing there?"

"A few minutes," Tidwell said. "You're deep down some rabbit hole. I've been trying to get your attention the whole time. What's got you?" he asked.

I wanted to tell him, wanted to get it over with and behind us. "Just in a funk," I said. *Coward!*

"I know what you mean," he said. "Tomorrow's Halloween. I hate Halloween. All the crazies come out of the woodwork."

That's it! They were attacked on Halloween. "Yeah, some of the worst murders take place on Halloween." Come on, Tidwell, take the bait. I waited, but he just stared at the wall calendar. "I don't know if it's the anonymity of the masks, or that evil just rises to the occasion," I added, trying to spur him on.

"Probably a little of both." He sat in his chair and sorted through some pages on his desk.

"Detective Tidwell, there's no good way to say this," I started. "I've been trying to find one all morning."

"Say what, Rhodes?" he asked with his back to me. "Does this have to do with the Ripley case?"

"No, sir. I'm really sorry about your family. I just found out." I could feel the air being sucked out of the cubicle. *Say something, please.* He didn't. "I googled you…"

"You what?" He turned and looked at me. "You just up and googled me for no reason?" Now he was angry. "And you just happened to find an old article about my family?"

"Well…kind of."

"Why didn't you just ask me?" I didn't have an answer. "Why would you do that behind my back?"

"I was told by a friend that you had a tragedy in your life," I said.

"A friend? You talk about me with your friends?"

I bit my lip. "Well, now that you put it that way, it sounds creepy." He shook his head in disgust. I watched the color of his face change from a pale white to a dark red. His jaw muscles pulsed as he gritted his teeth. A large vein on his forehead bulged. He turned away. "I was complaining. Okay? I was pissed that I had to give up on the Ripley case when I felt the killer was still out there."

"I knew it was about that case." He spun back around and rolled his chair up to mine, invading my precious space. "And that led to my family? You're unbelievable, Rhodes! What were you looking for? Some dirt on me so you could keep looking for a murderer we already have?"

"What? No!" I rolled my chair back the few inches I had left in the cubicle, but he made up the distance, pressing his knees against mine. *You want the truth. Here it comes.* "I was complaining that you didn't care enough to rule out all the possibilities before jumping to a conclusion. Okay?" I stopped. Something flashed in his eyes. He rolled back to his side of the cubicle and spun his chair away from me. "I was having a grand old pity party, okay? My old Lieutenant said we all have our own tragedies. He encouraged me to find out about yours. He said it might change the way I feel."

"Did it?" he asked in a defeated tone. "Did it change how you feel about me?" he asked. "Do you pity me now? Huh, Rhodes?"

"I don't know exactly what I feel," I admitted. "I just know I'm sorry you've had to carry that around with you these past three years." I started to say something more but thought better of it. There was a long, awkward silence.

"Spit it out, Rhodes. Don't stop now."

You asked for it. "Do I remind you of her?"

"Yes." Before I could ask another question, he got up from his chair and sulked out of the room.

Well, Abbey, that was awful. You are heartless. I turned my attention back to the file and ran over the evidence Detective Spence,

a member of our day homicide team, gathered on a case he was working. No matter how hard I tried, I couldn't wrap my mind around anything but Tidwell's tragic past.

I rose from my chair and walked to the other end of the room. "Hey, Detective Rollins." He was the lead investigator of the Cold Case Unit.

"What's on your mind, Rhodes?" he asked, not looking up from a toxicology report.

"Do you have the Tidwell case?"

"It's in evidence storage. Why?" He looked up. "Think you can solve a three-year-old case no one else can? We put everything we had into that case." I could hear the resentment in his voice. Why not add someone else to my "hate me" list? "Go ahead. Knock yourself out," he said. "They're listed by date. October 31, 2020."

"Thanks." I left for the evidence room, not really knowing why. Was I going to try to solve the unsolvable case, or was I just looking for more information about Detective Tidwell and his family? I signed in and walked through the rows of shelves until I found a box that read, "Tidwell—October 31, 2020."

I moved the box to an empty table and pulled up a chair. As I laid out the pieces of evidence, I studied the photos, read the reports, and quickly realized why this was a cold case. The DNA matched nothing in our system. Even though they had prints, the murderer had no priors. The only thing they had to go by was the unique way he staged the bodies.

I grabbed a picture. I looked so much like his daughter it was frightening. It was like looking at my own murder pictures. He had to face me each day being constantly reminded of his dead daughter. She was my age too. I finally returned the box to its shelf and signed out of the storage room.

Upon returning to my desk, Detective Tidwell asked, "Where have you been?"

"Evidence room," I said, busying myself with the folder on my desk.

"Anything I need to be aware of?" he asked.

"No. I was just checking up on something." I purposely sifted through several pages to make some noise. "It turned out to be nothing."

"Hey, Rhodes, Sorry I jumped on you earlier. It's just a bad time of year for me," he said. "We good?"

"Sure. Detective Tidwell?"

"I keep telling you, just call me Tidwell or Sam. No need for formality."

"Okay." I would never call him Sam. He was a senior detective. I wanted to ask him so many things, but I knew it wasn't the right time. I wanted to know more about his family. I wanted to ask why he stayed on if everything reminded him of them. I wanted to talk more about Mark Ripley's murder...tell him about Mr. Cook...tell him about the poor girl named Skylar. Instead, we sat in silence, pretending to study the cases set before us.

Chapter Nineteen

6:20 pm—Home of Brandon and Melissa Cook

Another secret interview. I couldn't help myself. I couldn't cut the switch off even if I wanted to. I knocked and waited. I knocked again. I could hear stirring in the house. Someone finally unlocked the door and opened it. "Detective Rhodes?" she asked. I nodded and held out my badge for Melissa Cook to confirm I was the one they were expecting. "Please, come in."

"Thank you." I followed her to a room with a couch, a love seat, two recliners, and a forty-two-inch television. Everything was out of date. I glanced at the couch, which had dark stains on the fabric, and decided to sit on the loveseat. I could tell the recliners were a "his and hers" set, both facing the television.

"Brandon, Detective Rhodes is here."

He muted the television and rocked forward until he could get his feet on the ground. He followed Melissa to the couch and sat. "What can we do for you, Detective?"

"First, I appreciate your taking the time to meet with me. I'll try to keep this brief."

He glanced over at the screen, then looked back at me. "We'll answer what we can. You say this has to do with Pastor Mark's death?"

"Yes." I took out my phone. "Do you mind if I record this? That way I don't have to take notes and can concentrate on the two of you."

Melissa looked at her husband before answering. "We don't mind. What does his death have to do with us?"

"More than likely, nothing," I said. I always liked to put them at ease first. "I just like to cross my t's and dot my i's." I looked at my notes, which had nothing to do with either of the Cooks, flipped a page or two, and then pretended to find the right entry. "It says here that you were receiving counseling from Pastor Mark. Is that true?" Of course, that was from Faith's mouth, not my notes.

"Yes," he said. "We'd seen him for six sessions."

"May I ask what you were trying to resolve?"

Melissa looked at her husband again. This time, she waited for him to answer. He cleared his throat and finally said, "We were having marriage problems." Melissa put her hand over his.

Were? I'd follow up on that later. "Let me be blunt, Mr. Cook." I leaned forward. "I have a witness who claims you threatened Pastor Mark at the end of your last session." I paused and watched their reactions.

He nodded. "I did. He pushed me too far, made me see a part of myself I didn't like."

"So, you threatened to kill him?" I asked.

He lowered his head and stared at his hands. Why did he look at his hands? "I'm ashamed to admit it, but yes. I threatened his life. I lashed out in anger and said stupid things I regret terribly."

Melissa put her arm around him and kissed him on the cheek. "A few weeks ago, he wouldn't have owned up to something like that. He would have lashed out and deflected blame on someone else."

Owned up to? Deflected blame? Words from their sessions, I'd bet. I nodded and then focused on Mr. Cook. "Is that why you killed him?" I asked.

He looked up, his face full of bewilderment. "Killed him? Me?"

That was not exactly a denial. He looked at his hands again. *Why does he keep looking at his hands? Guilt?* I waited. I didn't have to wait long.

"No. I didn't have any reason to kill him," Brandon Cook

answered. "Why…if it wasn't for Pastor Mark, we'd probably be divorced or on our way to one."

I tilted my head. I ran that sentence over in my mind before saying, "I'm confused. You're giving him credit now, but you threatened to kill him just over a week ago?"

He showed a look of confusion on his face too. "I know. It doesn't make sense." He turned to his wife and smiled. "It took someone with balls…Oh, I'm sorry." He grimaced.

"I've heard worse," I said. You'd be amazed at what was said in front of me in the Army. I had to admit I liked it…not the language…being treated as one of the guys. "Go on."

"Well, Pastor Mark didn't mince words with me. I guess he knew I needed a big push." Brandon paused, seeming to consider his words carefully. "I needed to change. I kept blaming Melissa for all of our troubles." He turned to her again. "Pastor Mark and I both knew I was the main issue, my thick-headed pride." He looked back at me. "He called me the next day to check on me and ask if we could meet one on one."

"Did you?" I asked, making a quick note in my book. "Meet with him?"

"Yes, and it made all the difference. I'm sorry he's no longer with us. The world needs more people like him."

"What do you mean?" I asked.

"Preachers who really care…care enough to say the hard things instead of all this Pollyanna crap." Brandon looked down at his hands and played with his wedding band. "I just wish someone could have said those things years ago. And the difference is…I could tell he cared about us." He turned back to his wife. "I guess I didn't make it easy. Did I?"

She shook her head and wiped a tear that formed in her eye. "No. You didn't." She looked at me. "We owe Brother Mark everything."

I smiled despite my doubts. Maybe Mark Ripley was the exception. Maybe he was genuine. Maybe he just didn't have enough time to mess up yet. I secretly hoped it was the positive. "Well, I appreciate your time," I said, standing up and closing my notebook. "You've told me everything I needed to know."

We said our goodbyes, and I drove away. Nothing made sense. The more I heard, the more I realized no one had a good reason to kill him. Another thought struck me at that moment. I'd hoped Sarge didn't catch wind of this.

Chapter Twenty

Back at Homicide the next morning, I sat alone in our cubicle. I leaned over the partition and asked, "Hey Spence, have you seen Tidwell? I can't find him anywhere."

He pointed to a circled date on the calendar attached to Tidwell's cubicle wall. "It's the thirty-first of October. He always takes this day off."

"Oh." I turned back to my own side of the cubicle. This was all starting to make sense. I took the opportunity to pull out an extra copy I made of the Ripley murder notes. I rolled back to the hallway and looked in all three directions. Satisfied no one was looking for me, I rolled back to my desk.

I couldn't say exactly why I thought Alvaro Garcia was innocent. It was a gut feeling. Was it just because he told me so? How many criminals say they're innocent? Nearly all of them. But he swore on his patron saint. That's not something a Honduran Catholic would do lightly. Every single piece of evidence pointed to him. Every motive and probable cause solidified his guilt, and yet Alvaro, like many of the others, claimed Pastor Mark reached out to him and wanted to set things straight, to put the incident behind them. And the time he was in the building was the bare minimum it would take to pull off the murder. Everything would have to be perfect. And there's no way he had time to clean up.

I looked at the names of the other suspects. Owen Jenkins

had multiple witnesses confirming his alibi for the murder window. The only time unaccountable was the middle of the day, and even that wouldn't have been long enough for him to leave the site and return in time. Duke Stearns disagreed with the pastor, didn't like his vision for the church, but had an odd sense of respect for the man. Besides that, he was on a truck run in Kentucky, verified by GPS. Jonathan Williams had the strength to do it, but he too had a solid alibi. Two of his roommates swore he was home throwing up that morning and the previous day as well. Food poisoning. None of the other staff members had reason to kill the man.

Quentin Green had moved on from the broken real estate deal. He too had a solid alibi for that morning. The Cooks seemed genuinely grateful for Pastor Mark's blunt advice. That left Alvaro, who not only had a motive but the means (strong man with large hands) and the opportunity. The neighbor put him at the church during the murder window, and Alvaro raced away. He claimed it was because of the blood he discovered, but his vehicle was the only one there besides Mark's. And the killer cleaned up the mess. So, either Alvaro did it all, or he walked in right after the murder before it was cleaned. That would mean the murderer was still there when Alvaro came in. No way that happened.

I put my head in my hands. I hated to admit I was wrong. Sarge was right. I just needed to let go…put it all behind me. I needed a distraction. My phone rang.

"Rhodes."

"Hey Rhodes, it's Olson. Remember me?"

"Very funny," I said. "I've only been gone three months."

"Really?" he feigned surprise. "It seems like years."

"Aww." I leaned back in my chair and put my feet up on the edge of the desk. "How are things in the East?" He caught me up to speed with my East Precinct buddies. At one point I said, "I miss you guys. It was so much fun at East." Then I sank down in my chair realizing that came out a little too loud for our quiet office. Embarrassment burned my face.

"We're getting together Saturday morning at that climbing course in Franklin, and everyone wanted to know if you'd come."

I tried to speak softer. "Like what time morning? Not like crack of dark early?"

"No. We'll let you get your beauty sleep. Lord knows you need it."

"Hey!"

"Just kidding. Like you need any more sleep."

"Well, Olson, that was the nicest thing you've ever said to me. Of course, I'll come." I pushed the files back into the folder and chit-chatted a bit before saying, "I can't tell you how much I need this. It's been a rough week. It will be nice to see the gang again."

We talked a little more, worked out the details, and said our goodbyes. Sounded like fun. I needed fun.

A head popped up over the top of my cubicle. "Sounds like a date."

"Spence!" I pushed his head back over the top and into his cubicle. "We're just good friends."

"Sure, Rhodes. If that makes you feel better." We both laughed. It was the first time I'd laughed at homicide. It felt good.

Chapter Twenty-one

11:23 am—Office of Barbara Humphrey, Doctor of Psychology

Sam Tidwell slumped in a chair across from his psychologist, Dr. Barbara Humphrey. He stared out of the window to his right. The skies overcast, a light drizzle in the air. A perfect day for depression.

The third anniversary of Kathy's and Molly's murders hit him just as hard as the first two. In many ways, that day also marked the end of his life. His house had become a museum more than a home. Even though they didn't live there the last few months of their lives, his wife and daughter kept many of their clothes and keepsakes at their original home with Sam. After their murders, he refused to touch any of it, feeling as if leaving it intact kept their memories alive. Instead, it kept them in limbo, neither alive nor dead.

He settled into his new reality without family and was going along unhindered until the day Abbey Rhodes strolled into Homicide and upended his world. He thought she was either an apparition or a sign that he'd finally lost his mind. Turns out, it was neither.

At first, it was just her looks that made him uneasy. Lately, it was her mannerisms and her willful defiance of the norm that triggered feelings from the past. His new partner had no qualms about challenging the status quo, and because of it, something stirred deep within him. Combine her presence with the third anniversary of their deaths, and he felt as though he stood on a precipice about to fall, completely out of balance and control.

"She asked if she reminded me of Molly."

"How did that make you feel?" she asked.

"I don't know."

"Now, Sam, let's go back to the precise moment she asked the question. What was the first emotion you experienced?"

He thought for a moment before answering. "It was true. I'd been struggling with that since she came to Homicide. It's uncanny how much they look alike."

"Sam, you are stating facts. I want you to express emotions. Given they do look alike, how did you feel when she asked?"

"I don't believe in reincarnation, but this…this is causing me to doubt."

"And how does it *feel*, Sam?"

He turned his glance from the window to his psychologist. "When she said it, I felt betrayed."

"Good. It only took you half of a session to dig in. Now that's related to an emotion. Betrayed and angry? Betrayed and disappointed? Betrayed and… ?"

"Angry. Not at her, but at the person who gave her that information."

"Okay, now we're getting somewhere. Do you know who told her?"

"Yes. I pressed her on it later. It was Matthew Daniels. He was her lieutenant at East. She says he told her so she might be sympathetic to me and my lack of fire." He looked back outside. "They're both right, you know. I have lost my fire. I still do a good job, but I'm running on auto-pilot."

"If the statement is true, why do you feel betrayed?"

Sam sensed something different. He knew he was almost there. Over the past three years, he'd gotten to the edge. He'd come to the knowledge but refused to risk *feeling* the loss. Over and over again he did the mental dance, getting to the edge only to shut down at the last second. This time he had a reason to go forward.

"No one had the right to steer her into my past," he said. "It's my past!" He scratched the side of his face. For some reason, his beard itched.

"What do you think was his purpose?" she asked.

"I don't know. I suppose to get her to see me differently."

"Differently how, Sam?" He didn't say anything. "Come on, Sam, don't stop now. We're getting somewhere."

"I don't know. Pity?" She let him sit with the question in awkward silence. "Maybe compassion?"

"Those sound like questions, not answers or even opinions."

"I suppose he wanted her to give me some grace." Dr. Humphrey nodded and raised one eyebrow. "I know. I don't give myself any grace. Never have."

"So, what is it about this girl?"

"She. She—I don't know. That's why I pay you." He pounded his fist on the arm of the chair, but quickly retreated emotionally and became stoic once again.

"Don't you quit on me, Sam Tidwell. Stop running from the truth. How does Detective Rhodes make you feel?"

"I'm not sure what you're asking. Are you implying I have some strange fantasy about this girl?" He gripped the arms of the chair so tightly his knuckles turned white and his hands blood red.

"I'm not implying anything, Sam. I simply asked how the girl makes you feel. Does she stir an emotional response from you? Your defensiveness and your grip on that chair tell me she does. It also tells me you are confused about that feeling."

He reflected pensively as he stared out the window. It began to rain. "She's a beautiful girl." He used the reflection of the window to see if Dr. Humphrey had any physiological response to that. "She looks a lot like Molly, but…" He turned. He suddenly understood. It wasn't really about Molly. "She reminds me of me, of me in the past, when I was young and unafraid. When I was tenacious and undaunted."

"Really?" She leaned forward and waited for him to face her.

"Would it be safe to follow the logic in that statement, Sam? Would it be safe to say you are the opposite of those qualities now?"

He pulled a hangnail from his left thumb until it snapped free. He watched as a spot of blood took its place. He grabbed a tissue from her desk and put it on his thumb. "Probably. I suppose that makes me afraid, indecisive, and weak. All true. I just want to coast. Just do my job. I just want to make it to retirement without any problems. She can't take that from me."

"Now, Sam. We both know you could retire now. You have plenty of money. From what you've told me, you still have all of the life insurance money, and you'll get a full pension." She leaned back in her chair. "This girl stirs something in you. Tell me, Sam, what are you afraid of?"

"Being obsolete." He didn't have to think about it. It haunted him day and night, even more than the deaths of his wife and daughter. "I like the way this girl thinks. She challenges me. But I'm afraid of opening up again…of caring. I just don't want to…" His voice trailed back and he looked out the window again.

"Get hurt?"

He nodded.

"Sam, you know you can't have it both ways. Don't you?"

He nodded again.

"Then you need to decide what you want more, safety or relevance."

He remained silent for several minutes. He picked up a wooden carved elephant from the corner of her desk. "I want to be safe." He set it back down. "If I open up now, I risk a flood of things I don't want to feel anymore."

"If that's your decision, you already know how to do that. You've had three years of practice."

She didn't disagree with him or push him to the better, more difficult choice. Disappointing. "Okay, truth is I'm sick and tired of hiding, going through the motions, just existing."

"If you say so." She said it flatly, not like she was proud of him, not like it was the wrong decision…just acknowledging he said it.

He spoke more of Abbey and her desire to pursue every possibility in the Ripley case, even though there was a clear and logical suspect. Dr. Humphry asked why he thought Abbey did that. She asked if that's what he used to do. She asked if he meant what he said about no longer hiding? Then, before their time was up, she asked what he planned to do about his new resolve.

"I suppose I'm going to open my eyes and see the bigger picture." He nodded and sat up on the end of his chair. He had an epiphany. "I remember when I first came up and no one wanted to hear what the rookie had to say." There seemed to be excitement in his voice now. "I'm going to encourage her hunches until we prove them to be wrong." He paused. This was the hardest part to admit...the part that made him vulnerable to pain. "And I'm going to believe in her, even if no one else does." He stood and walked toward the door but stopped suddenly. "And I'm going to make her believe in me." Now he sounded like a little kid. "You know, doctor, I needed someone like her to kick me in the pants. It's not like I didn't know these things before...not like I didn't know what I needed to do." He smiled. "I just needed the nudge to step over the line."

As Dr. Humphrey walked him to the door, she said, "Sam, you had your mind made up before you came today, didn't you?"

He smiled.

"This is the most progress since you first came to me three years ago. To be honest, I've seen you mostly stagnant. Today, you decided enough is enough. Be careful, but not too careful. This girl is good for you, just be sure not to project Molly onto her."

Chapter Twenty-two

Thursday, November 2, 6:45 pm—Harmony Apartments

Home at last. The clock moved so slowly today; I nearly fell asleep on my keyboard. Tidwell was strangely quiet the past two days. I guess he was still mad at me. I changed into my comfortable sweats and opened the refrigerator door, looking for something appealing to eat. The intercom buzzed. "Who in the world?" It buzzed again. "Hello?"

"Can you buzz me in? My hands are full."

"Who is this?" I asked.

"Detective Tidwell." I didn't know what to do. "Rhodes, are you there?"

"Uh…yes. Sorry." I buzzed the door. "Twelve-o-seven."

"Gotcha."

What was he doing here? Had he found out about the Cooks? Maybe he went down to the evidence storage and found out why I was there. I made a quick sweep of the apartment to make sure everything looked clean and in its place. Of course, it was. I'd never gotten out of the habit from the Army. I paced back and forth. It seemed like it was taking forever for Detective Tidwell to get there. The doorbell rang, and I rushed to open it.

Detective Tidwell stood in my doorway holding a large box in his hands and two pizza boxes stacked on top. "Uh…come on in." I was confused. "How did you find me?" I asked.

"I'm a detective." He was unusually chipper. "Where can I put these?" he asked.

"Oh, yeah. Sorry. I don't have a kitchen table. Just a couple of bar stools and the bar." I grabbed the pizza boxes and set them on the bar area. "I'm confused."

He set the big box on the bar and opened it. He reached in and pulled out a six-pack of beer. "Can't have pizza without beer."

"Um…I don't drink." I had my reasons.

"Mind if I do?" he asked. "If it bothers you, I'll just take them home later."

"No…no…go ahead. I just don't like taking anything that dulls my senses and…"

"Hey, no need to explain." He opened both pizza boxes. "To be honest, I haven't even asked if you were vegetarian or not, so I brought a meat pizza and a veggie pizza."

I tilted my head and watched as he grabbed a slice of the meat pizza and took a bite. "I don't mean to be rude, Detective Tidwell, but what are you doing here?"

"Okay, first of all, we need to dispense with formalities. Please, call me Sam. Is it okay if I call you Abbey?"

What's with the first name basis? Was he hitting on me? "You're kind of creeping me out, to be honest."

"Can I sit down? I'll explain everything." I motioned to one of the bar stools. He sat and took a deep breath. He began wringing his hands together. I could tell he was nervous but in a giddy sort of way. "I owe you an apology."

"You owe *me* an apology? For what exactly?" I took the seat beside his. "I'm the one who put my nose in your personal business."

"Honestly, it's about time someone did," he said. "Everyone has pretended as if nothing happened for far too long, walking on eggshells for fear of sending me off a mental ledge." I raised an eyebrow. "I've been coddled far too long. You were right. I have lost my fire." He forced a smile. "I need you to help me get it back."

"Are we talking about work?" I asked timidly. I was still terribly confused.

"Of course, we're talking about work. What else would I be talking about?"

I let out a sigh of relief. I didn't realize I had been holding my breath. "What's this have to do with your visit tonight? Couldn't you have said this tomorrow? Like at work?"

"I could have, but I was afraid I'd chicken out again and slip back into the rut if I waited. You know, go back into the old safe habits. Besides, it's taken me two days to act on my resolve." He took another bite, then popped the tab on his beer. "I want to get back to my younger self, the one who kept at it until the right person was put away." Even though he said it with a full mouth, I understood most of it.

"But, Alvaro..."

"You don't think he did it. I just need to know why."

This was a trick...to get me out of Homicide. "Sarge warned me about doing anything with the case. He said it's closed, and I need to move on." Good, safe answer!

"He doesn't have to know." Detective Tidwell pointed to the box. "This is everything we gave to the D.A. I called in a favor and borrowed it off the record for a few days."

"What?" I was shocked. "Why would you risk your career over this?"

"Let me be perfectly clear, Abbey. I still think Alvaro Garcia did it, but I want to listen to your hunch before I let it go completely. Are you up for a private investigation?"

"You better believe it!" I grabbed a slice of the veggie pizza and pushed everything out of the way to make room for the evidence. "I'm not sure I'm comfortable calling you Sam. You're older than my parents."

"Parents? That's another thing we need to do, Abbey. We need to learn about each other's past. No more surprises."

Wasn't ready for that yet either. Baby steps. "Let's start with the case and work from there. You're going to have to give me time and a little grace on the other stuff."

He smiled.

Sam and I finished eating and moved everything to the floor in front of the couch. We made a timeline of events, put the characters in their proper sequence, and placed the diagrams and photos above the timeline. The pieces of evidence went to either their left or right, just within reach of one of us.

"According to the testimony of the neighbor," I began, "the murder occurred between nine and ten-ten."

He checked the notes. "That's right. Pastor Mark was seen entering the building at nine. Alvaro, himself, admitted to seeing the bloody room. He peeled out of the parking lot at ten-ten." He adjusted the timeline on the floor. "So, for the sake of argument, let's say Alvaro is telling the truth. First, how can that be proven?"

"The pathologist said five minutes would be pushing it to do all that was done to the pastor. Add to that the time it would take to find the mop and bucket, fill it with soapy water, mop the area, and then dispose of the bloody water, and I think you'll find it impossible for Alvaro to do all of that."

"Okay, but you're assuming the witness's times are accurate and precise."

I searched for the officer's notes on the canvassing that recorded that conversation. "Here it is." I scanned the conversation. "The church's neighbor says he just started a recording session in his studio at nine when he noticed the pastor pulling into the parking lot." I looked through the notes and stopped immediately. I tapped the note with my finger. "The neighbor took a smoke break at ten, right as the pickup pulled in, and was pissed when the truck made so much noise pulling out that it bled through the sound insulation and ruined that part of the recording. That was at ten-ten."

Sam nodded. "That's pretty precise."

"So?" I asked.

"So, we run his defense for a while."

"Are you kidding me?"

He shook his head, and I smiled. Now this was going to be fun.

"He had no more than ten minutes from entering and exiting the driveway." Tidwell said as he grabbed a notepad and pen from the box. "But we only have his word that he went there to meet with Pastor Mark."

"We could verify the call from Mark's phone setting up the meeting that morning," I said. "It won't tell us the content of the call, but it would prove they made contact."

"Nice try, but that won't work. Alvaro said the call came from a woman at the church. And as far as we know, the pastor wanted to chew him out for ruining the baptism."

"True." I slumped…another strike for Alvaro. We looked for anything…anything that would tip in Alvaro's favor. It just wasn't there. "We need to find the murder weapon," I admitted. "Without it, he's cooked."

"Don't give up yet." He looked at his watch. "Let's get a good night's sleep and try this again tomorrow night."

"Okay by me." I stretched before getting up. "Just leave everything like it is. That'll save us time tomorrow." It took him a little longer to get up from the floor. "And, Detective…Sam…"

"Yeah?"

"Thank you."

We both smiled. What a miracle.

"You're welcome, but don't be surprised if I bring a folding table and chairs tomorrow. We old people struggle getting down and back up off the floor."

I laughed and said goodnight. It was the first time I saw a glimmer of light…a spark of a fire in his eyes.

Chapter Twenty-three

Saturday, November 4, 10:00 am—Soar Adventure Tower, Franklin

I arrived at Soar Adventure Tower in Franklin and parked in an open spot. Olson was the first to greet me. He waited for me to get out of the car and then gave me a high five and a brief side hug. "This is official East Precinct recreation, but we all agreed that you're still a part of the family."

"Aww," I said. "Did T make it?" I asked, looking for my old partner.

"Yes. She's getting her harness on right now. Twelve of the day shift plus Lieutenant Daniels made it today. We all get our points."

We walked to the entrance, and I was greeted by my former day-shift squad. "Hey, Fleming. Haven't seen you since last week."

"Miss High and Mighty," he said, acknowledging my presence. He bowed.

"Funny." I screamed, "T!" I ran past Fleming to my former partner and only Sudanese friend. We did our secret greeting, a series of odd handshakes and high-fives. "Still working on that book about your escape from Sudan?"

"Yes," she said with a strong accent. "So many stories about the lost boys. I want to tell the girls' side of the story." I hugged her again. It was so good to see her.

"You know you're late?" A familiar voice.

"Well, I guess you better write me up." I hugged Lieutenant Daniels. "Thanks for including me today."

"Any progress with your partner?" he asked. I nodded, but

before I could say anything, others came over to say hi. They pulled me through the entrance to the man in charge so I could get fixed up with my harness. "Okay, everyone, this is official-unofficial time. The point is to get to know each other better and to foster trust. "It's on me. You have access to all the options of the climbing tower, and then we'll close the day off with a round of miniature golf, for those of us who are older and less agile."

They collectively thanked him.

A young blond-haired man extended his hand. "I'm Chase Martin. I've heard so much about you."

"Exaggerated, I'm sure," I said, not knowing at the time what he meant.

"I hope not." He winked for some reason.

"I've passed by this place quite a bit," Olson said, "and I've always wanted to try it out." He grabbed me by the arm and said, "Race you to the top."

"You're on!"

We ran through the obstacles in our path, through the rope climbing section, and up to the higher level. We were as agile as ninjas. At least that's what we told ourselves. Clipping our harnesses to safety ropes, Olson and I pushed ourselves to and over the first set of boardwalks and to the hand-over-hand part of the climb. We were neck and neck, until he slipped, and I took advantage of his momentary lapse. One more obstacle in my way. I came to a series of ropes hung in loose "U" shapes. Knowing I was a few steps ahead and had time to spare, I transferred cautiously from one loop to the other, letting the natural sway of the ropes assist me.

Olson, on the other hand, rushed through the obstacle and lost his footing a second time. He discovered the beauty of the harness and the safety clip as he fell from the obstacle. I made sure he was safely swinging below before taunting him and finishing the final part of the climb.

The rest of the group paired up and followed suit with us, seeing who could best the other. After a while, we set our competition aside and leisurely enjoyed the course. The new guy, Chase Martin, kept following us and asking all sorts of strange questions. He waited at one of the pedestal platforms as I came his way. I tried to make a good impression on the new guy. I had a reputation to maintain. I showed my agile form by swinging hand over hand on the rope ladder. "So, are you and Olson an item?" he asked as I neared the platform.

"What?"

He repeated the question and added, "He talks about you all the time. They all do."

I was huffing and puffing as I said, "No, we're just friends."

"Sure you are," he said, winking. As I swung closer and closer, he said, "I'd like to be friends too."

I still didn't catch his drift until it was too late. As I grabbed the last rung of the rope ladder, he reached out for the rope, but he cupped my breast instead. He winked again.

Suddenly, it all made sense. I screamed, "Jerk!" and turned loose. I fell to the end of my security line with a snap. Suddenly and without warning, I was fourteen again, running for my life… my shirt torn open…my trust dashed…my world crashing 'round me. The whole terrifying event of my rape flashing before my eyes. I must have dangled for several seconds, screaming and flailing at an invisible enemy, for several officers were coming to my aid, trying to contain my spasms.

They told me later that Olson grabbed Martin by his harness and shouted, "You little prick!"

I heard Chase Martin's reply as he said, "It was an accident." I'd heard that line before. I thought that was all behind me.

"You did it on purpose!" Olson pushed Martin to the edge of the platform.

I glanced back up to the platform. Martin pointed down to me as I was unclipping and climbing down the last two levels of the tower. "You don't talk about her all the time just because she was a good cop. Seriously?"

Olson pushed him off the edge. I heard the snap of his line as he hit the bottom of his tether.

I was back as an adult in the present, my past safely pushed back down in my mind. I ran to the car. Lieutenant Daniels intercepted me, grabbed my arm and asked, "What happened?"

"Let go!" I locked the doors and covered my face. I couldn't let anyone see me like that. I didn't want to see anyone. I needed to be alone, back safe in my apartment, where I could lock the world outside. I pushed the button, but the car didn't start.

I got out and searched for the key fob while everyone else was at the bottom circled around Martin. I leaned against the car for support. My mind was spinning.

Olson described Martin's actions and accusations. T punched Martin, and everyone else jumped in to separate the two. "How could you?" she screamed as Fleming held her back. "She's my friend."

Chase Martin wiped his bloody nose and smiled. I tried to turn away, but I couldn't. He stared at me with such contempt. His whole countenance darkened. "You all act as if she's so innocent." He turned to Lieutenant Daniels and said, "And I'm sure I know how she promoted so quickly to Homicide." He spit the blood from his mouth and asked, "Didn't she live with you?"

Lieutenant Daniel's face turned blood red. A vein bulged in his right temple. "You better take that little innuendo back, Martin. You're already facing a hearing about this incident." I wanted to get out and stop the inevitable, but I was frozen in fear, a small child alone in the darkness.

"Deny it if you want, but we all know you were doing her in the night while your wife was asleep."

Olson held Martin's arms behind his back. "Where did you get this crap?"

"Oh, come on." He looked from face to face for any sign of affirmation or support. Martin got none. He looked over his shoulder at Olson. "Just friends? I bet."

"We like her because she's nice…to everyone," T said. "And she was great at the job."

Martin smiled. Lieutenant Daniels moved inches from his face. "This is a Metro Nashville Police Department activity. Your behavior is unacceptable." He gritted his teeth and said, "You can either face a formal investigation, or you can be smart and pack your things. Either way, you have no place at East."

"Let me go!" he screamed. With a nod from Lieutenant Daniels, Olson let go. "Your loss. I was sick of this place anyway. I can go private and make twice the money with half the headache." He pushed away from Olson and spit another wad of blood at T's feet, before walking to his truck. He looked directly at me and said, "Pretend if you want. You'll never convince me."

I looked away and noticed the fob lying on the ground beside my back tire. I snatched it, jumped back into the car, and drove off. Both Lieutenant Daniels and Olson tried my cell, but I let it go straight to voicemail. T texted, and I turned off the phone. I couldn't drive fast enough.

Chapter Twenty-four

3:05 pm—Harmony Apartments

I hated to leave the shower. It was a place of safety and warmth, but I slipped on my robe and wiped a clear spot on the mirror with my arm. The room was so full of steam it fogged back up. I wiped it again and stared at my reflection, proving to myself I was no longer fourteen and vulnerable. I rubbed the chill bumps from my arms. Strange. I was standing in a fog of steam, yet I had chills. As I opened the bathroom door to let the steam out, I could hear the buzzing sound of the intercom. I wanted to ignore it like I did my phone, just turn it off and enjoy the silence. It buzzed over and over again. I clicked the switch for intercom.

"Come on, Abbey, I know you're there. Your car's in its space." He buzzed a couple more times. "I can stand here all day annoying you, or you can buzz me up."

"Leave me alone." I didn't want to see anyone…not like this. "Just go away. I'm fine."

"No, you're not. I can hear it in your voice. I'm not going away until I see for myself that you're okay."

"Fine!" I buzzed the intercom. When he got to the twelfth floor, he rang my doorbell. I still didn't answer, so he knocked and knocked on my door, making a scene for the whole hallway to see. "Okay, Lieutenant, come in." I grabbed him by the arm and pulled him inside.

The first words out of his mouth were, "You're soaking wet."

"Of course, I…" I looked up. "What did you just say?"

"I said you're soaking wet. You're dripping everywhere." He pointed to the puddle forming at my feet.

"You're a genius!" I turned and ran to the pile of papers on the floor. I flipped through pages, asking "Where is it?"

"Where's what? You're not making any sense, Abbey." He followed me to a small table with two chairs and a mess of papers all over the table and the floor. "Are you having another breakdown?"

"No! I'm looking for our notes with the pathologist. I have the official report, but I don't see my notes from our conversation."

"Abbey, did you steal a case file?"

I looked up and pushed the wet hair out of my face. "Not exactly. Sam brought it over."

"Sam? Sam Tidwell, your apathetic partner? You're on a first-name basis now, and he's been to your apartment?"

"Yes. It's kind of all your fault, really." I gave him an exaggerated smile like a little girl needing her father's approval. "You told me to dig into his tragedy. Well, I did, and now we're like best buds."

"Uh-huh…and?"

"And he brought the Ripley case over as kind of a peace offering."

"That's the Ripley case? You were told to let that go."

I just shrugged my shoulders and turned back to the mess. "Here it is!" I searched for the line and then read it aloud. "Sam said, 'We know at that point someone picked him up, carried him to the baptistery, and threw him in the water, which, to me, means that person got in the water with him and choked him, probably under the water, until he was dead.' And she said, 'That is consistent with our findings.'" I looked up at Lieutenant Daniels and tilted my head, awaiting his confirmation and praise.

"I don't get it," he admitted.

"What did you say when you entered my apartment today?"

"I said you were soaking wet, which you still are by the way."

"Exactly!"

"Abbey, you're going to have to spell it out. I'm not following you." How could he not follow the logic? "I don't know the details of the case. What am I supposed to be seeing?"

"He would have been soaking wet."

"Who?"

"Alvaro!" I flipped through the pages, looking for the testimony of the neighbor with the studio. "He makes no mention of Alvaro being wet."

"Maybe it was just an oversight," Lieutenant Daniels argued. "You know how witnesses are."

"Yes, but this one has OCD."

"How do you know that?" he asked.

I showed him the interview, how precise he was, how detailed the information was, and exact the times. "He's got to be OCD. He wouldn't miss a detail like that." I scanned the report. "Please have his phone number."

"You better make sure if you're going any further with this. You've already violated several protocols."

I waved him off. "Oh, you and your protocols." He was such a rule follower. *Sometimes you just have to break a rule. Sometimes life demands a change.*

"Rules are made…" he began.

"I know, I know…to be followed…to protect us. You've told me a hundred times before," I said, still focused on the neighbor's testimony.

"I can see what good that lesson did."

I ignored him, even though I sensed his deep disappointment. "I was also taught to be Ever Vigilant," I said bringing the Army to my defense. "I should have caught this before. Ah ha!" I got up and ran to the bathroom to retrieve my phone. I dialed the number. He answered, and I introduced myself and said I just wanted to clarify part of his testimony. He grumbled but agreed. I read the report verbatim, and he said, "Yes." Then I asked him how clearly he saw the man coming out of the church. To that, he described precisely what Alvaro wore, what he looked like, and the truck he drove.

"Were his clothes wet?" I asked.

"Excuse me?" he said.

"The man who got into the truck. Were his clothes wet?"

"No. They were dusty gray like someone who works with concrete or construction."

"One more question. Did he enter the church the moment he drove up?"

"No. I told this to the officer. He sat in his truck for nearly five minutes. He got out right before I went back into the studio."

That wasn't in the officer's report. That only gave him five minutes total. I could barely hold back my excitement. Alvaro was dry. He couldn't be the killer. "And you said there were no other cars in the parking lot during that time."

"That's correct."

"Thank you. You are a great help to the case." When I hung up, I danced and jumped around so much, my robe began to open.

"Abbey, for goodness sake, cinch that robe and get dressed!"

I kissed him on the cheek and ran to the bedroom to get dressed. "I can't wait to tell Sam!"

When I returned to the living room, I was in jeans and a sweatshirt. I told Lieutenant Daniels everything that had happened over the past week and a half, including details I'd already told him the other day. I was so giddy about the new details I could hardly contain myself. Justice!

Then, after I said all I wanted to say, Lieutenant Daniels turned the conversation back to the incident at the adventure tower. "I'm sorry about what Chase said and did. He acts without thinking, but that's over now."

"I don't want to talk about it." I looked away and crossed my arms over my chest, suddenly feeling violated again.

"You need to," he said sternly.

"It's over, and I'm past it." Of course, I wasn't. I'd never be over it. I pretended to busy myself with the case.

He took the papers from my hands and said, "Look at me,

Abbey. I know what happened to you in Guatemala. Don't shut yourself off again." I looked away. He didn't know everything. Besides, Guatemala was in the past. I couldn't let it ruin me again. That's why I ran…to the Army…to Germany…to a new life. But Lieutenant Daniels was persistent. "Listen, if you'd rather talk with Sherry that's okay. We'll go there right now."

"No. I don't want to talk about it…to anyone." I was getting angry…pushing everyone away…pushing him away.

"Don't!" he demanded. "Stop walling up."

I turned and snapped at him. "The idiot intentionally grabbed my breast, okay. But maybe I overreacted." My face and heart hardened. I took a step back and turned to the window. "Okay, it triggered the rape, and I had to get out of there as fast as I could."

"I let him go."

"Dealing with the Ripley case, having to be in a church again, and then for him to do that…"

"It's okay Abbey. You don't have to do this alone." I nodded. I knew he was right, but I wasn't ready. He put his hand on my shoulder. "You know we're here for you, any day, any time."

"I know. I just can't deal with the past right now."

"Can I do anything?" he asked.

I shook my head and pretended to smile as if it was all good. "You sure?"

"Yes. Thanks for checking on me. I took a long run. I ran until I couldn't run anymore. Then I came back and soaked in a hot shower." I put a loose strand of hair behind my right ear. "Good thing I'm not renting a room in a house with a small hot water tank anymore."

We both laughed. Those were better memories. Once he was sure I'd be okay, Lieutenant Daniels left me and went home.

Chapter Twenty-five

Sunday, November 5, 9:55 am—Living Water Church

After calling Sam with the news, I decided to attend the Sunday morning service at Living Water Church to observe possible suspects. I slipped in five minutes before it started and stood in the foyer. Although the ushers offered to help me find a seat, I stood fast. I just wanted to spectate. I stared past the pulpit to the baptistery, where just two weeks ago Mark Ripley baptized someone. Little did he know it would become his own water grave the next day.

The sanctuary was relatively full. To my right, I could hear the chatter of two rows full of youth. Down the opposite side and two rows from the front, I could see Susan and her two children. At precisely ten, one of the elders ascended the steps to the pulpit. He welcomed everyone, turned their attention to the visitor cards in the pew racks, and gave a few general announcements.

"As I'm sure everyone is aware, we said our goodbyes to our pastor a week ago Saturday. The elders have arranged for pulpit supply for the next two months as we delve into the process of finding a new pastor." He looked at Susan. "Although we will never truly replace Pastor Mark, we are thankful he set in place a leadership structure that will keep us steady for quite some time. Susan, Hannah, and Danny, we love you and are delighted that you are considering staying with us."

I moved to the back corner, opposite the youth section, and watched the various reactions to what he was saying. I located

Duke Stearns and Owens Jenkins. Neither seemed moved one way or the other. As the minister of music and the praise band took their positions on the stage, I did catch the two men stealing a glance at one another. Obviously, neither cared for modern musical instruments, especially the drums. Most of the congregation, however, seemed quite moved and sang out with joy.

In the corner of my eye, I saw Jonathan standing with the youth, which consisted mostly of girls. Skylar stood to his immediate left. She sang, but it was evident Jonathan was the object of her worship. Not uncommon for a lonely, neglected young girl to look up to her minister. He represented safety. Wish that had been true for me.

Jonathan continued to sing. He seemed unaware of my presence. I slipped into an empty spot in the back pew and watched people throughout the service. I struggled with the words of praise about a God who cared for and loved us. I fought the chill running up my spine. Being in a church for investigation was one thing; attending the service was quite another.

I made it through the funeral last week but had that moment where I forced myself to stare at the baptistery window. I came today to study the crowd, but the moment the guest speaker began his sermon with an analogy my father had used many times before, I was thrust once again back to Guatemala and my childhood.

I found myself driving away with no conscious memory of ever leaving the service. Two thoughts emerged: *That's terrifying. How'd I get here?*

I drove to East Precinct and idled in the parking lot for half an hour. Once I felt the old familiar calm returning, I chose to drive through my old patrol routes. I let my mind slip away from the Ripley case. The other two active cases facing my homicide day crew filtered in. Before long, I was driving the route on autopilot and mentally scouring the facts of each case. Although nothing new rose to the surface of my thoughts, I succeeded in pushing the memory of my father and Guatemala back into the dark recesses of my mind.

Lieutenant Daniels was right. I hadn't dealt with the cause of my PTSD, and it was coming back with a vengeance. He said if I didn't learn how to own it and control it, the memory would control me. He'd advised me over and over to see a counselor. Somehow, I would have to trust another and share every detail of my past to help me believe it didn't define me. But even Lieutenant Daniels didn't know the whole truth. I could never trust anyone with all of it…never. I couldn't even forgive myself for what I'd done…how could I expect anyone else to?

I pulled out onto Shelby Avenue and looked at the clock in the car. Sam was going to be at the apartment in fifteen minutes. I headed home so I could change into comfortable clothes before he arrived.

Chapter Twenty-six

1:30 pm—Harmony Apartments

I met Detective Tidwell at the lobby door of my apartment building. "I'm so sorry I'm late. I got caught up in something and just got back."

"Not a problem. Did you end up verifying the neighbor's testimony with Owen Jenkins?" he asked.

"Yes. He said Alvaro was dressed the same when he left work as he was when he came back, clothes full of concrete dust from cutting that morning. He said that's when he had to let Alvaro go for taking off without notice."

As we rode up the elevator to my apartment, Detective Tidwell said, "Well, we better have someone else to offer the D.A. when I tell him Alvaro's not our man."

The elevator stopped, and I led the way to my apartment. Once there, I ran to my bedroom and changed. We sifted, once again, through the evidence and testimonies. "Okay," he began, "who do we have as viable suspects?"

I sorted through the list of names, dividing them into two piles. In one, the people we thought generally liked Mark Ripley and affirmed his plans. In the other, anyone who had an ounce of distaste for the man or his mission. "As I see it," I said. "We have Duke Stearns, Owen Jenkins, Quentin Green, Brandon Cook, the former pastor, and the children's minister Mark let go. All had viable reasons to hurt him."

"Okay. Let's look at what we know." Sam Tidwell flipped

through his notes. "The murderer has to be strong enough to haul Mark Ripley up the baptistery steps and hold him under the water until he drowned."

"And his hands have to be strong enough to fracture his hyoid bone," I added.

"You said, *his*. Are we ruling out the old children's minister? Wasn't that a woman?"

"Yes. Carol Hodge. I suppose we should."

"Why was she let go? I don't have that in any of my notes?" he asked.

"According to Susan, for pushing gender issues and sexual orientation discussions with the children."

"Wow! I guess that's the world we live in now." Sam shook his head. "Why are we ruling her out?"

"Because she's five-one and eighty-eight pounds," I said. "Unless she has superhero strength, she's not our murderer." We both laughed, which lightened the mood for a while. "Out of the list we have, Duke Stearns, Owen Jenkins, and Jonathan Williams each have large strong hands and have keys to the church."

Didn't they all alibi out?" he asked.

I looked at my notes. "Yes. Duke Stearns was on a truck run that was GPS verified. Owen Jenkins was on the construction site from five-thirty in the morning until nearly four that afternoon with only a short unverified time. He even ate lunch on-site. Owen has multiple people who can verify his story. We've questioned him twice already."

"What about the youth minister? Didn't he have an alibi too?"

I looked through my notes. "Yes. His roommates said he was home with food poisoning Saturday afternoon through late Monday night. I checked with the church and his other employer, and Jonathan was out sick that Sunday and Monday. Faith said that's why she gave him a ride to the leadership meeting Tuesday. She didn't want him to have to ride his bike having been sick three days before. We've questioned him twice. He's cooperated at every

point of the investigation, and he has an alibi. His roommates swear Jonathan was sick."

"Still, that's the weakest of all the alibis. Roommates can cover for one another. Rule those three men out and we're just left with the developer, the husband, and the former pastor?" he asked. "Why's the old pastor a suspect?"

I explained the comments Susan made about his jealousy of Mark's success. Jonathan mentioned him in his interview. I looked through my notes. "Concerning the move to a Spanish service, Jonathan said, 'It was a bold move, but a good one; it's not something the previous pastor would have risked.' Maybe the former pastor was upset about that. Susan also said several people from the church mentioned the former pastor calling them, attempting to undermine Mark's changes. She gave a physical description of him. He's older and has suffered from chronic health issues. More than likely, even though he might want Mark Ripley out of the way, he wouldn't be able to physically pull off the murder."

"What about Green and Cook?" Sam asked.

"Physically, they could both do it," I said. "Unfortunately, both seemed to be in favor of the pastor and his ways. And both men have alibis, although Cook's is his wife."

"That's as weak as Jonathan's roommates. What you're really saying is we have nothing." Sam was blunt in sharing his disappointment. "We should have just left it alone. I don't know what I was thinking."

"But Alvaro's innocent," I said. "Come on, Detect...Sam. That's going to take me a while to get used to." I smiled and added, "We can do this." I sifted once more through the evidence. "It's probably right in front of us."

"We'll have to get back into that church and look at everyone again as a suspect," he said. "But you and I both know, if Sergeant McNally catches wind that we've gone behind his back and reopened the case, we'll both be busted." He was trying to support me, I could tell. He was making an honest effort to reignite his earlier passion and drive, but I could sense his apprehension and fear.

"What about the woman who called Alvaro? Do you think that was Faith? We could ask her about the meeting between Mark and Alvaro." My phone rang. "Hello. Oh, hey, Susan. Yes. I was there this morning, but I had to leave suddenly. No. I didn't want to disturb the service." I cringed. "This Wednesday? I don't think I can."

Sam suddenly perked up. "Is she asking you to attend Wednesday services?" he whispered. I nodded. "Do it." I shook my head. I couldn't go back to that or any other church. It brought up too many bad memories. "Come on, Abbey," he begged. "This is our chance to get back in the church unofficially."

I mouthed, "No! She's been getting nosey." Turning my attention back to Susan, I said, "I don't know, Susan." Sam put his hands together like a man begging for his life. *Ugh!* I gave in, rolled my eyes, and mouthed, "You owe me." I agreed and told Susan I would meet her there. Susan begged me to come early for supper and eat with her and the kids. They hosted Wednesday night suppers at the church. "Okay. What time?"

I hung up and made it clear I did not want to do this. Detective Tidwell told me that if we were going to have any chance of freeing Alvaro and discovering the true suspect, I'd have to get in with the people. Knowing we had no other good leads, I surrendered. Sam agreed to talk with the D.A. in the morning and Sarge right after that. He said he would tell Sarge it was his idea, come what may.

"Tomorrow," he began, "we get on those two other cases and help our team out. We'll pick this back up Thursday night, and you can fill me in on your church meeting."

We straightened up the evidence box, and Sam left. My shoulders shivered as I thought of going back to the church. I put my air pods in and started my music playlist of good country music… anything to keep my mind from sinking back into the past.

Chapter Twenty-seven

Wednesday, November 8, 5:25 pm—Living Water Church

I was dreading this all week, but I faced my fears anyway. A man's life depended on it. I opened the side door to the church and walked in. I could hear the commotion from the foyer, even before I opened the interior door. People filled the hallway, chatting with one another, and I squeezed between them. There to my right was the baptistery changing room where someone attacked Mark Ripley. A black plastic construction tarp covered the doorway.

So many people walked past, oblivious to the scene that once lay behind that barrier. This was a nightmare. I feigned a smile as I made my way into the fellowship hall where Susan promised to be waiting.

The moment I entered the fellowship hall to my left, a little boy ran over and hugged me. Ah, a familiar face. "Hey, Danny." I peeled him off my leg and looked for Susan, who was already heading my way.

"So sorry, Abbey. He's really attached to you for some reason." She laughed. "No pun intended."

"It's okay." It wasn't, but I put on a good face. I could handle children. Adults were another story…especially men. Time to focus. I was here for an undercover investigation, to look for more suspects. "I can't believe you've jumped right back into things here."

"It's cathartic," Susan said. "I'm having a harder time staying home."

"I understand." With Susan by my side, I had all the information

I needed on anyone I saw. I gave myself a mental pep talk. *You can do this. Just breathe.*

Susan introduced me to everyone. I was truly shocked. The fellowship hall was full of families with children and teenagers. The meal wasn't elaborate, but it was good…and it was free. They had a donation basket on the table, and by the looks of things, there was enough in there to cover the meal for everyone. Maybe that was the way church was supposed to be. As I was eating, I noticed the back door to the fellowship hall opened. Jonathan walked through carrying a bike helmet. *That explains his biking shirt that Tuesday.*

He noticed me and made his way through the crowd. "Hey, Detective Rhodes. Nice surprise."

Before I could answer, Susan said, "I twisted her arm. The kids have been dying to see her again."

He knelt by the table. "Hello, Hannah." She looked down at her plate. "Going to give us a try tonight?" Hannah shook her head. "Oh, well," he said, sounding very disappointed. "You know you're welcome anytime."

He whispered to me. "Any luck finding Mark's murderer?"

"Not yet. We interviewed everyone who had access, and we verified all alibis," I said. "This probably isn't the place to discuss it right now," I added, motioning to Susan with my eyes.

"Oh, right. Well, I better go mingle with my youth."

After he left our table, Susan explained that Hannah had an issue with men. She'd been sexually abused in their foster home by the man who was supposed to protect them and care for them. Susan was surprised Hannah took so easily to Mark, but they had some special bond. She shied away from everyone else until I came over that night. "You can't imagine what she's gone through," Susan said, rubbing Hannah's back.

Oh, I could imagine…more than she knew. "I'm so sorry." I leaned across the table and whispered, "Not all men are like that, Hannah." Just that moment, Skylar entered the fellowship hall with raven black hair and blue highlights. She walked with her head down and sat in a chair just outside of the group of youth eating at a cluster of tables. She chewed on the edge of her sleeve. "What's her story?" I asked.

"Oh, poor girl." Susan leaned forward to whisper. "Mark always suspected something was going on with her. She too has all the signs of being abused, but we never could prove anything." She looked over at Jonathan. "He's been so good with her. Skylar trusts him implicitly. He makes her feel safe."

"Who, Jonathan?" I asked, trying not to turn around and be obvious that we were discussing her.

"Yes. He and Mark talked about it. Jonathan thought something was going on with her father. She was...and is...terrified of the man."

"Have you ever met him?" I asked.

"No. But Mark was going to talk with him while I was out of town. I don't know if he ever did."

"When was this?" I asked. The color in Susan's face disappeared. I realized it was the week of Mark's murder. "Do you know if he's a big man?" I asked, suddenly putting the two things together.

Susan shook her head. "Jonathan would know."

Skylar passed us on her way to the hall. She glanced at me and then looked away. Even though Skylar had her hair down, I noticed the fresh bruising on her cheek. I followed Skylar to the ladies' room. I pretended to go as well. Skylar walked directly to the sink. I headed into one of the stalls and peeked through the crack in the door. Skylar bent over, turned the cold water faucet on and soaked a handful of towels. She pulled the right side of her hair back and put the wet towels to her face, which was freshly bruised from the end of her hairline to the tip of her jaw. She worked her mouth back and forth. Skylar wet the towels a few more times before drying off and positioning her hair for the best coverage.

I flushed and stepped out of the stall. "I don't think we ever met, but I saw you at the funeral. The name is Abbey Rhodes."

The girl lowered her head. "Skylar," she whispered.

"I couldn't help but notice your face."

The girl darted out of the bathroom and disappeared into the crowd. Oh, her father was not going to get away with it this time!

When I returned to the fellowship hall, I found Jonathan and started another conversation. "Do you ride your bike all the time?"

"Just until my car is fixed," he said. "They've been waiting for a part for three weeks. Why? Are you going to interrogate me again?" After an awkward period of silence, he smiled and said, "Just messing with you, Detective."

"Oh. Well, at least you'll stay in good shape," I said. I made small talk for a while, pretending to be interested in his ministry at the church. Once I felt like I'd created enough dialogue to slip it in casually, I asked, "Which house did you say was Skylar's?"

He stepped into a side classroom and pointed through the window. "That's her house there, right across the little bridge."

"Oh, that's cute…the bridge, that is. Does it belong to the church?"

"Yeah. Not many people know it, but we own that little spot just across the creek too." He pointed to a forty-foot square patch of green grass on the other side of the little wooden bridge. "It's a dry creek, only flows when it rains."

"I guess it's not a dry creek this week," I said.

"No. It's still dry. We haven't had rain down here for over three weeks. I should know; I ride my bike all the time."

"But it stormed half of last week," I insisted. "The thunderstorms were pretty heavy a couple of times."

"Rain never got here," he said. "Sorry to be rude, but the kids are heading upstairs. I can't afford to leave them unattended."

"Sure. Go."

Glad that conversation ended quickly, I went back to my table and finished my dinner. I saw Faith and went over to her table. Faith smiled and greeted me. "Mind if I ask you a question?"

"Not at all, dear," Faith said with a broad smile.

"Can you tell me about the meeting with Pastor Mark and Alvaro?"

"What do you mean?" she asked.

"Alvaro said a woman from the church called him to set up the meeting."

"Wasn't me," Faith said with a straight face.

"What about the email from you to Pastor Mark Sunday night?"

"Detective, I don't know what you're talking about."

I scrutinized her face. "Does anyone else have access to the email here?"

"Other than the pastor," she said with a gloomy face, "just me. The staff all have their own accounts."

"Then the email had to come from you," I said.

"Come on." Faith took me by the arm and led me to the church office. She logged into her computer and pulled up her email history. "See here?" Faith clicked the sent email from that Sunday evening. "What in the world?"

There it was, and it was timestamped 8:07 pm. It was addressed to Mark Ripley's personal email address telling him Alvaro Garcia wanted to meet with him tomorrow morning at ten to apologize for this morning's misunderstanding. At the bottom of the letter, it read, "Your Servant in Christ Jesus, Faith."

"I thought you said…" I began.

"I swear, Detective; I did not send that email."

"But it is on your computer and has your name at the end of the conversation."

"I can see that," her voice full of disbelief. "But I did not send that email. I was visiting Mrs. Jones Sunday night. She invited me for supper, and we talked until nearly ten o'clock." Faith looked up at me. She knew I was skeptical. "Come here." She led me back into the fellowship hall to another table. "Shirley, can you tell this detective where I was two Sunday nights ago?" The woman confirmed Faith's story. Faith was not at the church that night, and she wasn't anywhere near a computer.

I was more confused than ever. What other woman from the church would Alvaro Garcia and email Pastor Mark from the church office desk arranging a meeting between two parties, leading each to think the other initiated it? And what was the point of that?

Susan signaled for me to follow her to a woman's Bible study. The sign on the door read, "Experiencing Grace and Forgiveness." Just what I needed. I was still looking for suspects, and in light of the new information, a woman was involved. What better place to look than an all-women study? I noticed Hannah following too. "Doesn't she go to her own class?"

"Not yet. She still doesn't feel safe. And I'm afraid we've taken backward steps since Mark died. She won't leave my side."

"I can understand that," I said. I was surprised Susan was able to attend. "You can sit by me," I told Hannah. The girl nodded. So, for the next hour, I forced myself to stay seated. They talked about grace. They talked about giving grace and love just as God had given His to them.

The woman read a Bible story about a man who owed a great debt but was forgiven. And yet, that man refused to forgive a tiny debt someone else owed him. God was the master who forgave the great debt we owed, she explained. We need to be more like Him. At least that's what she was saying.

I bit my lip so hard at one point, I tasted blood. Then, just when I didn't think it could get any worse, they spoke about forgiving someone who'd hurt you in your past. Each woman took her turn sharing a difficult situation…an event or a person where it was difficult to give grace and forgiveness. Faith spoke of her father who made her feel useless.

"I know it's going to be hard," Susan said, "but I'm trying to forgive Alvaro for…" She wiped a tear. "Well, you all know." They nodded.

I didn't know whether to tell her Alvaro was innocent or to just scream, "You don't have to forgive the murderer…ever!" I swallowed my anger, just as I'd always done. A flood of negative thoughts cascaded over me…thoughts of hate, anger, and criticism took over my soul. Now, that was the church I remembered. A bunch of self-righteous hypocrites pretending to be right with God and acting as if they could forgive and forget anything. But I heard the private talk around the kitchen table. I knew better. Don't tell me I needed to forgive the man who raped me. I grew up in a missionary family whose father was nice to everyone on the outside but would talk about them around the dinner table. He put on a smile when everyone else was around and was cruel to us when they weren't. I had a father who took my rapist's word over mine. I had my family turn their pious backs on me and kick me out on my own. At fourteen! Hypocrites…the whole lot of them.

I saw visiting groups of church people come to my father's ministry house week after week. They put on the façade of God's children but acted differently when they thought no one was looking. I'm sure all the groups weren't that way, but in my mind, the fakers tainted my memories and feelings toward the rest forever. I was all for doing the right thing. I fought for justice every day of the week. But these people spoke of fantasy…a modern-day *Peyton Place*, and we all know that ended disastrously.

Every once and a while, I stole a glance at the clock. It seemed to be stuck in the same place, never moving, never freeing me from this hell on earth. Just when I was about to stand up and scream, I felt a hand grab mine. It was Hannah's. She scooted her chair closer and put her head on my shoulder. Hannah sensed it too. We were sisters born of tragedy…kindred spirits with major trust issues. I leaned my shoulder towards her and savored the moment. Finally, someone who understood. I noticed a tear falling from Susan's eye.

Chapter Twenty-eight

I excused myself the moment the study concluded. Having discovered earlier that the youth activities lasted at least another half hour, I decided to make a quick visit to Skylar's house. I figured that would be just long enough to confront her father about the abuse.

I headed for the bridge. Before crossing over the creek, I looked down. Jonathan was right...bone dry. *Nashville weather is so weird.* I crossed through the side of Skylar's yard and rang the front doorbell. I heard it ring and could see a man sitting in a recliner in front of the television, so I rang again. When he still didn't respond, I knocked. I was not going to be ignored.

"Go away," he shouted.

At that point I pounded on the door. I could see him snap the footrest in place and get up from his chair. He opened the front door and said, "Listen, little girl. Piss off." He was huge, easily six-two, six-three, but in the high two hundreds in weight. He wasn't what you would call "cut," but I could tell he was strong. His shirt was stained with whatever he had for his last two meals...at least.

"Are you Skylar's father?"

"Who's asking?" He looked over my shoulder.

"I'm here about the bruises on her face."

He stepped out onto the porch and shut the door. "You have no idea what goes on here, little girl."

"I have a general idea," I said. "Why don't you tell me your version?"

He looked over my shoulder again as if he expected someone

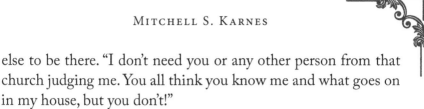

else to be there. "I don't need you or any other person from that church judging me. You all think you know me and what goes on in my house, but you don't!"

"What makes you think I'm from the church?" I asked, somewhat surprised he thought I was a member of Living Water.

"Cause you're the only people stupid enough to trespass on my property and butt in my family's business." He moved a little closer.

He'd already pushed my button calling me *little girl* twice, and now getting all up in my face…I was two seconds from kicking his face in. "And what is this, exactly?" I asked, pointing to his position and posture. Before he could move, I stepped the remaining distance between us. "Is this your attempt to intimidate me?" I asked.

He scowled. "It's worked for everyone else, 'cept maybe that last little guy." He leaned in and whispered in my ear, "But I hear he got his." The fumes from the alcohol were so strong, his breath nearly knocked me over.

Oh, I wanted so desperately to deck him right on the spot, but I relaxed my hands and took a deep breath. "And what might you know about that?" I asked, now clenching my teeth. I may have just stumbled upon the killer without meaning to.

"Oh, you know, you hear things." He was smug, and it was killing me. I could take him to Central and question him there, but I decided on the sure arrest, letting my friends from East Precinct haul him in tomorrow for child abuse.

I took a step back to get away from his soured breath and body odor. He thought I was backing down and smiled smugly. I looked directly in his eyes, even though he was six inches taller. "I'm not from the church," I said, "but I will tell you this. Lay another finger on Skylar, and I'll give you a taste of your own medicine."

He laughed aloud. "You think you know me."

"Bullies are all alike," I said. "Nothing but hot air."

He stopped laughing and put his finger in my face, "You got three seconds to get off of my porch."

I smiled. "Or what?" I dared him to say it.

Instead, he lifted his left arm and cocked it for a hit, but I struck him like lightning; he was on his knees gasping for air before he could swing it forward. I spun, landing a kick to the side of his head. I was so mad, I left him dazed and lying face down on his porch.

I crossed the bridge and walked to my car. I tried to convince myself that it was justified. After all, he technically swung first. But in reality, I knew I'd crossed the line. I was an officer of the law. Oh well, he'd just have to forgive me. I couldn't wait to see his smug face in the morning when they hauled him in for child abuse.

Chapter Twenty-nine

Thursday, November 9, 9:57 am—Skylar's home

I confessed my actions to Sergeant McNally the next morning and asked if I could be there when the officers from East arrested Skylar's father. Although he wasn't pleased with my continuing connection with the people of Living Water, he granted the request. I touched base with Lieutenant Daniels and met his officers from East at Skylar's house.

After receiving a warrant for his arrest, they drove to the house and parked in the cul-de-sac in front. I agreed to stay in the back, but I desperately wanted to see his expression when he saw me with the police. They knocked and received the same response Skylar's father gave me the night before. His car was still in the drive, and they could see the television on. After pounding a few more times, he finally answered the door. The officers could smell the fumes of his breath the moment the door swung in.

"We have blood!" Fleming shouted looking at his shirt and hands. Two other officers grabbed Skylar's father, put him up against the wall, and made sure the blood wasn't his. His knuckles were bruised and skinned. After clearing him of any significant injuries, they searched the home for the source. Two officers searched for Skylar.

T shouted out, "I have a girl down."

Oh, no, no, no, no! What had I done? "Is she alive?"

"Yes. Barely."

I could hear T calling for an ambulance. I shouted at Skylar's father and went after him. Fleming whisked me out of the house and demanded I stay behind the cars. All the while, Skylar's dad swore he didn't know what happened…that he didn't do anything. He called me and his daughter all sorts of foul things, blaming me for stirring things up. Maybe I did. I listened as they read him his rights. Off in the distance, I could hear a siren. It took an eternity to arrive.

I leaned against the car with my head in my hands. "It is… it's all my fault. It's all my fault." After T secured Skylar's father in the back of her cruiser, she tried to calm me down, assuring me I'd done the right thing. I wasn't so sure.

The EMTs attended to Skylar and rolled her out on a gurney. She was bloody and swollen from multiple beatings. I asked which hospital and said I would follow. I called Sergeant McNally, who okayed the request and mentioned that he and Detective Tidwell were discussing the new developments in the Ripley murder. I couldn't tell whether he was pleased or angry with me. To be honest, I didn't really care.

Once we arrived at St. Thomas Hospital—Midtown, I followed the EMTs as they pushed Skylar through the intake process. I asserted myself, using the clout of my badge to gain access and stay by Skylar's side even though I wasn't family. I explained that her only parent was arrested for beating her. She had no one else.

Skylar remained unconscious. By the looks of it, her father beat his daughter literally within an inch of her life. I was no doctor, but I could tell he either broke or dislocated her jaw. He'd also broken Skylar's left arm. I could see the fracture pushing against the flesh. I wondered what he damaged internally. Despite T's efforts, I blamed myself for the excessive beating…because of my visit the night before. I'd shamed him and beaten him at his own game of intimidation and force. He took his revenge on Skylar.

I scanned the monitors. Skylar's vitals declined…heartbeat weak…blood pressure dangerously low and dropping. A phlebotomist rolled her cart into the room, checked the wristband, and

proceeded to extract two small vials of blood. A doctor entered on her heels and announced they were taking the girl for a CT scan. As soon as they had the results, they would make a plan.

I sat in the corner of Skylar's ER room and waited. About ten minutes later, my phone rang. "Hey, Detective…Sam. I'm still getting used to it." He gave me the surprising news that Sergeant McNally complimented us on our tenacity. I described my encounter with Skylar's father the night before and informed him of our newest suspect. "Obviously, Mark Ripley followed through with his promise, confronting Skylar's father about his daughter's injuries, 'the little man' was Mark Ripley. Skylar's father even admitted he'd heard Mark Ripley 'got his.'"

Sam said, "That's good news. Let's see if he has an alibi for the twenty-third. He certainly had motive and opportunity."

I described his personality and hatred for all women, especially his daughter. "No doubt, it's probably related to his wife's disappearance in some way," I added. "And Sam, you should see the size of the man's hands. He could easily crush Mark Ripley's throat if he wanted. And he would have no problem hauling him up the steps."

"Okay," he said. "I'll call East Precinct and see if I can get a transcript of their interview. I imagine they'll turn this over to Youth Services, seeing the girl is still a minor. She's fifteen, right?"

"Yes." I saw a stretcher go by. "I wish they would bring her back from her scan and let me know something."

"She'll be all right, Abbey. Kids are resilient."

"I don't know, Sam. He did a number on the girl." After hanging up, I closed my eyes and listened as the doctors, the front desk people, and the ambulance teams carried on various conversations. I tuned in to hear updates on patients. None concerned Skylar. I stirred to a strange sound, opened my eyes, and watched as a tech began to clean the room and remove everything associated with Skylar. "Excuse me?"

"Oh, I'm sorry. I didn't see you there."

"Where's Skylar?"

"The young girl that was in this room?"

"Yes." I tried not to show the frustration in my voice, but I couldn't help it. It was a stupid question.

"Are you family?"

I showed my badge. "I brought her in. Her father's in custody, and she has no one else."

The young girl looked toward the desk and then back to me. "I guess it's okay. They took her into surgery straight from her CT scan. She won't be coming back here."

"What happened?"

"I don't know."

"Where will they take her?" I asked, now on my feet.

"I don't know. Honest."

I thanked her and gave my cell number to the desk nurse and asked him to call me once they knew something about Skylar's status and room. I knew I couldn't do anything there, and I hated hospitals almost as much as I did churches. I drove straight to Central to find something productive to do.

I just opened the door to the homicide room when I got the call. I listened to the list of injuries, some old, but most current. The doctor said, "She suffered a ruptured spleen. Unfortunately, we were unable to save the baby."

"The baby?" Skylar was seven weeks pregnant. That was right around her birthday. "Thank you, doctor." We were talking about physical and sexual abuse. That poor girl. She still could have been fourteen when it happened to her. I grabbed the nearest chair and flopped down on it. I felt the tsunami of my past roaring upon me, preparing to sweep me back in time. Thankfully, a gruff voice, pulled me back to the present.

"You look like crap, Rhodes." Sergeant McNally meant it as a gentle tease, a conversation starter, but I knew it was true. And I was thankful for the interruption.

"Hey, Sarge. I know I haven't built up enough days yet, but I need to take a couple." I glanced up. My eyes, like my mind, were distant and sorrowful. "This girl has no one, and I want to be there when she wakes."

"Keep us in the loop," he said. "I'll tell Tidwell and the others."

I could barely push up out of the chair. I staggered across the hall into the women's restroom and looked in the mirror. I hadn't realized I'd gotten blood on my shirt and cheek. I didn't even remember touching Skylar before they took her. Maybe it was in the ER. It didn't really matter. Skylar would be unconscious for a while. That gave me time to go home, take a shower, eat a bite, and put on comfortable clothes. I'd probably be spending the night at the hospital anyway.

Chapter Thirty

2:45 pm—Harmony Apartments

I wiped the steam from the mirror. That was the one complaint I had about this new apartment. Everything else was pristine and state-of-the-art. The bathroom exhaust wasn't. Of course, it didn't help that I ran the water as hot as I could tolerate and took long showers.

I wiped it again. I didn't recognize the face in the mirror…the eyes hollow and tragic. My world was crumbling, and no matter where I turned, everything triggered the past I tried so desperately to escape. After two years of keeping it in check, my PTSD was becoming a regular occurrence, and my paranoia heightened. Unless I did something soon, I knew I would plunge head-on into the dark abyss of depression once again. I dried off and donned my robe.

Back in the bedroom, I reached to the back of the closet and dug out the present from my sister. I threw it in the trashcan and screamed. I needed to open it and deal with it, but I couldn't bring myself to do it. I should have opened it the day my brother-in-law reached out to me in Germany and said Miriam was ill. She'd contracted some unknown infection in Central America, and it never cleared. I kicked myself for avoiding the funeral. And yet, I kept the present Miriam had given for my eighteenth birthday, the day I became an "adult."

Just open the stupid thing and get it over with! I retrieved it from the trash can and tore off the wrapping before I could chicken out again. Inside the small box, I found a CD and a book. "Oh, thanks, Miriam, just what I always wanted, Christian books and music." Sarcasm, of course. I flipped over the CD and read it aloud, "WOW 2017." It was a compilation of the top Christian songs from 2017, the year I turned eighteen. The book, *If I Run* by Terri Blackstock. I read the blurb. "Yeah, that sounds familiar. What are you trying to tell me, Miriam?"

So far, so good. I opened the card. Within a "Happy Birthday, Sis" card, Miriam had written a three-page letter.

Happy Birthday, Hannah Leah.

I know you've been waiting for this day for a long time, and I do understand why…more than you can imagine. You weren't the only one trapped. I want to say, 'I love you.' I also want to say, 'I'm so, so, sorry!'

I know I only compounded your humiliation and hatred for God by taking you to get an abortion against your will, but you were only fourteen, and I was your big sister. Being thirty at the time, they just assumed I was your mother, and I took advantage of that. Maybe one day you can find it in your heart to forgive me, and we can be sisters again. I got so caught up in trying to protect Dad's ministry, that I forgot to protect my little sis.

What happened to you was horrific, and no one should ever have to experience it. Rape, especially by someone who professes to be a minister of God, not only violates your body, but it destroys your heart and your spirit. I know that now. When that group leader took advantage of you, he stole your innocence. When he lied to Dad about raping you, he stole your soul and love for God. For that, he will pay. But I know the hardest part was when Dad took his word over yours and blamed you for being so well-developed at your age and for wearing shorts and a t-shirt, being a temptation. And to make matters worse, Mom and I just stood by and did nothing.

I guess that was the day you first felt alone. In many ways you were. Again, I'm sorry. I know this tragedy affected the way you see the church and God. Don't let it. Don't let the lies and the abuse of one youth minister take that from you. Don't give him that power. Part of God's love is that He gives us free will, and that includes sin...even against others.

Now, about the gifts. I want you to find the song, "If We're Honest," and let that be "our" song. It's really about both of us. We're both broken. Don't let your fears and your past define you. You have to own them, or they will continue to own you. As you probably already figured out, the book could be your story. I know you feel trapped, and you dream of being a cop who can rescue people like yourself. Maybe these gifts will inspire you to take charge of your past, your present, and your future.

I really do love you and desperately ask you to forgive me.

Miriam.

PS – Take the CD out of the trash and listen to it.

Despite the pain surging through me, I laughed at Miriam's final comment. She knew I'd throw it away. *A CD, Miriam. Really?* I scolded myself for the criticism. I knew my sister was trying to mend the rift between us. I promised Miriam at that moment, I'd download the album. *Oh, Miriam, I'm sorry I didn't open it earlier. We could have talked.*

I cried so long I lost track of time. I cried hard, a full-body cry; it was long overdue. I had a long way to go with the healing process, but for the first time in ten and a half years, I felt like I'd taken a step in the right direction. Maybe there was a purpose to this case...maybe there was some grand scheme of healing. With Susan's Hannah and now Skylar, I began to understand I wasn't alone. Maybe I could use my pain to help other victims.

I washed my face again, put makeup on, and left for the hospital. I wondered if I could find Skylar's mother. How long ago had she given up and left? Was she married again? Did she have a new name? Would she even want to know about her daughter if I could find her? Those were all questions for another day.

Chapter Thirty-one

Friday, November 10, 6:23 am—St. Thomas Hospital Midtown

I stepped out of the elevator and cupped my hand over my cell phone to block out the ambient noise. I listened as Lieutenant Daniels explained the case against Jamison Watson, Skylar's father. The man admitted he may have gotten a little heavy-handed with her last night, but said she provoked the beating. When the officer described, in detail, the wounds Skylar suffered and the baby she lost, Jamison laughed and said, "That little witch had it coming." He remained adamant he'd never touched his daughter in any sexual way, and he continued to claim Skylar provoked him into last night's beating. He said, "You don't know what she's like. She's downright evil."

When confronted with the judge's order of his DNA for a paternity test, Jamison opened his mouth wide and said, "Go for it! You'll see."

"Oh, he makes me want to vomit!" I said. "I wish I'd hit him even harder." I glanced both directions of the hospital hallway to see if anyone heard me.

"Be thankful he considers women the weaker sex, Abbey. Otherwise, he would press charges against you."

"The judge's order for the paternity test," I began, "how can they do that if the child died?"

"They'll take a sample from the fetus," he said. "I know it's not pretty, but we need to know for sure."

I wondered how Skylar was doing. In many ways, we were the

same. Someone took advantage of her too. She lost her child too. Young and vulnerable. I wished I could be in her room to protect her and comfort her if she woke, but I realized Skylar needed rest and was getting the best of care.

"They'll do it this morning sometime," Lieutenant Daniels said. "We should know soon. If the baby was his, we'll slam this door shut."

I noticed a long pause…too long. "And if it wasn't?"

"We have another case on our hands. I hope the D.A. will go for attempted murder, because Jamison said two or three times, on camera, that he wished he would have killed her this time. Then he called her a tramp and an assortment of other choice titles not fit for one's own daughter."

"That's what I like about you, Lieutenant."

"What's that, Abbey?"

"You're such a gentleman, even when it comes to trash like Jamison Watson." He didn't say anything, but I could tell he was smiling on his end of the phone. "Promise you'll let me know the instant you have any news?"

"You know I will. By the way, I met with your Detective Tidwell. I gave him copies of all we had so far on Mr. Watson. Oh, and Abbey, Detective Tidwell had a lot to say about you."

"Oh, great. I wonder which blunder he made fun of."

"Oh, no, Abbey. It was all good."

"Really?" That excited me. It was remarkable how a good word could brighten my day. I was beginning to get close to him and hoped it was mutual. Funny. The only two men I let close were father figures to me. I wasn't sure if that was twisted or normal with my history. I looked at my watch. Still too early to call Sam.

I went to the nurse's station and asked if there was any update on Skylar. My heart sank when they said there'd been no change in the night. At that moment, the doctor came out of the Intensive Care Unit. He looked at me and said, "Detective Rhodes?"

"Yes."

"We're going to keep Skylar sedated for a few days, so she can heal more efficiently. There's no reason to stay here. We can notify you when anything changes."

"I feel like she needs someone here," I said.

"You're free to stay if that makes you feel better," he said, "but you could use the rest too, I'm sure."

I nodded. He was right. I was so tired; I'd run out of fumes.

"I promise, we'll let you know."

Even though I felt guilty for doing so, I left.

Chapter Thirty-two

8:03 am—Homicide

Instead of going home and getting rest, I headed back to Homicide. After grabbing breakfast on my way, I sat in my chair and forced myself to eat. I'd lost my appetite. When had I eaten last? Everything was a blur. I looked at the stack of paperwork in my bin and sighed. So much had happened in the past two weeks. I wanted to talk with someone about my sister's letter, but I didn't feel safe doing so. To say I had trust issues was like saying the ocean had a little water. Even Lieutenant Daniels, who knew a lot of the story, would look at me differently if he knew everything.

I was just now getting close to Sam. I could take Lieutenant Daniels' advice and see a counselor, but that thought still creeped me out. Sitting in a room divulging my innermost thoughts and secrets to a stranger…no matter what his credentials and training…screamed of folly. Better to keep it to myself. I didn't like being vulnerable, surrendering control and power to someone I barely knew. That was also true for the people I did know—like the Daniels. Trust, once it is broken, takes forever to recover. For the time being, I decided to keep it all to myself. I held it in this long; what was another week or two?

"Hey, kid, I thought you were at the hospital?" Sam put a sack on his desk and dropped a thick folder on mine. "Everything they have on Jamison Watson is in there. You weren't kidding; this guy is a creep."

"Did you talk with him?" I asked, swiveling around in my chair to face him.

"No, but I watched the interview. I'm not a psychologist, but that dude is a psychopath. He has a general disregard for the safety and well-being of anyone, especially his daughter." Sam turned his chair to face me and sat down. "He blames her for his marriage failure, for their financial woes, and for cutting him off from friends, and for everything else wrong in his life. He must truly despise women. I'm surprised he didn't hit you when you asked about Skylar."

"Well…he tried. My reflexes were faster. I hit him hard and put him on his knees before I left." I turned away to hide a tear that trickled down my left cheek. "That beating he gave Skylar is on me."

"No, it's not!"

"Jeez, Sam. Give me a heart attack."

"Sorry. I didn't mean it to come out so loud." He lowered his voice. "Jamison would have given it to her sometime. At least now it's over."

"Maybe." I filled Sam in on what Lieutenant Daniels had told me this morning. I left out the part about Sam's compliments. "The sexual abuse and rape charges all hinge on the paternity test, but right now they have him on Domestic Assault, Aggravated Assault, and Aggravated Child Abuse. As you know, he admitted to those."

"We'll let them take care of their case. We need to take care of ours. You're right about the size of his hands. He could wrap them completely around the preacher's neck. And he seemed plenty strong to me. He works in a warehouse stacking and unstacking bags of mulch and gravel all day." I halfheartedly listened and was still staring at the carpet. Sam nudged me. "Come on, girl, don't quit on me now. We have motive, means, and opportunity for this guy. Let's find the evidence to nail this jerk to the wall." He nudged me again. "What's wrong with you?"

Without saying a word, I rose from my chair, walked down the aisle and out of homicide.

"What did I say?" he asked as the door closed.

Fifteen minutes later, I returned to my desk. "Sorry about that, Sam. This case is really getting to me. We need to solve it, so I can get on with my life." He didn't say anything. I slowly turned in my chair. "You need some air. Want to walk in the woods?"

"Excuse me?" he asked. "Are you okay?"

"Yeah. Why?" I grabbed my jacket and headed out. "I want another look around the church for the murder weapon." When I realized Sam hadn't moved, I hollered over my shoulder, "You coming or what?"

We drove to the church in silence. When Sam pulled into the drive, I said, "Park as close to the creek as possible."

"Okay." He turned the car off. "Before you get out of this car, tell me what in the world we're doing here."

I smiled. "I'm just following your orders."

"Oh, no. You're not turning this around on me." I unbuckled, but he snagged the seatbelt before it went three inches. He held me in place. I didn't realize he was so strong. "What gives?" he asked.

"You said we needed to find evidence and nail him, so what are you waiting for?" I pulled the belt from his hands and opened the car door. "I think the police searched too quickly, assuming the murder weapon would have been thrown from this side of the creek." I pointed to the house across from the church. "That's the Watson place." Then I pointed across the back section of the parking lot, the fenced-in area. "That bridge crosses the creek. We'll start over there."

We got out and walked to the little creek. "If I tossed it, I would have thrown it in the creek, way upstream. That way the water would degrade the evidence," Sam said.

I smiled again, remembering something important. "It hasn't rained here in three weeks. Jonathan said they didn't get a drop from the last two storms. If they assumed the weapon was thrown

from the church's side, they would have looked at the bottom or in the opposite bank. No one gave a thought to it being thrown from this side. Why would they?"

Sam pulled out a coin. "Heads I get the bank. Tails I take the creek." I nodded. He flipped the coin. Sam caught the coin and flipped it into his opposite hand. "Of all the bad luck." He stuck it back in his pocket.

"Aren't you going to show it to me first?" I asked.

"Why? You think I'd cheat to lose? That's absurd." Sam used the side of the bridge to steady himself as he slid down the bank to the bottom of the dry creek. "I'm too old for this."

"What? Mid-fifties?" I laughed and then said, "You're only as old as you feel."

"Don't make it any worse, girl. I'm old enough to be your father."

"Maybe, but you're nothing like my father."

"We have to talk about that one day," he said. Sam grumbled as he looked at the weeds, the sticks, and the debris. "Anything could be down here."

"Well, let's hope there is a piano bench leg."

I searched from the Watson's side of the creek bank, while Sam painstakingly made his way through the debris at the bottom.

I took a few more steps, moved some sticks, and tossed them aside. "My theory is the leg was used as a weapon of opportunity. Jamison saw Mark pull into the church, walked across the bridge, and entered through the door the preacher unlocked for his meeting with Alvaro." I moved another pile of limbs. "He followed the pastor, who rushed into the changing room and locked the door. Jamison kicked it until the lock broke. Jamison saw the piano bench leg leaning against the doorway, he seized it and swung away."

"Sounds feasible," Sam said, ducking under a fallen log.

"Did you know Jamison Watson is left-handed?" I asked.

"Yes, I did." Sam said. He stumbled and fell over a big limb.

"Are you okay, Sam?" I jumped over two clusters of branches

and directly to the creek bed, immediately helping him to his feet. "Why don't we switch for a while?" I got no argument from him. With a push from behind, Sam made it up the far bank. "Where was I?" I asked.

"Left-handed."

"Oh, yeah. Remember our theory about the blunt force trauma to the right side of his head and the blood splatter?"

"Refresh my memory," he said. "God, this place has to be full of snakes."

"They're actually more afraid of us than we are of them. Besides, it's too chilly for snakes this time of year." Even though that was true, I started looking a little more thoroughly anyway. "I theorized he was hit in the head by a left-handed swing, which the pathologist confirmed. Well, most of Skylar's wounds were to her right side too."

"His left," Sam added.

"Exactly! And when he was going to hit me the other night, he reared his left arm back." I was having fun despite the conditions of our search. "Then I think he ditched the club…oh, that sounds like a bad joke." I laughed anyway. "I'm on a roll."

"Are you on something?" he asked. Sam stopped to observe my balance.

"Nothing but a lack of sleep," I said. "And I'm a little bit giddy because I think we're getting close." Sam watched as I continued down the creek bed. I don't think he believed me.

"Abbey, stop!"

"You don't have to be rude. I'm just a little chatty," I said.

"Don't move!" I froze with my right leg suspended in the air. My first thought was a snake. I scanned the area in front of me. "Look on the bank to your right." I did. Lodged in the brush, just at eye level…the leg of a piano bench.

"I see dried blood! Quick, Sam, get an evidence bag and a pair of gloves."

He went to the car and retrieved the crime kit from the trunk.

Now that we had the weapon, we had the killer's prints. It was only a matter of time.

Chapter Thirty-three

3:45 pm—Homicide

I paced outside our cubicle. "That's ridiculous! It's going to take how long?" I tossed my phone to the desk.

"Abbey, sit down. You're going to wear a hole in the carpet." Sam looked at the transcripts of Jamison's interview. "Sometimes it takes weeks to get them processed."

"I can't stand this!" I flopped down in my chair. "How can you sit there and be so calm?"

He didn't even look up. "Years of practice." He smiled and pushed his reading glasses up on the bridge of his nose. "It comes with time...knowing nothing I do will speed them up." He set the paper down and turned around in his chair. "Use the time to be productive. Prepare for good news...prepare for bad. Either way, you're ready."

"What's that mean? Prepare for good...prepare for bad? It sounds like something from a fortune cookie." Irregular sleep and lack of a steady diet were wearing on me.

"Maybe that's where I heard it," Sam said. He glanced over at me. I slumped in my chair and put my feet on the desk. "Sit up and at least act professional," he snapped. "You look like a bored schoolgirl."

I huffed and sat up straight; proving his accusation to be true. "Finding the murder weapon was such a high." I turned my chair and rolled it up to Sam's desk. "Now, it's like...like...post-partum depression. I hate waiting." I noticed the transcript in his hands. "Did they even ask him about the murder?"

"I don't think so," Sam said. "I haven't found anything yet." I was looking over his shoulder, which bothered him, so Sam tore the back four pages free and handed them to me. "Look these over."

"Thanks." I started to read my portion of the transcript.

"At your desk."

I made a pouty lip and rolled back to my side of the cubicle like my feelings were hurt. Back at my desk, I scanned the document.

Unfortunately, neither section contained a reference to Mark Ripley's murder. We would address that when, and if, the prints belonged to Jamison Watson. If the prints weren't Jamison's, Sam hoped they belonged to someone else in the system. The good news…he wasn't going anywhere. Jamison had motive, means, and opportunity…not to mention the murder weapon discovered thirty-five feet from his back porch. Shame it was on the church's property. I hoped he was the murderer. Then we could bury him for good.

"Prepare yourself," he said. "That piano leg has been out in the elements for nineteen days. We don't even know if the prints will be legible or not."

"They have to be." Every time I thought we were close, something came up to dash my hopes. Without the prints, we were stuck with circumstantial evidence. If they were legible but turned out to be someone other than Jamison's, we were once again back to the proverbial drawing board.

I thought of Skylar. What would she think about the turn of events? If it was her father, did she know? Suddenly I realized in all the excitement, I forgot to inform the church about Skylar's condition. I called the church, but no one answered. I tried again.

This time Faith answered. "Living Water Church." I decided to keep the miscarriage a secret for now, but informed Faith that Skylar's father nearly beat her to death. I gave the number for the nurse's desk. Faith thanked me and promised to let Jonathan know.

As Sam and I were preparing to call it a day, Lieutenant

Daniels called. "Abbey, the paternity test was negative. In fact, it was zero percent."

"Wait, shouldn't it be at least twenty percent?" I asked. "Assuming it was his grandchild?"

"Yes. Eighteen to thirty-two percent match according to the doctor. Now have a greater problem. Skylar's not his biological daughter, and we've found no adoption records."

I was stunned. Selfishly, I was hoping for a rape conviction. Someone else had gotten Skylar pregnant. Who? "So, Lieutenant, who will look into the rape now?"

"You assume it's rape. Don't let your past blind you from the truth. What if it was consensual and they're both underage?"

I wasn't projecting my past on Skylar...was I? "This doesn't make any sense. The church people all said she was a loner, that her dad barely let her out of the house." I had more questions than I had answers. I took a deep breath, counted to ten, and then let it out slowly.

"Abbey, are you still there?"

"Yes."

"Let me handle it. For now, we'll gather all the evidence we have against Jamison. The D.A. should still have a solid case for multiple charges."

"Okay. Thanks." I hung up and passed on everything I'd just learned. Sam was as surprised. Now, I would have this hanging over my head all weekend as we awaited the results of the fingerprints.

Chapter Thirty-four

Sunday, November 12—Nashville

On Sunday afternoon, after studying the Ripley case all morning, I put on a pair of sweats and walked the streets of Nashville. I had to uncloud my head and get a fresh look at the case. The best way to do that was to get fresh air. I was missing something, something I believed was right in front of my face.

I had a bad feeling about Jamison Watson. Where was his ex-wife, and why couldn't we find a trail of information? If she remarried, there had to be a divorce. If she got a new job, there had to be a social security trail. I could understand a woman who lived with Jamison keeping a low profile. Jamison was a true scoundrel. I was shocked when Lieutenant Daniels learned Jamison kept a steady warehouse job. He looked like a jobless bum. Instead, he was just a drunken jerk.

No doubt he abused his daughter and would pay for it. Now that the paternity test ruled him out not only as the father of the baby but as the father of Skylar too, I doubted Jamison cared enough to leave his home, go to the church, and kill Mark Ripley. The man barely moved to answer his own door. A man like Jamison would have no need or reason to haul Mark Ripley's body to the baptistery. That would be a meaningless gesture for him. Jamison, like Alvaro Garcia, filled the trifecta: motive, means, and opportunity. In my gut, I knew neither man did it, even if I secretly wanted it to be Jamison Watson. So, where did that leave us?

I skirted the roundabout with colored telephone poles sticking up in every direction. A poor excuse for art! I turned up Korean Vets Boulevard. Passing the Music City Center, I followed John Lewis Way to my left. When I came to Walk of Fame Park, I found an empty bench and sat down. I didn't need the evidence or the paperwork anymore. I was blessed with a great memory. I guess that was also a curse. Anyway, what I needed was a break from the case.

I pulled out my phone, hit the app for iTunes and searched for the song Miriam had asked me to hear. Of all times to have a memory lapse. *What was it? "Honesty?" No. "Let's Be Honest?" No. "If We're Honest." That's it.* I typed it in the blank for search. The song by Francesca Battistelli popped up. I hit the pay button and watched as the song downloaded and gave me the option of opening it. I synced my earbuds and hit play. I listened and thought of Miriam.

I hit play again…and again…and again. I couldn't believe it. I ran as fast as I could back to the apartment and looked up the lyrics. *Oh, Miriam.* I copied them and printed them. I just stared at the words. *Why didn't I open that present years ago?* I took a piece of tape and stuck the song on my bedroom wall where I would see it every day. I just stood there and stared at the lyrics. They spoke to me; they spoke to that broken part of me.

I knew I was broken. Was Miriam admitting as much? Honesty, integrity, and discipline…the traits of a soldier. I struggled so hard to prove my integrity, not realizing I was living a lie all this time. It was easy to point fingers at others…not very easy to look in the mirror. Maybe I could finally have peace with Miriam. We'd come to terms…better late than never. My father was a different story altogether. Fingers pointing to him were justified.

As I played the song one more time, I thought of Skylar. Did she know he wasn't her father? I made a note to search for her birth records on Monday. But Skylar was pregnant…by whom? Was it from a random encounter? Did she have a boyfriend? I knew most of these questions wouldn't be answered until Skylar regained consciousness.

Even though the walk's purpose was to divert my mind from the stress, my thoughts turned to the case. My skepticism raised its ugly head. Mark Ripley lived that song; look what it got him. Then I thought of all the other church people…and of course, my thoughts were negative. What secrets must they be hiding? Was Susan as innocent and sweet as she seemed? What about Faith? Was she just a smiling facade covering a world of hurt? What woman made the call and used Faith's email to send Pastor Mark a message about Alvaro? Nothing added up. Oddly enough, the two men that seemed to have the most distaste for Mark Ripley didn't even try to hide their feelings. Maybe they were the most honest of all.

Who had the most to gain from Mark's death? Faith Jones gained nothing but the unknown of a new pastor and boss. Duke Stearns gained his power back, possibly. He also could steer things back to the old way. Same thing for Owen Jenkins. The elders gained nothing but a battle with the original members for the direction of the church. The minister of music and worship, the new children's minister, and the missions coordinator all came because Mark and his vision. They had nothing to gain and everything to lose. Maeve Kennedy was totally on board with Mark…unless she gave Sophia that passage to provoke Alvaro. No. He didn't kill Mark. Jonathan was working with Mark to help Skylar. Why kill an ally? On and on my thoughts rambled.

So, who did that leave? Quentin Green, the former pastor, and the former children's minister. What if the old pastor and children's minister coordinated the death with someone else? Other than revenge, they gained nothing. Revenge led the old pastor to discredit and undermine Mark Ripley, but those are both passive-aggressive means to an end, the church getting rid of Mark, not making him a saint (as close as Baptists would…building something in his name). Quentin Green seemed genuinely pleased the church was thriving.

"Ugh!" I felt like pulling my hair out. Thankfully, my phone rang before I had the chance. It was Susan Ripley. I couldn't deal with her right now. I let it go to voicemail.

She texted a message. "Thanks for bonding with Hannah. It means the world to me for her to have someone." I didn't respond. Instead, I microwaved some leftovers from Maggie's house and sat on the couch. *What am I missing?*

I decided to try a different strategy. I would search all the church leaders to see where they came from, if they had social media accounts, and whether they had any skeletons in their closets…especially since I was now on the theme of honesty. I searched every leader. Some were easier to find than others. Some barely made a footprint on social media. Others had multiple accounts. The younger the leader, the more I could find. I decided to search Susan Ripley. Other than a few inner-city mission pictures, her social media accounts were focused on her family. Squeaky clean once again.

Some leaders such as two of the elders, the new children's minister, and the missions coordinator were as clean as a microchip lab…almost too clean. The third elder was a former marine with distinction. Although I could find pages upon pages of his history, he seemed heroic and exemplary. The only thing negative about Owen Jenkins was an article accusing his company of using cheap materials and hiring illegals under the table. Two other articles cleared him of the first charge but could never say for sure whether the second was true. Even if these accusations were legit, it wouldn't make him a murderer.

Duke Stearns had a Facebook page, which surprisingly was devoted to cats and gardening. Who would have figured? Faith Jones was related to a famous studio guitarist in Nashville. He played with many of the greats. Her social media sites focused on her late sister. That left Maeve Kennedy and Jonathan Williams. Each had a detailed and complex social media presence and past.

My eyes were burning, and I couldn't read anymore for the night. I printed several pieces on each of them. Maybe Sam could see something I didn't. I collected the printed paper and set it by the front door, so I wouldn't forget it in the morning.

Chapter Thirty-five

Sam was already sitting at his desk when I walked in. "Bad news, Abbey."

"I don't need any more bad news," I said.

"There's a backlog on the prints. We may not get them for a month."

I set the box on the desk. "What else is going to go wrong in this case?"

"Hey, patience. It's not going wrong; it's just delayed." He looked at the box. "What did you bring me today?" I handed it to Sam and watched as he opened it. "What's all this?" he asked, pulling out two bound stacks of paper. "Is this for the Ripley case?"

"Yes. I took a different approach. I searched their personal lives for red flags."

"Maeve Kennedy?" he asked. "What gets you about her?"

I pointed to a printout where Maeve was charged with domestic violence. "If you look at the first part of the paper, it says it was justified as self-defense."

"So why flag her?"

"Look at the weapon of choice," I said. "She beat him with a wooden club…a broken chair leg." Sam raised an eyebrow. "Sound familiar?"

"Eerily so," he said. "Did you read all of this?"

"Not yet. My eyes wore out."

174

Sam pulled out the second set. "Jonathan Williams. Baseball player."

"He's certainly fit enough to be one."

He slapped his desktop. "I knew I recognized him!"

"You know him?" I asked, looking at the article with Sam.

"J.J. Williams. Jonathan just didn't ring a bell for me, and he's aged five years. He played for the University of Louisville. He was a top recruit and a rookie of the year candidate until he got in some trouble. The university swept it all under the rug, but it was enough to end his short and promising career." Sam turned to face me. "He led the NCAA in home runs and was third in average. The pros were all after him."

"What happened?" This piqued my interest.

"The case was settled, and a gag order put in place before the details ever came out. Most speculated it had to do with either a prostitution ring used to recruit top talent or the fondling of a minor. Either way, he just disappeared."

I took a handful of sheets from Jonathan's stack. "How does a guy like that end up as a youth minister? Even if the case was sealed, he'd have to carry that reputation with him. Nashville's not that far from Louisville."

"One would think," Sam said, "but these things have a way of seeping through the cracks."

I read more of the article. Nowhere did it say he was guilty, but it certainly smelled rotten. And, if he was this promising of a player, something major had to happen to bring all of that to a halt, especially if he had the attention of the pros. "What if he's the one involved with Skylar?" I asked.

"Oooh. He would have access and persuasion over her." Sam leaned back in his chair. "We better be certain of it before we ruin another career of his. One question and he's done as a minister."

"But if he's guilty?" I asked. "He needs to be removed from that church and put in jail. Skylar's only fifteen. He's what… twenty-five…twenty-six?"

"Before you jump to conclusions, you need to do the work. You're letting your emotions dictate the results instead of the facts, Abbey." He sounded just like Lieutenant Daniels.

"So, what do you suggest?" I was hot. "Let a suspected rapist run free?"

Something triggered Sam, and he did an emotional one-eighty. "Stick to homicide!" he barked. "That case belongs in Sex Crimes Division." I could tell he was irritated with me. "Do the same thing you would for any other case. Follow the facts and find the right suspect. Don't focus on who you want to be guilty, Abbey." He saw my look and said, "Yes, you were right about Alvaro. Yes, you were right about Skylar's dad abusing her. You may even be right about Jonathan Williams. But do the work assigned to you!" His thundering voice shocked me into submission. "We're homicide detectives, and we investigate homicides. End of story." Heads were popping up from every cubicle.

He spun around in his chair and dug into the first case file he could grab. The silence was deafening. I wanted to say something, but I knew he was right. I'd gotten so attached to Skylar and Susan's family, I felt personally responsible for bringing justice, and I let myself be sucked into areas that didn't belong to us. Trusting others wasn't a strength of mine. But he was right. The team was larger than us. "No more contact with Living Water Church unless it's official business," he added.

Sam got up from his desk and walked the few steps to Sergeant McNally's cubicle. He handed Sarge the articles I printed on Jonathan Williams and asked him to pass them on to Sex Crimes. Then he left the building.

I sat alone, completely embarrassed. I deserved that. I opened my team's case file and read the material inside. I desperately wanted to have something to offer Sam when he came back, whenever that might be.

Chapter Thirty-six

Thursday, November 16, 2:15 pm—Behavioral Health Services Division

I sat in the corner of the waiting room of Metro's Behavioral Health Services Division, professional counseling services offered to members of the police force. I'd waited long enough. I desperately wanted to flee, but knew it was time I heeded Lieutenant Daniels' advice. I crossed and uncrossed my legs. I'd seen a study where they could analyze a person on when he had his legs crossed or uncrossed. I couldn't remember what it meant, though. I grabbed a nearby magazine and flipped through it, only to set it back down.

"Detective Rhodes."

"Yes." I stood and pulled on the collar of my sweater. "I'm Detective Rhodes."

The woman extended her hand. "I'm Dr. Grissom. Come in." The counselor signaled for me to enter her office and take a seat. She shut the door and pushed a button on a device that made ocean wave sounds. "It's white noise, so what we say in here, stays in here."

"Oh, okay." I looked at the two options before me, a wing-back cloth chair or a leather loveseat. I wondered what it meant if I chose one over the other. I opted for the chair, assuming the loveseat was for couples' therapy. "I appreciate you fitting me in on such short notice."

"Thankfully, I had a cancellation."

"What now?" I asked.

"I read over your intake information, but it was all rather vague." The counselor sat behind her desk, which was nothing more than a fancy acrylic table with a laptop and a lamp on it. There were no drawers, and I could see clearly to the other side. Dr. Grissom was dressed professionally in a maroon skirt version of a business suit. Her light brown hair pulled tightly into a bun. She pulled her glasses off and set them on the desk. "Why don't you begin with why you're here...what you hope to achieve."

"Okay." I thought about it. That was a loaded question. Start small. "I'm having trouble trusting others."

"Professionally or personally?"

"Yes."

"I see." The counselor closed the laptop and focused on my face. Was she studying me like I did suspects? "Why don't you tell me a little more."

"I...I seem to be having the same issue with you, to be honest," I said.

"I assure you that I will keep everything you say in confidence. My office already explained the exceptions, which are judge's orders, danger of harm to self, and danger of harm to others. Beyond that, what you say stays between us."

"No offense, but I don't know you. So, how do I know your assurance is legitimate?"

"That's a fair question. Let's start with something simple," Dr. Grissom said. "Tell me your name and what you do."

Easy enough. "Abbey Rhodes. Homicide detective for Metro."

"How long have you been with Homicide?"

I crossed my legs again. She didn't even break eye contact to notice. Good. I could stop worrying so much about my body language and unintentional signals. "Just over three."

"Oh my, you're new to this." She opened the laptop and said, "Will it bother you if I take some notes?" I glanced at the laptop. I didn't know which was the right answer...how it would look... what the counselor would think. Before I decided how to answer,

the counselor closed the laptop again and said, "I'll be fine without it. Let's just talk today."

For the next forty minutes, I talked about my job. Questions about family and personal life made me anxious and were avoided. I discussed the difference between my experience as an MP and an officer of Metro. I admitted I was still trying to get the hang of Homicide and had issues of following tangents that were not homicide related. I also admitted I had deep boundary issues and would often retreat if something seemed emotionally dangerous or embarrassing.

Then, I spent the final five minutes explaining the phrase "Ever Vigilant," which I adopted from the Army as my own personal motto. "We were trained to always be on the lookout for the unexpected. To be on high alert constantly, therefore, nothing ever took us by surprise."

"Isn't that exhausting?" the counselor asked.

"I don't know. I've lived that way since I was fourteen."

"What happened when you were fourteen?"

"I'd rather not talk about it." I began chewing on the nub of a fingernail.

"How long have you lived on your own?"

I didn't answer. It was complicated. Not something I wanted to talk about. The counselor redirected her questions to the Army or the force. I perked up when I spoke of my Army experience or my three years at Metro's East Precinct. I admitted it was like starting all over at Homicide. At the end of the session, I scheduled another meeting with Dr. Grissom, surprising both of us. I shook her hand and left for home feeling hopeful.

I parked in my spot and entered the building from the back. I bypassed another mixer in the lobby bar and headed right for the elevator. I recognized the man standing with his back to me. "Aaron?"

He turned and smiled. "Abbey. You remembered me?"

"Of course. I can't be a snob all my life," I said with a smile. It was real.

"Just for part?" he asked, joining the sarcasm.

When we entered the elevator, he pressed the button for our floor. "Only when it's convenient," I said. "Seriously, I owe you an apology. I work police homicide for Nashville, and the job is wearing on me."

"You're a cop?" he asked.

"Was a cop. Now I'm a detective."

"I must say. I wouldn't mind being arrested by you." He put his face in his hands. "Sorry. That sounded better in my head."

"I'm flattered." The door opened, and I headed to my apartment. "Nice talking with you, Aaron. Goodnight."

"Goodnight, Abbey."

I opened the apartment door, shut it, and then leaned back against the door. He was cuter than I remembered!

Chapter Thirty-seven

Friday, November 17, 8:57 am—Nashville Downtown Detention Center

The moment I walked into Homicide, Sam told me to grab my things and come with him. We had an appointment with Jamison Watson at the Nashville Downtown Detention Center. I hadn't mentioned the Ripley case since the first of the week and tried my best to fall in line with my team and the many investigations they had going. I was cautiously excited to interview Jamison Watson and even happier that it was Sam's idea.

The door locks released, and the guard brought Jamison Watson into the room and handcuffed him to the table. "This really necessary?" he barked. The officer didn't say a word. The moment Detective Tidwell nodded, the officer left us alone in the little room, which had a gray metal table and four heavy metal chairs.

Sam opened the file. "Mr. Watson, my name is…"

"Your little sweetheart and I already met. Isn't that right, little girl?"

"As I was saying," Sam continued. "My name is Detective Tidwell, and my associate is Detective Rhodes."

"Funny you didn't mention you were a cop the other day, sweetheart." He stared at me, glancing first at my face but then lowering his gaze to my breasts. I tried not to react. His eyes remained there. "You look better in the light."

"Mr. Watson," Sam continued even though he knew he didn't have the man's undivided attention, "we're here to ask you a few questions about the Pastor of Living Water Church."

"He's dead," he said. He winked at me and then licked his lips.

It took every ounce of control I had not to jump over the table and kick him in the face. "That is why it's called a murder investigation," I said. "We are from Homicide after all."

"Oh, you're smart and beautiful." He continued to stare at my breasts. "I didn't think that was possible."

I stood. "I think you'll get more accomplished if I leave, Detective Tidwell."

"No!" Jamison Watson was shaking his head vehemently. "She goes, I shut up. She stays, I talk."

I sat back down. "I'm here. Now pay attention to the questions, or I leave."

He nodded.

Detective Tidwell asked, "Is it true that you've waived your right to have counsel present?" He nodded again. "And you've been advised of your rights?" Jamison nodded once more. Detective Tidwell proceeded with his line of questioning. "Is it true that you live across a creek from Living Water Church?"

"Yep, and I wish they'd stay on their side and leave me alone." He looked at me and winked. "All except you, sweetheart."

"Is it true that you have issues with the church people, including some who have come to your residence?" Sam asked.

"I just said that, stupid."

"Who specifically would that be?" Sam asked.

"That fat lady, the buff guy, and the small one," Jamison said.

"Do you know who those individuals are? Do you have names?" Sam asked.

"The fat lady, Maple something. That buff guy who does things with the kids Skylar's age, his name is John something. She talks about him all the time. The last one was that dead guy… the preacher."

"Did they anger you?" Sam asked.

"The woman was just plain stupid. They all are." He smiled at me. "Except you, little girl. The guy that works with the kids was

182

a wimp. He shut up the moment I stepped in his face." Jamison leaned down to the table so he could scratch his cheek. "The last little guy pretended to be concerned about Skylar. I didn't buy that, and I told him so. He had some guts, though, that little guy. I could tell he was afraid of me." Jamison jerked on the handcuffs and laughed when we both jumped. "You afraid of me too?"

"Do you want to harm me too?" Sam asked. "Would that make you feel better?"

"It might." He laughed. It was an obnoxious laugh that filled the little room and showed his decaying teeth.

"Did it make you feel better to beat Skylar?" I asked.

"I told you before, that conniving little witch had it comin'. Should have known she'd get pregnant. Just like a dog in heat. That's what women do." This time he glared at me. It's like he flipped a switch and became Mr. Hyde. They say the eyes are windows to the soul. His were dark, menacing, and downright evil. "That what you want too, girl? To get pregnant?" He looked to Sam. "He get you pregnant?"

Sam laughed. "Is that all you think about, Mr. Watson? Beating people and degrading women?" Jamison glared at him too, but he didn't say anything. "We're here to ask you a few questions that matter, Mr. Watson. If you can't do that, you can return to your cell. Just don't waste my time." Sam was stern and direct. He was matching Jamison's intensity, testing his theory about the real man…a "man" who would abuse a petite young girl. When he noticed a slight movement back in his seat, Sam said, "You decide, Mr. Watson. What's it going to be?"

"I'm still here." His voice was quieter, less antagonizing. "Ask your stupid questions."

So, he would only respect a person who could stand firm in the face of his menacing temper. "Did you kill the pastor of the church?" Sam was tired of dancing around the issue.

"No. I should have, but someone beat me to it."

"Why?" Sam asked.

"He couldn't control his people, and they stuck their noses in my family business."

Sam tried various ways of tripping him up, getting him to make a mistake, but the man didn't even seem to care to deny anything he'd done. Jamison insisted Skylar deserved it, that we didn't know what she was like. He didn't shy away from his hatred of women either. Nothing seemed to issue the response we came to get.

"Where's your ex-wife?" I asked.

"Wouldn't you like to know?" Jamison said.

"Did you know Skylar's not your daughter?" I asked. Jamison didn't flinch. "Is that why you hate her so much?"

"Guard."

I slapped a copy of the birth certificate on the table. "That's not your name."

"Guard!" Jamison Watson was done. "I want out of here!" I'd hit him below the belt…again.

Chapter Thirty-eight

Back at Homicide, Sam and I agreed that Jamison Watson had the desire and ability to kill Mark Ripley, but he was probably too lazy to do so. If Ripley had presented himself again on Jamison's doorstep, he would have hurt him or even killed him. But Jamison Watson was not the kind of man who would go to the church, kill the pastor, and then go to the trouble of throwing him into the baptistery.

"I'm confused. Alvaro is in the clear, and he was the most logical suspect," I said. "But we have no other cars entering the parking lot that morning."

"That still makes me think Jamison did it," Sam said. "All he would have to do is walk across the bridge."

We looked back at Mark Ripley's phone records. We read the texts beginning on October 20, three days before his death. Nothing seemed out of the ordinary. Most were group texts to his leaders, either keeping them informed of the activities, scheduled events, or reminders of meetings. A few short texts to Susan expressing his love for her and his loneliness without her and the kids. A text to another pastor, asking about a community event opportunity. Another to the Director of Missions setting up a time to meet about the Spanish service he hoped to begin soon. The phone records were a waste of time. Nothing new.

"He was a busy man," Sam said. "I'm impressed."

"I know. The more I hear about him, the more I wonder why anyone would want him dead."

"I keep coming back to the way he was killed," Sam said.

"Someone went to an awful lot of trouble to do it that way. Why not just keep beating him until he was dead? Why drag him all the way up the steps, get in the water with him, and drown him."

"It has to be someone with anger issues or a deep, deep, seething hate of Mark Ripley. There's also something about the baptismal water."

"Okay. Let's go back over what we do know." Sam grabbed his notes. "Strong. Probably left-handed."

"And someone within walking distance. Do we have addresses for the church leaders?" I asked.

"I'm sure we can get them from the secretary," Sam said. "But you're assuming it was one of the church leaders. What if it was someone from the church congregation? We need to get a list of all the original members, anyone who was a member before Mark Ripley came to the church. And what if it was just random? Someone who found an open door and made themselves at home only to be discovered by the pastor."

"Not if Duke locked the doors and they stayed locked until Mark Ripley got there," I said. "If it was random, I don't think they would have bothered with the baptistery. I'll call Faith and have her send us a list of addresses and names of members prior to his first Sunday."

I called Faith, and she agreed to email both lists by the end of the day. I also asked if there was a way of determining which members lived within walking distance of the church. Faith explained that would have to be done by hand. Their church records were not in a database that facilitated that kind of search. When they were a smaller congregation, she could have done that easily. They grew so much in the past two years; it was nearly impossible. The church didn't even have addresses of all the new members.

I wanted to call the hospital and check in on Skylar. I also wanted to see what Sex Crimes had done with the tip on Jonathan Williams. If he was the father, I'd kill him. I busied myself with something else. *Can't go down that road. Not now.*

186

As if on cue, Spence stepped into our cubicle and asked for a second set of eyes to look over something. I reached out and grabbed the papers. I studied the report and looked over the testimonies. I flipped back and forth a few times and said, "I don't know if it matters, but the times don't match."

He leaned in. "Where?"

I pointed to the eyewitness report and then back to the gas attendant's testimony. "The attendant says the robber shot the customer at two a.m. Over here, the neighbor said he woke to the sound of gunfire at one." I turned back a page or two. "Did the gas station have video recordings?"

"Yes." Spence added, "But the date and time stamps were off. I'm not sure who's right. Good eyes. Anything else?" I looked it over again and shook my head. Spence thanked me and went back to his desk.

"Hey, Spence?" Sam asked.

"Yes."

"What did you determine on the Smith case? Was it suicide or homicide?"

"Suicide," he said. "We couldn't find any sign of foul play."

"So, it's closed for us?" Sam asked.

"Yes."

Sam closed the file and put it in a metal bin. My phone rang. It was Susan Ripley again. I let it go to voicemail. "Who was that?" Sam asked.

"Susan Ripley. She keeps calling me."

"Why don't you answer?" he asked.

"I'm trying to cut myself off from them and keep this on a professional basis. She keeps inviting me to her home and to the church." I let out a heavy sigh. "This is hard, Sam. I went so long keeping everything in…trying so hard to be vigilant of my emotions, to keep them in check. But this case…this case just hits too close to home. I'm having a really hard time adjusting to…" I stopped. I wasn't exactly sure how to describe my feelings without revealing another page of my past. It was still too raw, especially after Miriam's letter.

"You don't have to explain anything to me. Trust me. I understand."

He did. This case opened the floodgates for his past too. Murder and rape all in one case. There was a reason he turned Jonathan Williams over to Sex Crimes so quickly. I could tell his emotions were running wild too. My uncanny resemblance to Molly started it all. Skylar's rape escalated the pain. He wasn't ready to face anything else right now. We had more in common than met the eye.

My phone rang again. It was Susan Ripley. This time I answered. "Detective Rhodes."

"Oh, Abbey, thank God. I was beginning to think you were avoiding me." Susan sounded desperate.

"What's going on?" I asked.

"Hannah's been having these horrible nightmares. She wakes up screaming at the top of her lungs and can't be consoled. The doctor's calling them night terrors. There's nothing he can do but refer her to a counselor."

"That sounds awful. I'm so sorry." I put my hand over the phone and explained it to Sam. "It sounds like good advice."

"She's already seeing a counselor but is having trust issues."

"That's normal for an abused child," I said. I knew firsthand. I lived with the trauma and still had trust issues.

"She keeps asking for you." I didn't respond. "I know you're terribly busy, but if there's any way you can find a few moments to come talk with her, I would be in your debt." I swallowed at a lump forming in my throat. "Please, Abbey. I don't know where else to turn."

"Okay. I'll stop by tomorrow morning around nine. Does that work for you?"

"Yes. Thank you. You are such a godsend to our family." Susan hung up.

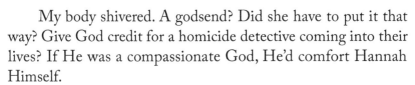
My body shivered. A godsend? Did she have to put it that way? Give God credit for a homicide detective coming into their lives? If He was a compassionate God, He'd comfort Hannah Himself.

"That didn't last long," Sam said.

"She hung up first." Even I heard the tightness in my voice.

"I meant keeping a disconnect with the people from Living Water Church."

"Oh, shut up." I hit him playfully on the back.

Chapter Thirty-nine

Saturday, November 18, 9:00 am—Ripley home

I pulled into the driveway at the Ripley home right at nine. I grabbed the soccer ball from the passenger floorboard and got out of my car. It was a brisk November morning, barely in the mid-forties. Great day for soccer!

I didn't even have to ring the doorbell. Susan opened the door before I reached the front porch. Danny was right on her tail. I braced for the hug, which was almost a tackle. I rubbed his head. His eyes lit up when he saw the soccer ball. "Is that for me?"

"Sorry, little man," I said. "This is my favorite ball. I got it in Germany."

"Where's Germany?" he asked.

I smiled. "Too far to go get another one, I'm afraid." I looked behind Susan, but Hannah wasn't there. I tilted my head and looked into Susan's eyes, a way of asking without having to ask.

"Still in bed. Maybe you can coax her out."

"I think I have a better idea," I said. "How do we get to the backyard? That is your fence, isn't it?"

Danny grabbed my free hand and yanked. "Follow me." He dragged me through the house to the back door. "Come on!"

"I'm coming. I'm coming." I nearly stumbled, rushing through the back doorway. "It's huge!"

"The nice thing about the older lots in East Nashville is the size, measuring a full acre."

190

I was impressed. "How could you afford this?" I cringed the moment the words crossed my lips, and I tried to recover by saying, "None of my business. Sorry."

"No," Susan said. "It needed a lot of work. That's how we got it so cheap."

I tossed the ball out in the middle of the yard, which only had three trees, two large, older oaks and a Chinese maple. They'd lost most of their leaves, but enough remained for me to identify the species. A small swing set with an attached clubhouse sat near the back corner of the lot. Other than that, the space was wide open. Danny retrieved the ball and ran it back to me.

"Come on, little man. You know you can't grab the ball with your hands in soccer."

"I know." He put it on the ground. "I didn't know we started."

"Okay," I said. "Kick it to me."

Danny kicked the ball. I scooped it up with my right toe and proceeded to bounce it off of one knee then the other, back and forth. I finally kneed it up high in the air and waited for it to come down far enough to direct it back to Danny with my head. "Oh my gosh! Are you like a pro?"

"No, but I've played it all of my life…as long as I can remember."

He hit it back to me. "Show me something else," he begged.

I noticed the blinds of one of the back windows moving. I saw Hannah looking through the bottom three slats. Time to put on a show. I dribbled with my feet, crisscrossing, feigning kicks, and tossing the ball over my head by gripping the ball with both feet. "How's that?" I asked. I looked over at the window, but Hannah was gone. *Nice try.*

"Do something else," he said. "Please!"

I continued to show him tricks with the ball. I said, "Watch this," and ran forward and performed a ball flip, throwing it against the tree when I landed. It bounced right back to me. It was one of my favorite tricks.

"Where did you learn that?"

I turned. It was Hannah. I set the ball on the ground and kicked it to her. "Everybody plays soccer in Central America."

Hannah kicked it back to me. Over her shoulder, I could see Susan crying. "You're really good," Hannah said in a soft voice.

"Thanks. I worked hard at it." The three of us made a triangle and kicked the ball back and forth. Occasionally, I would do something to amaze Hannah and bring a squeal from Danny. After an hour, Susan came out and got Danny. He left reluctantly, making it clear to everyone he'd rather stay with us. After he left, I sat in one of the swings and said, "I need to rest. You guys are wearing me out." It was time to see what was bothering her.

Hannah took the other seat. "Why did you say your name was Hannah?"

I wondered when this question would come up. I'd rehearsed the answer many times. "It is…well, technically it was."

"I don't understand."

I couldn't tell her everything, so I chose my words carefully. "I've only told one other person this." Then, I explained to Hannah that I too had been taken advantage of by an older man. "He made me feel special." I said, "He gave me something and said it would relax me, but it did more than that." I explained how I tried to escape his grasp. Tried to scream. Tried to fight back, but it was no use. He was too strong, and we were too far from home. "I felt ashamed and dirty."

Hannah nodded.

I continued. "The worst part was when I ran home and told my dad. I expected him to hold me and wipe my tears away, to tell me everything would be okay. I expected him to scold and punish the man who hurt me. Instead, the man had already visited my father and said that I had torn open my shirt and tried to seduce him. I didn't even know what that word meant. He warned my father that I would lie, saying he'd done something to me, because I was so embarrassed when he refused my advances.

"That was the story my father chose to believe. That was the story my father shared with the other leaders—the visitors—everyone. He accused me of dressing provocatively and showing off my over-developed body. He called me a tease and said I was dead to him. When I cried and ran to my mother, she turned her back on me, too. Even my older sister, Miriam, kept quiet.

"From that time on, I stayed out in the neighborhood and learned to survive on my own, only sneaking in one of the vacant mission group homes occasionally to eat or sleep when I could find nowhere else to go. No one seemed to care." I didn't tell her about the man who took me in and provided for me.

I stopped and looked around, making sure neither Susan or Danny was listening. Through misty eyes I said, "I found out I was pregnant." Hannah's eyes widened. "I was going to tell my parents, to say, 'See, I told the truth.' But my sister intervened. She took me to a doctor that…" I paused and took a deep breath. How could I explain that to her? Hannah put her hand on my knee.

"Did you get rid of it?" Hannah asked. I nodded and let the tears roll unabashedly. "Did your daddy ever find out?" I shook my head. I gave Hannah a side hug. For once, someone didn't judge me.

I took a deep breath and let it out slowly. "The day I turned eighteen and was considered an adult, I changed my name from Hannah Leah Abelard to Abbey Rhodes. Everyone called me Abbey anyway." I chuckled. "Who names their daughter after a woman who gave up her kid and a wife the man never wanted?" Hannah shrugged her shoulders. "Anyway, I picked the name because my father hated the Beatles."

"Who?"

I laughed again. "A rock and roll group. One of their albums was called *Abbey Road*. I did it to spite him. Three months later, I graduated from high school and left for the Army. I picked the place as far from my home as I could, Grafenwöhr, Germany." I noticed Hannah's confusion. "It's at the other end of the world." I took a few cleansing breaths. I'd made it this far. Might as well go the rest of the way.

"Everyone believed the reputation they heard of me was true. That I wanted men to do that to me. I didn't. But there was no convincing anyone of the truth. So, I let them believe what they wanted all the way up to the day I left." I put my hand on top of Hannah's. "I was alone. I've tried telling myself I like being alone, but I don't. It just made me feel safe…makes me feel safe." I wiped a tear from Hannah's eye. "You're the only person in the world that knows the whole story." It wasn't exactly the "whole" story, but she knew more than anyone else…even Lieutenant Daniels. Hannah leaned in and put her head on my shoulder. "Do you want to tell me your story now?"

Hannah nodded. It took a while, but through a lot of sniffles and tears, she told her story. She told of their parents' involvement in drugs, of their going in and out of rehab, of all the empty promises and neglect. Her schoolteachers were the first to notice when she came wearing the same clothes over and over, without being cleaned. She remembered the day DCS came and removed the two from their home, which was six inches deep in trash and refuse. Hannah complained of being bounced from one foster home to the next. Then she got really quiet. She looked up and said, "If I tell, do you promise to keep it a secret?"

I nodded. "For as long as you want me to. Mark already took care of the legal parts. The man is in jail. He can't harm you anymore."

Hannah told every last detail…how he got her alone…how he got on top of her…how much it hurt. At least I was fourteen. She was just eleven. Then she broke the last little part of my heart, saying, "He made Danny watch." Hannah and I sat in the swings leaning on each other and swinging as one.

Susan sighed as she opened the door. "You two must be starving."

I looked at Hannah, and she nodded. We walked hand in hand to the house. We had our own little secrets and were bonded for life. Susan thanked me repeatedly. I told her Hannah did as much for me as I hope I did for her. I finished lunch and started out the door

Danny ran up and said, "Here. You almost forgot your special ball."

I rubbed the top of his head. "You guys hang on to it for me. That way I have to come back." Susan smiled and wiped a tear.

Chapter Forty

Monday, November 20, 9:45 am—Homicide

Back at Homicide, Sam and I prepared for the interview with Maeve Kennedy. We dug into her past and discussed how we would spring it on her in the midst of a follow-up on the Ripley Case. We wanted to see why she used a similar weapon.

"Do you want to take the lead this time?" Sam asked.

"I'd like that. Thanks." Then in mockery of his earlier attitude, I stiffened and pretended to be Sam, adding in a deep voice, "If you have a question, don't be afraid to ask."

"Point made," Sam said.

Maeve Kennedy arrived and took a seat in the interrogation room. We asked if she wanted anything to drink, and she nodded. The administrative assistant returned with a Diet Coke as Maeve requested. I adjusted my skirt and sat down. Sam joined me. I began, "Ms. Kennedy, we appreciate your cooperation as we continue the investigation of Mark Ripley's murder."

"Anything I can do to help." She took a sip of her drink.

"I assume by now you know Alvaro Garcia was released and cleared of all charges?"

"Yes. Praise God. I know Sophia is so happy."

"I also assume you realize that puts us back at the beginning looking for the real murderer?" I asked, staring deep into her eyes. Maeve nodded and looked at both of us. I could tell she was starting to put two and two together. "That returns us to a position where everyone is a suspect."

196

"I hope you're not implying that you suspect me?" Maeve asked with deep offense in her voice. "I was a close friend and fellow minister of the Gospel with Pastor Mark."

"That's what we have in our notes. Isn't it, Detective Tidwell?"

"Oh, yes," he said with just a hint of sarcasm. "We have nothing but praises from you in our notes."

Maeve leaned back in her chair and crossed her arms. Her eyes narrowed, but she remained stoically silent. "We just have a few questions about you, Maeve," I said. "Something has come to our attention that…well, how do I put it…that seemed to connect to our crime scene." I decided to put a little lie out there first and see how Maeve reacted. "Your fingerprints are on our crime scene."

Maeve relaxed. I could sense a sigh of relief. "Of course, they are. That's the women's changing room. I was back there helping the women during the baptism."

That's interesting. "So, you were back there when Alvaro made his wife leave in such a hurry that she walked out in one of the church's robes." Her body tensed again.

"I thought you just said Alvaro was cleared?" Maeve asked, tilting her head to the side and trying to interpret my body language.

I remained remarkably calm and neutral. Sam seemed to be enjoying my line of questioning. "Oh, *he* is." I put just enough emphasis on "he" that Maeve wasn't sure if she or Sophia was my suspect. I looked down at my notes and gave a long, uncomfortable pause between questions.

I looked up. "I'd like to know a little about June ninth of twenty-nineteen." Maeve didn't say anything; she didn't have to. I observed the immediate reaction to the date. "You see," I began, still staring at Maeve, "our murder weapon is remarkably similar to the one you used to strike your ex-husband." Sam set a picture of the piano bench leg on the table between us. Still no verbal response. I turned it up a notch. "Do you think men deserve a piece of their own medicine?"

Maeve leaned into the table so hard, it slid into us. She

pointed her finger at me and went off, "Don't you dare compare Pastor Mark with that pig of a husband I had." Her voice intensified as she leaned in even more. "Did you know that he beat me every day? Did you know that he abused me verbally *and* physically? He destroyed me emotionally and spiritually as well." She pointed to me again. "You would never understand that, Detective."

"You'd be surprised." I leaned into the table.

"Oh, I'm sure. You have a perfect body, perfect hair, perfect teeth...probably a perfect life too."

Sam cut in. "I admire your attempt to redirect the conversation and to project your anger on my partner, Ms. Kennedy, but we're here to investigate you, not Detective Rhodes."

Maeve immediately went silent. We both took notice of her reaction to his input. It subdued her almost instantly. She scooted back and pulled the table back into position. Maeve nodded, "Yes, sir."

I motioned for Sam to continue the interview. "Mark Ripley was beaten with the leg from the church's piano bench." He gave a moment for the significance to sink in. "Gauging from your reaction, you can see our predicament." He turned the copy of the article around so she could see it. He slid it next to the picture. "You used a broken chair leg to beat your husband, nearly killing him in the process."

"I used that leg because he'd just broken the chair over my back." She was angry but soft-spoken. She did not raise her voice to Sam. "It was available to use in my defense. I was terrified and desperate," Maeve said in a soft whisper. "Hardly the way I felt with Pastor Mark." Her head gradually lowered until her chin rested on her chest. "If you'll look at pictures of me back then, I was thin." Her lip began to quiver. "I was attractive—like you, Detective Rhodes. My ex-husband starved me so I would look pretty...at least in his eyes." She looked up and with a wave of her hand, she motioned to her large figure. "Now look at me. I still have image problems."

After wiping a tear, Maeve said, "But you know what? Mark

and Susan Ripley loved on me and built me back up. They prayed for me and with me. They studied with me and helped me find my passion…working with women. They taught me to use my brokenness to help others who are broken too."

I immediately thought of Miriam's song. "I understand," I said. We're all broken in some way.

Maeve sat up straight in her chair and said, "They also taught me I was made in the image of God, and He loves me just as I am."

"I think we have all we need," Sam said in a sudden shift. "Thank you for your honesty."

As soon as Maeve left, he said, "She's not the killer."

"Yeah, I'd figured that out the first time I met her, but we had to be sure. When's the worship leader's interview?"

"Not until this afternoon," Sam said.

I grabbed my things and headed out the door. Broken people made me think of another young girl abused by men. "I'm going to call the hospital and see if there's any change in Skylar."

Chapter Forty-one

Friday, November 24, 10:12 am—Homicide

At the end of my Wednesday jog, I bumped into Aaron and was totally shocked when he asked me out. I was even more surprised when I accepted. Then Thursday, as I had done for the last three years, I spent Thanksgiving with Lieutenant Daniels and his wife, Sherry. I was in a great mood. That feeling was short-lived.

"Rhodes," Sergeant McNally's voice thundered over the cubicles. "In my office."

Great. "Yes, sir, Sergeant."

Homicide stationed the sergeants just outside of the detectives' wing. Each sergeant had a cubicle to himself. "Have a seat, Rhodes."

"Yes, sir." I didn't know if I should take the offensive, beat him to the punch, or just play ignorant and wait for him to call me out? I wasn't certain, so I opted for plausible deniability. I let the sergeant go first.

"How's the Ripley case going?" he asked.

"Still waiting on the fingerprint analysis," I said. "Also, we're waiting for Skylar Watson to regain consciousness to see if she happened to see anyone toss that bench leg in the creek. It was within view of her bedroom window."

"I'll make a call to forensics to see if I can't speed up that analysis. In the meantime, I want you to look into another homicide for me. It's connected to your case."

"Should I get Sam…Detective Tidwell?" I asked as I began to stand up.

"Sit down," he said. "Not yet. I want to discuss it with you myself." I pursed my lips and gave him a half nod. I didn't understand. "I want you to take the lead on this, since you have ties with the family and the church next door."

"I don't understand," I admitted.

"In light of Jamison's comments, they've changed Katy Watson's case from missing person to homicide." I perked up. "According to Lieutenant Daniels of East Precinct, Jamison Watson has been bragging to his cellmate that he 'offed his wife,' and he should have done the same with her girl.

"How did we come to that knowledge?"

"His cellmate was requesting a transfer to another cell. Jamison threatened him several times and nearly broke his jaw. When speaking with the sheriff about the cell change, he gave that little tidbit as a bargain. Jamison didn't deny it." He picked up the file from his desk and handed it to me. "Don't go getting all emotional with this one, but you know the situation better than most. I know you've taken a personal interest in the girl."

"Yes, sir. Thank you, sir."

"Take Tidwell with you, but I want you running lead."

"But he won't…"

"I already told him he will," Sergeant McNally said with a menacing grin. "Go see Deborah for any paperwork you need. I think she's already filed for a search warrant of the house and the lot, just in case."

I took the file and returned to my cubicle. I wasn't sure what to say…to be apologetic…be reluctant…or just act as if nothing changed. I grabbed my coat and asked, "Are you coming, Sam?"

"On your heels, Detective Rhodes." I shot him a glance, and he smiled.

We stopped to see Deborah, one of the admins for the homicide and cold case units. The search warrant had yet to be granted. "I'll call you the moment it comes in," she said.

Sam drove to the Watson house and parked in the driveway.

"This is so strange," I said.

"Leading?" Sam asked.

"That too. It's just strange how this case has morphed into a multilevel case of deception, abuse, and murder. Now, the missing mother is probably dead too? This is my first real case with Homicide as a real detective…not just an observer. It's like we tipped over one domino and the whole thing is tumbling." I looked at Sam before I got out of the car. "Don't you think that's strange?"

"I don't know," Sam said. "I've had some like it in the past, but it is rare." He shut the driver's door and locked the car. "It would have been so easy and neatly wrapped if Jamison was the father and if his fingerprints end up on the leg."

"I'll be honest," I said. "I hope they are." I looked at Sam and asked, "Is that bad?"

"If it is, we're both guilty," he said. "What's the plan?"

I pointed to the street adjacent to the Watson house and said, "We'll begin here and ask the neighbors if they remember Katy Watson. If they do, we'll follow up on details and a timeline of her disappearance."

"Sounds like a plan."

"Then, I suppose we speak to the church members and the neighbors on that side of the creek after that. Hopefully, by then we'll have the search warrant for the house and the yard."

We made our way down the street going up one side and then back down the other before moving on. As we suspected, most of the people were gone during the middle of the morning. A few people answered their doors, but they knew little of the Watsons. Some of the residents moved in within the past year and had yet to interact with their neighbors at all. One older woman had a peripheral knowledge of the Watsons.

"That man is as mean and nasty as a snake. I don't blame her for leaving him," she said. "She always seemed so nice. We exchanged waves when we were both working in our gardens. She had such beautiful flowers." The woman looked at the house now. "Look at it. Weeds, weeds, weeds, and he doesn't lift a finger."

"You said she would plant flowers?" I asked. "When's the last time you remember exchanging waves?"

The woman put a finger to her wrinkled cheek and thought. "Well, I supposed it was during all that COVID hoopla. I remember wearing my mask, but she wasn't wearing hers. She had the prettiest smile."

"Do you remember if it was the beginning of the COVID pandemic or the end?"

"Let's see," she began. "Two seasons ago. That must have been near the end of it, I suppose." She stopped to fix a little Pilgrim man that fell off the pumpkin. "Yes, it was a year ago this last spring."

"And that's the last time you remember seeing her?" I asked.

"Yes."

"Just curious," Sam said. "Do you remember seeing her pack up a car and leave?"

"I never saw her again."

We thanked her and made detailed notes. Down the road from the home, we heard a similar story, praise for the woman and detest for the man. They spoke highly of Katy's friendliness. This person remembered a time he hit her. "It was right on the front lawn. She was down on her knees planting something." The woman pointed to a part of the lawn within view from the front porch. "I was standing right over there," she said, pointing to some shrubs in the front corner of her lot. "He came barreling out of the home, screaming at the top of his lungs. By the time Katy looked up, his hand was coming down on her face. He hit her a couple times and then drug her by her arm back to the house."

"Did you call the police?" I asked.

"No," she confessed. "We didn't want to get involved."

No one on the other streets beyond theirs ever heard of the family. We made our way over to the other side of the creek. I knocked on the door of the man who cleared Alvaro. I introduced myself, but he couldn't talk right then, spouting off a strict schedule that he must keep. He told me when to return.

Just as Sam was about to protest, I tapped his arm and said, "We'll be back then, thank you." I explained his OCD and said it would be more productive to work into his schedule. We went from house to house with no luck. Either no one was home, or they didn't know anything about the Watsons. We walked up the street side of the church's driveway. At the first house on the left, a woman answered.

We displayed our shields and introduced ourselves. Sam said, "We'd like to ask you a few questions about the family that lives on the other side of the creek." I pointed to the house.

"Isn't that the home where the little girl was hurt?" she asked.

"Yes."

"I recognize you," she said to me. "You've been down here a few times."

I nodded and said, "Yes, ma'am." I hated the term, but she seemed to like it.

"That poor girl. No wonder she walks with her head down all the time." I agreed. "What is it you want to know?"

"Do you remember his wife?" I asked.

"I never met her personally, but I remember seeing her all the time."

Sam's countenance lifted. "When is the last time you remember seeing her?"

"Oh, it's been a little over a year ago," she said. "Near the beginning of summer."

I elbowed Sam. "What was she doing?"

"Trying to protect herself," the woman said. "He chased her out of the house all the way to the creek."

"Tell us more," Sam said. "What did she do?"

"Not much. They yelled at each other and then went back into the house," she said, pointing across the bridge. "Her little girl was watching from that window there, her face smushed against the window."

My stomach churned. "Skylar saw it?"

"Oh, yes. That poor little girl saw everything. We called the police, but the woman insisted it was all a terrible misunderstanding."

"Do you happen to know when you called?" I asked.

She thought for a moment and said, "Yes. First or second week of June, two summers ago."

We both noted the date. We thanked her for her time and started to walk away. I stopped and turned back. "By chance do you remember anyone coming to the church on Monday, October twenty-three?"

"Is that the day that preacher died?"

I nodded.

"Unfortunately, I was out of town visiting my sister. She had her gallbladder removed, and I had to stay with her for two weeks. I'm sorry. I told that to the policeman that asked. I'm sure he told you."

"Yes, I'm sure he did," Sam said. "It's probably in our notes. Thanks again."

She said that she was always outside when it was warm enough. She fed the turkeys and the deer. That's why she knew so much.

As soon as we got far enough away from her house, Sam said, "A regular Gladys Kravitz."

"Who?" I asked.

"You know; the nosey neighbor from *Bewitched.*"

"Oh, I love Nicole Kidman," I said.

"Thanks for making me feel old." Sam walked away.

Having canvassed the rest of the neighborhood with no more positive results, I decided to call it a day and return to Homicide. With the two testimonies narrowing the date of Katy Watson's last public appearance, we decided to find the corresponding police report. The records corroborated both stories. The only call made was June 9, 2021. After that, nothing. "You'd think there would be more disturbance calls, especially if he beat Skylar regularly."

"Do you think he killed Katy, or do you think she managed to get away?" I asked.

"I don't think a mother would leave her daughter with a man like that if she could do anything about it. I bet she's dead and buried somewhere near the house,"

"I know I would have killed him," I said. "I only spent ten minutes with him before I knocked him on his…"

"No," Sam said, before I could finish my sentence. "You'd never have married him in the first place because he targets weak women, women he can intimidate and control."

"Thanks—I guess."

"Any word on that warrant?" he asked.

"Not yet. I'll check again." I started back down the aisle toward Deborah's desk. Before I took five steps, I spotted Deborah with a folded piece of paper in her hand, coming our direction.

"I have the warrant."

I grabbed my coat and then noticed the time. "How did it get to be five o'clock?" I asked. "Did we eat?"

"I did," Sam said. "About two hours ago." He grabbed his coat. It's your call. Head back there now or wait to search it in the morning."

"Tomorrow's Saturday, Sam."

"We can wait until Monday, if you prefer."

"No. I just didn't want to make you come in on a Saturday," I said.

"Like I got something better to do," he said with a smile. "See you at nine." He started down towards the door. "Oh, and Abbey…"

"Yes."

"Have a good date."

"What? How did you know? I didn't tell anyone."

As he pushed through the door, he said, "Like I said before, I'm a detective, girl."

Chapter Forty-two

It was five-forty when I stepped out of the elevator. Aaron was ringing my doorbell. "Oh, Aaron, I'm so sorry. I just got off work."

He smiled. "That's okay. Let's go."

"You have to let me change," I insisted. "I'm not going to the Opry dressed like a businesswoman."

"That's perfect for the restaurant."

"Are you kidding? I've got to put on some jeans."

"Jeans? We're going to miss our dinner as it is. I thought we agreed to leave at four-forty-five?" He looked at his watch.

"We did," I said, pushing past him. "I promise, I'll just be a minute. You can wait on my couch." He followed me in. It was the first time he'd seen the inside of my apartment. I was yelling from the bedroom. "I did my best."

"Abbey, we're not going to have time to eat."

"I'm hurrying," I hollered. Five minutes later I came out in jeans, long sleeve dress shirt, and my new cowboy boots, holding my coat in hand. Thank God for the Army. No other woman could change that fast. "Seriously, Aaron, the concessions will be fine with me. It's the nature of my job." I gave him a puppy dog face and grabbed his arm. "If we get there in time, we can eat at the food court of the mall."

"Food court? That's not exactly what I had in mind for our first date," he said. "I really wanted to treat you to a nice dinner and then the Opry."

As we rode down the elevator and entered the parking lot, I

explained that I was a simple girl with simple tastes. If he wanted to please me, all he had to do was take me to the Opry. Food was food. It was the company that mattered. Looking at his reaction, I got the feeling Aaron's tastes weren't as simple.

It dawned on me at that moment that I didn't really know him at all. "What do you do as a career?" I asked.

"I'm an anesthesiologist," he said. "I followed my father's footsteps."

"Really? Should I call you doctor?"

"Please don't," he said. "This is why I didn't mention it before." We pulled off the ramp for Briley Parkway. "We should be there in ten minutes if you still want to eat at the food court."

"Of course," I said with enthusiasm. "Throw it down and head to the Opry."

"I can't tell if you're being sarcastic or serious." I just smiled. He parked nearest the Opry, and we entered the mall by the theater. We talked as we walked through the mall until we reached the food court. "What will it be?"

"Chinese," I said, spying the restaurant.

"That's not Chinese," Aaron said. "That's American fast food."

Shoot me down. "Okay." I looked around. "The Philly steak stop over there," I said pointing to the opposite side of the food court. He nodded, and we got in line. Aaron kept his eye on his watch. We sat down and began to eat.

He took a deep breath and let it out slowly. "I'm sorry. I have this thing with being on time. Surgeons don't like waiting for anyone including the anesthesiology team. I'm always early."

"I haven't lived by punctuality since I left the Army."

He tilted his head to the side and gave a thin smile. "I apologize; I didn't mean to be so uptight. I just wanted everything to be perfect."

"It's all good. Perfect isn't my style."

"I think you're perfect," he said softly. He held out his hand to shake mine. "Let's start over. My name is Aaron. I'm an anesthesiologist at Vanderbilt Medical Center. And you are?"

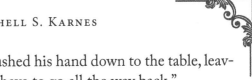

I giggled and gently pushed his hand down to the table, leaving mine on his. "We don't have to go all the way back."

"Okay. Tell me about Abby Rhodes. Where did you live before Nashville?" he asked. "You said country music is why you moved here."

"Ah. You listened. I'm not used to men doing that," I said. "I came here from Grafenwöhr, Germany."

"Germany? You don't sound German."

Just as a matter of pride, I started speaking fluent German. I went on and on until I could see the frustration building on his face. "I spent three years in Germany as a part of a military police brigade. Besides, I have a thing for languages."

"I'm impressed. Thank you for your service." He paused for a moment. "I lost my brother in Afghanistan."

"I'm so sorry." I moved my hand to his shoulder. "Older or younger?"

"My baby brother. It was his first tour. Our sister lives in Minnesota." He pulled out his phone and flipped through his pictures until he found one of the three of them together. "I'm the oldest." He showed me a few more pictures of his brother. "Are you the only child?" he asked.

"No. I had an older sister, but she passed away."

"I guess we have something in common," he said. "Misery loves company."

"We also have running," I added.

"What?" He looked lost for a moment. "Yes. We both run."

We changed to lighter subjects and finished our meal in time to walk over to the Opry House and find our seats before the beginning of the show. I clapped and cheered. I even sang with the songs I knew. I was in heaven. Aaron didn't seem as connected with the country scene as I was and didn't know as many songs. To be honest, he seemed to watch me more than he did the artists on the stage. I was hoping it was pleasurable, not judgmental.

Three hours later the elevator door opened, and we stepped

on board. I was still going on about the Opry. "I've wanted to go there all my life. Thank you so much."

"You're beautiful, Abbey." Aaron surprised me and pulled me close for an embrace. Then, he planted a big kiss on my lips.

I broke his hold and shoved him away. "What are you doing?" He pulled me by the hand, and I slapped his arm. "Why did you do that?" My eyes filled with tears, and my throat tightened.

"What did I do?" he asked. He reached out and put his hand on my shoulder.

I instinctively slapped his hand away again and pushed the number twelve several times as if it would make the elevator faster. I looked up at the numbers which seemed to be advancing in slow motion. "You just moved in on me." I turned on Aaron with fire in my eyes. "I guess since you bought supper and took me to the Opry, you feel you have the right to...to..."

He stepped back. "To what? Kiss you? I didn't buy any right," he said defensively. "I thought we were having a moment." He backed away and put his hands in the air as if surrendering.

The door opened and I ran to my apartment and slammed the door as soon as I cleared it. I ran to my bedroom and threw myself on the bed. I took out my phone and searched for Susan Ripley's number. I wanted to call someone, and she was the only name that came to mind.

I tossed the phone to the bed and cried in my pillow. After a while, I got up and grabbed my Army photo album from the shelf. I flipped through it while I rocked back and forth, back and forth. *It was such a good night. Why did he have to ruin it? You're just being stupid.*

I fell asleep arguing in my head.

Chapter Forty-three

Saturday, November 25, 9:15 am—Watson Home

The fire alarm continued to blare. No one answered the call. The Firehouse was empty. Suddenly, Abbey woke and realized there was no alarm. It was just her phone. She wanted to answer, but she could barely move. Her head pounded. Her mouth was dry—her lips stuck together. Abbey felt as though she was waking after a wild party where she had too much to drink, but Abbey knew that wasn't the case. She was four years sober and had the coins to prove it. She forced herself to grab the phone and answer.

"Are you okay?" the voice asked.

"Who is this?" Abbey tried to clear her head.

"It's Sam. I thought you said we were going to search the Watson house this morning."

"Oh, no. What time is it?" she asked, looking at her clock.

"It's nine-fifteen," he said. "Hey, if you had a rough night, we can do this another day."

"No. Give me thirty minutes, and I'll just meet you there."

"I've got a time-proven remedy for a hangover," Sam said.

"I don't drink, Sam." He didn't say anything. "Honest. I did have a bad night, though."

"Want to talk about it?" he asked. I'm sure he still believed I was drunk last night and just wouldn't admit it.

"Maybe later. Let me change, and I'll meet you at the Watson house." She just about hung up, but said, "Hey, Sam?"

"Yes."

"Are you by any chance still at Central?"

"Yes."

"Can you grab the warrant and the keys?"

"Sure. Meet you in thirty."

I stumbled into the bathroom and looked in the mirror. My makeup was smudged, and my eyeliner smeared all down my cheeks. I was still dressed for my date from last night. I cleaned up, brushed my teeth, put a little makeup on, and grabbed a breakfast bar.

Thirty-five minutes after the conversation with Sam, I was pulling into the cul-de-sac. Sam held up the warrant and the keys. I still felt like crap. We both put on our blue gloves and booties.

"You look rough, girl. You sure you didn't down a few? No shame if you did."

"No, Sam!" I snatched the warrant from his hands and said, "Just unlock the door."

He did. The house smelled like a restaurant dumpster. When we got to the kitchen, we both understood why. Jamison had stacked at least a week's worth of dirty dishes in the sink and left them. "Apparently, Skylar cleans up around here," I said, trying not to lose my breakfast. "There are maggots in that bowl. Gross!"

"Keep your focus. We're here looking for signs of Katy Watson's disappearance. Look for a purse or a makeup bag…anything that tells us she didn't pack and leave."

"Gotcha." I couldn't believe the mess all over the main floor. The kitchen, the den, and the bathroom. Jamison hadn't even flushed since his last time. "It smells like a port-a-potty. I can't believe she had to live in the mess too."

"I'll head upstairs and see what I can find. You search here and in the garage. Remember, anything that points to foul play instead of an organized departure."

Sam climbed the wooden steps and stopped at the landing. At first glance, it looked like a small rec room, two bedrooms, and a small closet. He searched the bedrooms first. The one to the left was obviously Skylar's. It was clean. The bed made without a wrinkle. The dresser clean with the exception of a myriad of little fantasy creature figurines. A few posters, all matching the fantasy theme. A PS5 and a forty-two-inch flat screen. Under her bed, Sam found several fantasy war games, the book *The Prince*, and a Macbook Air plugged into a charger. He opened the laptop only to find it required a password. Sam looked at the book and wondered what a young girl would be doing with a treatise of immoral political philosophy. He tossed the book back under the bed and put the laptop under his arm. "How does a neglected kid get all of this?"

He scanned her bathroom. Nothing unusual for a girl her age. She kept it clean as well. Skylar was nothing like her father. Of course, he wasn't really her father. Jamison supposedly lived in the next bedroom. Even at first glance, it looked like a married couple's room. If she left a year ago, why did Jamison keep her clothes in the closet and her dresser full of family photos…of seemingly better times. Skylar must have been around nine years old. All three of them were smiling. Sam glanced into the bathroom. All her makeup was still scattered on her side of the double sink. It looked as though she was still living there. Better thought…it looked like a museum. For some reason, Jamison wasn't using the master bedroom.

Sam looked under the bed, in the dressers, and in the corners of the room. Finally, he searched the closet. Her shoes, purses, clothes, and jackets filled her side of the closet. Each of the purses was empty. "Is that what I think it is?"

Sam squeezed into the back corner of Jamison's closet. He felt the wall immediately behind the shoe rack and ran his fingers back and forth across. "It is." He searched for a latch or a handle but couldn't find one. Then he had an idea. Sam pressed the center of the one-by-one square and the door sprung open. Inside the hidden compartment he found Katy's billfold, complete with credit cards, a driver's license, pictures, and an expired CPR card. "She never left." Why would it be hidden on his side? Maybe he wanted everyone to think she left. "What do we have here?" Sam reached in the back of the little compartment and found a diary. He flipped it open and read the first few lines. It was Katy Watson's diary. "Abbey, you'll never guess what I found." No response. He put everything back where he found it and took pictures, before adding it all to his collection of evidence.

"Hey Sam?" Abbey shouted.

He moved to the top of the stairs. "What do you need?" he asked.

"Let me see those keys." He tossed them down to her. Abbey glanced through the set and said, "Nothing here for a padlock."

"Why? What did you find?" he asked.

"There's a door in the garage that has a padlock on it. I haven't found a key anywhere down here. Did you see any keys upstairs?"

Sam came down to the main floor. "No, but I've just the thing in my trunk. We do have a search warrant." Abbey nodded and Sam retrieved the bolt cutter from his car and brought it back to her. "Show me the door."

I led Sam down the short flight of steps into the garage filled with lawn and garden tools. In the middle of the wall connected to the main part of the house, there was a 48" by 84" door with a key lock and a padlock. "For a man living with just a young daughter, this seems a little overkill. Don't you think?" I asked.

"Well, it won't be a mystery much longer," Sam said. He grabbed the two-foot orange handles of the bolt cutter and pushed them apart. Moving the blades on either side of the padlock, he squeezed the handles together and cut the arm of the lock in two. Sam pulled it free. He tried the door handle. "It's locked too. Look for a crowbar or something we can wedge into the door."

Just as he said it, I used a small screwdriver and a hammer from Jamison's toolbox and tapped the hinge pins out of their slots. "How's that?" I asked.

"I think you've done that before?" He took the tools from me and knocked the hinge pieces apart. The cool, damp air rushed past his face. Sam searched unsuccessfully for a light switch. "Got a flashlight?"

I used the flashlight app on my phone. It revealed a small room built under the main floor of the house. "That looks creepy," I said. "Go ahead."

"I'm going to get a real flashlight from my car." He came back with a large flashlight. It brightened up the small room.

"Still looks creepy," I said. I wasn't going first.

Sam stepped down two steps but stopped suddenly when the third step creaked eerily. He entered the small room with a low ceiling. I followed a couple of steps behind. I could see it had a concrete floor. Immediately to his left, hung a solitary bulb attached to the ceiling with a string hanging down. Sam pulled it, and the bulb popped. He scanned the rest of the little cellar with his light. I did the same on the opposite side of the steps.

"Sam, you still have those bolt cutters?"

"Right here. Why?"

"You are not going to believe this." I tapped him on the shoulder and waved my phone's light back and forth. "I can't believe it. He somehow got a freezer down here. And look. It has a thick lock on it."

"On the freezer? Talk about overkill. Two locks on the door and another one on the freezer."

"Yeah," I said, "and I don't think he's trying to keep his daughter from eating popsicles."

"Not even funny, Abbey." Sam made his way over to the freezer. "It's plugged in. Are you thinking what I'm thinking?"

"I'm afraid so. Cut it open." I shined my light on a small thin object. "I don't even want to guess what that sledgehammer is for."

He used the bolt cutters once again. As the lock fell to the cement floor, it echoed through the little room. I pulled open the latch and lifted the heavy door with both hands. "Well," I said with a soft voice that betrayed my shock. "I think we found Katy Watson."

Sam looked over my shoulder. "This case keeps getting darker and darker. Jamison filled the freezer with water and put his wife inside." Sam shook his head. "Look at her expression, Abbey. I think she was alive when he locked the door."

I stared at the frozen face of Katy Watson. You could see the terror in her gray eyes. Her face was contorted as if she struggled to keep her head above the water to breathe. It froze that way. "How in the heck are we going to get her out of here?"

"We call CSI. That's how," Sam said.

We went back upstairs and called it in. Sam and I used the time while we were waiting for CSI to search the rest of the house.

"How can someone be so cold-hearted and evil?" I asked.

"This guy is crazy evil. If he went to all the trouble to kill his wife this way and preserve her, I have no doubts he would kill Mark Ripley by throwing him in the baptistery and choking him until he drowned." He looked at me. "Any word on the prints since Sarge said he'd get them rushed?" I shook my head.

My phone rang, and I nearly jumped out of my skin. "Detective Rhodes. Really? Thank you. I'll be there in the next hour." I hung up and turned to Sam. "Skylar's awake." Sam handed me the bag of evidence. "Here, you take this and go see Skylar. I'll stay here until they take the body." I took the bag and tossed it in the passenger seat and headed to the hospital.

Chapter Forty-four

St. Thomas Midtown—Critical Care

I knocked on the door to her room. Skylar said, "Come in." She looked at me through glazed eyes and asked, "Who are you?" Skylar tilted her head back and forth. "I'm a little loopy from the morphine." She laughed.

"I'm Detective Abbey Rhodes."

"You're the pastor's wife."

"No. She's a friend."

"He died," Skylar said. She laughed and then cried.

"Skylar, we met in the bathroom Wednesday night." I pulled out my badge and showed it to her. "I'm one of the detectives looking into the pastor's death."

"Oh, you were the woman talking to Jonathan." She leaned back on her bed. "Nobody will tell me how I got here," Skylar said.

"Do you want to know?" I asked.

"Duh? That's why I'm asking. Are you stupid or what?"

It's amazing how a little painkiller will lower one's defenses and remove all filters. "You really don't remember?" I asked. Before Skylar could answer, I added, "Don't you dare say 'duh' again."

Skylar was taken aback. "Don't have to be rude."

"Your father beat you. He broke several of your ribs, cracked your cheekbone, broke your arm and one of your legs, and he ruptured your spleen."

Skylar looked away and stared out the window. "I don't want to go back there. He hates me…calls me an evil witch."

217

"You won't go back. I promise."

Skylar turned to face me. "Swear?" I nodded. Her face brightened with a grand smile. "You're really pretty." Skylar laughed again. "I bet you're really smart too…especially since you're a detective." She giggled.

"Your father is in jail." Before I could help myself, I asked, "Do you remember what happened to your mother?"

Skylar looked back out the window. She stared blankly for a long time before answering. "She left me…alone with him."

I walked around to the other side of the bed and positioned myself between Skylar and the window. "I have to ask you some very difficult questions. Are you up for it, or do you want me to come back another time?"

Skylar pushed a lock of hair behind her ear with her good hand. "Might as well get them over with." She couldn't or wouldn't meet my glance. Instead, she stared at the top button of my sweater. "Go ahead."

"Did your father ever sexually abuse you?" Skylar shook her head. "Are you being honest with me?"

"He never touched me that way. He said I disgusted him." The medicine was making it hard to judge her mood.

"Do you know if your father ever spoke of Pastor Mark before?"

Skylar nodded. "He didn't like him." She looked the other way to the window in her door. "I liked him. He was cute. I don't think he liked me, though."

Skylar closed her eyes and nodded off. "Skylar, can you wake up for me? I have just a few more questions. "Did your dad threaten to harm anyone at church?"

Skylar turned and looked me in the eyes. The medicine was causing her eyes to droop. They looked vacant. "Yes. He was gonna' kill 'em all." She laughed again. "I feel funny."

"It's the morphine, Skylar."

"I like it," she said. "You're pretty. Have I told you that already?" I smiled and nodded. If I didn't need the information so badly, the situation would have amused me. "It's Pastor Mark's fault."

"What is?" I asked.

Skylar fiddled with the straw wrapper on her tray. "He invited us all to church."

"Us all?" I snapped to attention. "Did Pastor Mark visit your mother? I thought she disappeared months before she…left you."

"No. Dad just wouldn't let her go anywhere…and no one ever came to our house." She lowered her head and began to cry. "It was so lonely."

"Did your mom ever visit Living Water Church?" I asked.

"I don't remember…she taught me to…to wait until dad was drunk or asleep and to slip away. That's what she did."

It was all starting to make sense. Living Water Church had invaded Jamison's domain, jeopardizing his power and his control over his family. And that all started when the Ripleys came to the church and turned it outward, reaching its neighbors and community. "Do you think your father killed Pastor Mark?"

Skylar paused for a long time. She picked at a loose string on her blanket. She closed one eye. I repeated the question. Without looking up, Skylar shrugged her shoulders. She opened the other eye and stared up at me.

"Okay." I took a long breath and let it out slowly. "You're doing great, Skylar. I just have two more questions for you. Do you think you can handle them?" She nodded. "Did you know you were pregnant?"

Skylar looked up suddenly. I could see the joy in her smile. Her eyes lit up. "I am? Seriously?"

"Didn't the doctor discuss this with you?"

"No. How far along?" she asked, putting her good hand gently over her belly. Skylar was smiling ear to ear.

"Skylar…I'm so sorry." The girl's smile faded. "You lost it."

Someone knocked at the door. Jonathan peeked his head in the room. "Oh, hey, Detective. I didn't know you were visiting Skylar. I'll just come back."

I looked from Jonathan to Skylar. I could tell from the longing in the young girl's eyes that she'd just identified the father. "No, no. Come right on in. I think Skylar has something she'd like to tell you."

"Really?" He stepped into the room and let the door close. "I think they have a rule of only one visitor at a time. Seriously, I can come back."

"Oh, no, Jonathan. You see I'm here on official business, so I don't really count." I turned to Skylar.

Tears streamed down her cheeks. "I'm sorry, Jonathan. I just lost our baby!" Skylar said, which she followed with a spine-tingling scream.

It surprised me. Jonathan's jaw hung wide open. His eyes opened wide. But then, I watched as something snapped. Jonathan's face turned stoic…distant. "Skylar, what are you talking about?" She tilted her head, questioning him. "Who did this to you?" he asked. "Was it your father?"

"Did you hear me?" she asked imploringly. Skylar reached out to him with her good hand. "We just lost our baby."

Jonathan stepped towards the bed. His voice seemed calm… almost methodic. "Skylar Watson, did your father have his way with you again?"

"She told me Jamison never touched her that way before," I said, coming to her defense. Skylar and I had two things in common.

"Of course, she did. That's how she's able to live with the horror." He turned to me and gave one of those looks that said, "Just humor the girl." He smiled. "She and I have had this conversation before."

"What? No. Jonathan, it was our baby. I haven't been with anyone else but you."

"Skylar, it's time to put that fantasy to rest. The detective here needs to hear the truth. You carry on like that, and I'll be in trouble."

"Oh, yes, you will," I said, moving my hands toward my cuffs. "Especially with a history like yours."

He turned on me and leaned in. His attitude darkened. "I've

lived with the damage of that accusation for years. There was nothing to corroborate those charges. They ruined my life!" he shouted.

A nurse popped her head in the door. "I'm sorry, but you two are going to have to leave. Skylar's blood pressure is rising, and she needs her rest."

"No!" Skylar screamed. "Jonathan, I need you."

"I was just leaving," Jonathan said and brushed past the nurse, knocking her aside.

Skylar grabbed my arm as I started after him. "We love each other."

"Skylar, he's ten years older than you. I'm sorry, but it's legally rape, even if you consented."

"No!" She was clinging to my sleeve, keeping me from following Jonathan. "We love each other."

The nurse intervened and pushed the button releasing the morphine. Skylar's body relaxed. "I'm sorry, Detective, but you'll have to leave."

"I'm trying."

Skylar finally relaxed her grip, and I ran through the door and down the hall. Jonathan was nowhere to be found.

I called it in and asked Sergeant McNally to notify the Sex Crimes Unit. "Skylar identified Jonathan Williams as the father of the child. He denied it and took off. Put out a BOLO."

Chapter Forty-five

Sam and I sat at our desks, laboring over the paperwork from Saturday's find. "Abbey, I think the paperwork is going to take us longer than it did to solve the murder." I didn't respond. "You okay, kid?" Still nothing. "Rhodes, are you mad at me?" he asked.

"No, Sam. I just want to get this paperwork done and move on to something else." I continued filling in the electronic forms.

"I hear you also solved the rape case."

"Yep."

"Hold back your excitement, Detective."

"Tidwell and Rhodes," Sergeant McNally barked. "The Captain wants to see you now."

"Yes, sir." We both stopped immediately and headed to Captain Harris's office. Whether it was bad or good, you didn't keep the Captain waiting.

Sam led the way and knocked on the door. Someone said to come in, so he opened the door slowly. "You called for us, Captain?"

"Sit." I glanced across the desk. Captain Harris was a thin, fifty-two-year-old Black man with distinguishing salt and pepper hair. He filled the back wall of his office with pictures of himself with various dignitaries over the years. I glanced to the sides, where the walls held his degrees, certificates, and awards.

"Yes, sir." Sam said. He and I sat in the two chairs opposite the Captain's desk.

"I just got off the phone with the Chief," he said.

We looked at each other. "Did we do something wrong, Captain?" Sam asked. I remained silent.

"Quite the opposite. He applauded your excellence on the Watson case. In his words, your efforts were, "swift and decisive.""

"Yes, sir. Thank you, sir. It was just dumb luck," Sam said.

"Whatever you want to call it, I like it when the Chief calls and it's good news. That doesn't happen as often as its inverse." He signed a few papers on his desk and slid them into the "Out" box. "Since you all seem to hear it when the news is bad, I thought you might want to hear a good word or two."

"Yes, sir," Sam said.

"Don't you speak, Rhodes?"

"Only when spoken to, sir." I finally met his eyes. I was still upset at myself for letting Jonathan slip away.

"That's not exactly what Sergeant McNally tells me, Rhodes."

"I apologize, sir, for my disrespect."

"Oh don't." With a wave of his hands he said, "For God's sake, would you two relax already? You're making me nervous." He signed a few more papers and slid them into the bin. "Rhodes, they tell me you also solved the rape case for Sex Crimes."

"Yes, sir, but I let him get away. I'm sorry."

"Well, Rhodes, we can't do everybody's job, now can we?" I didn't follow. "It's just a matter of time before he's caught. A man like that can't conceal himself forever. I'm sure they'll catch him." He put the cap on his pen and put it in his desk drawer. "I miss the days on the street, to be honest. Seems like I spend more time with paper or my computer than I do with the ranks anymore."

"Sir?" Sam asked. "Is there anything else?"

"Are you in a hurry, Tidwell?"

"No, sir. We do have to finish the paperwork on the Watson case."

"Tidwell, the paperwork will always be there. That's what I'm trying to tell you. Savor the job while you still have it. These days will be gone before you know it." I looked from the Captain back to Sam. Was I missing something? "Another month and you'll be officially retired."

"Sam?" I asked.

"Sir, I submitted the forms this morning to extend my time on the force."

The captain reached into the tray and pulled out the request. "Why should I approve such a request, Detective Tidwell? We both know you've just been biding your time here."

"Yes, sir. I have."

"Then why not go out on a case like this? Reminiscent of the old days. Right, Tidwell?"

Sam stared at the paper, but it was backwards. "If you would have asked me that two weeks ago, Captain, I would have jumped at the chance."

"But now?" the Captain asked. "You have a change of heart, Tidwell?"

He looked at me. "Yes, sir. I have." He turned back to the Captain. "Yesterday, my sister came over to my house and helped me clean out everything that was sad and depressing. Oh, I kept all the pictures and trinkets and things, but there was no reason to hang on to their clothes and personal items," Sam said. "It's time to move on."

"Another good reason to walk away now, Tidwell. Make a fresh start of everything."

I looked at Sam with pleading eyes. He couldn't leave now. We were just getting to know each other, and even though I hadn't told him about the counselor, I planned to. He had so much to teach me, and I was ready to learn. We made a great team. "You can't," I said. I didn't mean to say it aloud, but I did.

"And I don't plan to," Sam said. He turned back to the captain. "Did you sign it?"

"Yes. Even a crusted old Captain like me can see the fire's burning again. Glad to have you aboard, Detective Tidwell...the real you." He turned to me. "I don't know what you did to him,

Detective Rhodes, but I like it. I'm going to see that the two of you work together from here forward. I would make an analogy about how well you go together but it would be beneath my rank. Now, I'd like to see your career extended even further."

"Yes, sir. Thank you, sir," Sam said.

We stood.

"Rhodes, you stay here for a moment. Tidwell, you're dismissed."

Sam walked to the door, looked back at me. I was as clueless as he. Sam left for the Homicide room.

"I need to know the truth, Rhodes."

"Of course, sir."

"This whole mess with the church has done something to you, hasn't it?" I thought for a moment but didn't answer. *How do I answer that without getting pulled off the case?* "I don't know what it's triggered, but whatever it is, you've got Sergeant McNally worried. It takes a lot to do that, Rhodes."

"Yes, sir." I searched for the right words. "This case…everything about it…has really brought up some bad memories." I looked him dead in the eyes. "But I'm working on it, now, Captain. And I think I'm going to be okay."

He looked me over, studied my face. "We're keeping an eye on you, Rhodes. If you need help get it."

"I am, sir."

"Good. Now, tell me about the Ripley case. Where are we?"

"Still waiting on the fingerprint analysis to confirm Jamison Watson as the killer. His daughter thinks he did it. She says her father hated Mark Ripley's guts. And we know what Jamison Watson is capable of, sir."

"Dismissed, Rhodes. You'll have that analysis by the end of the day."

"Sir, Sergeant O'Malley already called, but it didn't help."

"Did he now? He picked up his phone and made a call to forensics. "Yes, this is Captain Harris. I want the results of the Ripley case on my desk in two hours."

Chapter Forty-six

11:42 am—Forensic Lab

We arrived at the Middle Tennessee Regional Forensic Lab and made our way to the autopsy room. "Dr. Coleman," I said, extending my hand to the pathologist.

"Detective Rhodes." She winked. "Sam."

"Will you stop that," he said. "You're going to make Abbey think we're an item."

"We're not? That hurts my feelings."

"I'm old enough to be your father," Sam said.

"You are not."

"Well…"

"I just love making him all jittery," Dr. Coleman said. "He blushes so easily. Relax, Sam, she knows we're old friends."

"You called us here?" I asked.

"Yes. Suit up and come back to the last autopsy room. And I have boots if you don't want to ruin your good shoes."

"Is that really necessary?" I asked.

"Well, we are thawing the ice and water is getting on the floor." She pointed out some spare rubber boots and we helped ourselves.

As we followed her through the swinging double doors, I gasped. "That's an image I won't forget easily." It reminded me of Han Solo's cryo-frozen features, but this wasn't special effects. It was real. Katy Watson's anguish was on display for all to see. "Was she really alive when he put her in there?"

"Unfortunately for her. Yes." Dr. Coleman pointed to a dark object near Katy's feet. "I have the preliminary findings. I also discovered this in the freezer."

"What is it?" Sam asked. Stepping closer, he leaned in, and said, "It's a book."

"Not just any book," I said. "It's a Bible."

"Who keeps a Bible in their deep freeze?" she asked.

"My dad used to tell me stories like that all the time," I said.

"Your dad?" she asked.

"He was a missionary. People in suppressed regions hide their Bibles in really strange places. Otherwise, they'd be easy to find."

Sam was still staring at the book. "Do you think Jamison shoved her in the freezer and tossed that Bible in there for spite?"

"It wouldn't surprise me. He hated that church for some reason." The water dripped continuously from the frozen block of ice, revealing more of Katy Watson's body.

"She could have used the freezer to hide it. Everything I know about Jamison Watson cries hidden lives. And Skylar said her mom had to sneak out to go to the church. It's just like him to make her pay by hiding her in the same freezer."

"It's odd, though," Sam said, using a tool to chip away at the ice. "I don't see anything else in the freezer…not a single item of food. That wasn't an easy place to put one either."

We all examined the melting block of ice. "He's right," I said. "It's almost like he got it just for her."

"You called us in. What was the cause of death?"

"Marrying an evil man," I said. "That's what I would write."

"First of all, we were able to match Katy Watson's image with her previous driver's license photo in the system," Dr. Coleman said. "It's definitely her. Death by asphyxiation."

"I thought she drowned," I said.

"As you can see, her head was above the water level."

"Then she froze. Right?" Sam asked.

"She ran out of oxygen long before she froze."

"If she suffocated, why is her head held up like that?" It creeped me out.

"From her position, the head was resting in the corner. Her legs contorted like they are, I imagine he broke them to fit her inside."

"The sledgehammer," I whispered.

"There wasn't much room for her to go anywhere." Dr. Coleman used a metal rod to point out the various body parts as she spoke. "She was in excruciating pain and in utter panic until she suffocated."

"This man gets darker and darker by the day," Sam said. "I hope he rots in hell."

"I hope we can pin the Ripley murder on him too."

"It won't matter," Sam said.

"It will to me."

"He'll die in jail," Sam said, "whether it's one life sentence or two."

"I hope they execute him," I said. "And I plan to visit him each month until they do."

"Don't give him another moment of your time," Sam said. "Jamison Watson would consider it a victory if you came to see him."

"If you two are finished, I have work to do," Dr. Coleman said. "Do you always banter like that?"

"Like what?" Sam asked.

Chapter Forty-seven

We headed back over to homicide and found a note on my desk reading, "As promised. Captain Harris." I opened the envelope. "It's the results from the fingerprints." I scanned the report. "Partially degraded from exposure to…" I looked further. "Jamison Watson is not a match." I tossed the report to the desk. "You've got to be kidding me. How are his prints not on the leg?"

Sam picked it up and read further. "One set matches Mark Ripley. The fingerprints in blood don't match either of them."

I was deflated once again. "This case is killing me!"

Spence popped his head over the top of the cubicle and said, "Poor choice of words, Abbey." I grunted and walked out. I suppose he thought that was funny.

Sam followed me out and said, "We have the murderer's prints and no one to match them to." I waved him off and continued down the hall. He ran after me. He finally caught up to me on my way to the vending machine. "You know what this means?" he asked.

"Yes. We're screwed." I put my money in the machine and hit E5.

"No." He put his hand on my shoulder. "We've just crossed another suspect off our list, which is getting smaller every hour."

I grabbed my cheese crackers and smiled. "We've been looking at this all wrong. We thought after Jamison was ruled out as the father the two cases were separate."

"I'm not following," Sam said.

"The Ripley murder and the rape. Any chance those mystery prints are in the system now?" I asked.

"Not without a clear owner to tag them to," Sam explained.

I grabbed the sheet. "What if Jonathan did both?"

Sam looked through the report. "You said our killer was left-handed. I saw him write something, and he used his right hand."

"Can we get a search warrant for his apartment?" I asked. "He is a fugitive."

"I like where you're going with this," Sam said. "Something in his house will have his prints."

I smiled. "So, my original theory is at least partially correct. He was struck by a left-handed swing." I demonstrated. "Right over left is a right-handed grip. Left over right is a left-handed grip. Whoever struck him was left-handed...or could be a switch hitter."

"The club was thrown from the Watson side of the creek. Why would Jonathan Williams go to the trouble of crossing the creek first?"

"He didn't," I said. "If Skylar was in love with Jonathan, she could have disposed of the evidence for him." I was smiling, and my eyes lit up. Everything was playing out in my mind, sorting and stacking into place like blocks.

"But that would make her an accessory," Sam said.

"Yes, an accessory that would never turn on him," I said. "What if Mark Ripley was at the church to meet Alvaro, but he caught Jonathan and Skylar together."

"Why would Jonathan risk being caught at church?"

I smiled again. The wheels were picking up speed in my head. "Because the church is closed on Mondays. Mark Ripley made everyone take a mandatory day off after Sunday."

"Go on," he said.

"I think Mark caught them, and Jonathan grabbed the bench leg because it was handy," I said. "He hit him once. When he saw Mark crawl to his feet, he panicked and hit him again."

"Okay, I'm with you. Keep going," Sam said, encouraging me to stay on the roll.

"Jonathan didn't know what to do until he heard the churning of the water in the baptistery. Then he tossed Mark in the water, thinking he was dead. When he discovered the pastor was still clinging to life, he…"

"Jumped in the water and choked him. And for good measure…"

"He stood on his chest until he was sure Mark was finally dead."

We stared at each other. This made total sense. "Okay," Sam said, "I'm going on the defensive. I'm going to punch as many holes in your theory as I can and see if it can withstand the scrutiny."

"Bring it on." I was confident. I was ready. The theory was sound.

"He had a key, so he could get in the church, but there weren't any other cars."

"He rode his bike," I said immediately. "He's been doing so for three weeks while they're waiting on a part for his car." I folded my arms across my chest and dared Sam to try again.

"If Skylar disposed of the evidence, why aren't her prints on the leg?"

"She either used gloves or she had her sleeves pulled over her hands. I've seen her several times chewing on the end of her sleeves."

"Okay, but Alvaro said he came in and saw the blood," Sam said.

"He must have surprised them…come in before they could clean up. Maybe that's why the cleanup seemed so sloppy. They were afraid someone else would come in while they were cleaning." I was getting excited, and I have to admit a little proud of myself. Every question had a sufficient answer.

"Well, let's stop wasting our time and get a search warrant for his apartment," Sam said. He smiled. "I'm really proud, Abbey. If you're right, the Captain's really going to love you." We turned to walk back to the homicide room.

My phone rang. I looked at the caller ID. "I need to take this."

Chapter Forty-eight

2:17 pm—St. Thomas Midtown

I could hear voices. I knocked on Skylar's door. "Come in."

I looked around. Skylar was alone. "Hey, Skylar. I thought I heard talking."

"Yeah. I talk to myself when I get nervous."

I gave her a gentle pat on the good arm and sat in the only chair available. "What did you need?"

"Thanks for coming." She pursed her lips, contorted them to one side, and then bit her bottom lip. "Did you talk to Jonathan? He hasn't called, and he's not answering his phone." Skylar grabbed her cup and took a sip of juice.

I noticed her trembling hands. "You're safe here."

Skylar put her hands behind her back to steady them. "My dad always made fun of me when my hands shook. He called me a baby."

"You don't have to worry about him anymore. He's in jail. You're safe. I promise."

Skylar pulled them back out in the open. "That's what Jonathan always said."

I decided to play it cool, see what I could find out. "So, how long have the two of you been an item?"

Skylar smiled. "I'm so glad to finally get this out in the open. I hated all the sneaking around." She looked off into the distance. I could tell she was counting the time in her head. "Just over a year.

We were just kissing and touching each other then. It's been two months since we started…," she said. "We started on my birthday."

"And you just turned fifteen September thirtieth, right?" I asked.

"Yep. I was crying to him about my mom being gone on my birthday again. My dad didn't even care it was my birthday. So, I went crying to Jonathan. He took me in his arms and said he'd make me feel special." Skylar was giddy. She finally had someone to tell.

"Where did you meet?" I asked. "Surely not at your house."

"Oh, no. My dad would have killed us both. Jonathan would text me, and we'd meet at the church." Skylar took another sip of her juice. It slurped as she ran out of juice and searched for the last drop with her straw. I grabbed it by the top and set it aside. I could tell Skylar was still on pain meds.

"So, you met in the church?" I asked, now picturing the two of them somewhere in the church.

"Yes. In the youth room." She had a wry smile. "We made love on the couches, on the pool table,…"

"I get it," I said, not wanting to hear another detail. "When did all of this happen?" I asked. "How did you arrange to meet when no one else was there?"

"I'm so glad you understand." Skylar sighed a pleasant sigh. "We met at first on nights when no one had meetings scheduled, but we almost got caught. Someone scheduled a meeting, and he didn't know about it." There was excitement in her voice. "Then we met on Mondays."

"On Mondays?" I asked, beginning to piece everything together. "Weren't you in school?"

She giggled. "Jonathan would call the school, pretending to be my dad, and say I was sick. Then he would call out of work and meet me there." Skylar looked over to me. "See how much he loves me?"

"It certainly sounds like he's obsessed with you," I said.

That made Skylar smile even bigger. She put a hand on her belly. "I was going to give him a baby."

"When's the last time you met?" Skylar started to answer but stopped herself. She turned and looked out the window. Her face hardened. "Did something happen?" Skylar remained silent, but she really didn't have to speak. It was written all over her face. "Skylar, were you there when Pastor Mark came in that morning?" She bit her lip and continued to stare out the window of her hospital room.

I decided to steer Skylar down a different path. "I need to tell you something. It's going to shock you, but I think you deserve to know." Skylar didn't turn. She didn't say anything. "It's about your mother."

Skylar turned and raised her right eyebrow. I could see she was sizing me up…trying to determine where I was going. "You found her?"

"Yes." I intentionally left it vague to gauge Skylar's knowledge.

Skylar stared at me, waiting for details. After a minute or two of silence between us, she asked, "Did you…tell her where I was?" There was neither excitement nor fear. She lay there with a blank expression on her face. Maybe she wondered if she could trust me. I could tell Skylar's wheels were spinning, which made me think the girl didn't know. "Maybe with dad in prison, we can live together again." It was almost a question.

"Skylar," I said softly. "Your mother wasn't alive."

It took a few minutes for it to register. Then Skylar became combative, in full denial. "You just don't want me to see her. Did he put you up to that? Why don't you want me to be happy?" Now, she seemed angry, as if everything were my fault. "You want Jonathan for yourself…don't you?"

"No. Skylar, your mother's dead. She has been for over a year."

"You're lying! Get out of my face, liar!"

The nurse came in and ushered me out. On my way, I turned and watched as the nurse did her best to calm Skylar before she had a full breakdown. She kept screaming that everyone was out to get her, to take her happiness. Then, as I was waiting for the elevator, I heard Skylar scream for Jonathan to come get her. The nurse must have pushed the button for pain medicine because Skylar's voice faded away.

When I got to my car, I wrote everything I could remember as closely as I could to Skylar's exact words. At the end of my notes, I wrote, "Check with her school and his fulltime employer for the same Mondays off. See if they were both out the 23rd. Also, destroy Jonathan's alibi."

Chapter Forty-nine

7:51 pm—Harmony Apartments

I stepped off the elevator and smiled. Some-one had tied a card and a helium heart balloon to my door handle. I opened the door and took them inside. *Please let it be.* It was. Aaron had designed and printed his own, "Please forgive me" card, complete with a long apology for treating me like an object to be won. At the bottom was a hand-written note, saying, "Please give me another chance—Aaron."

His timing was perfect. I ran down the hall and rang Aaron's doorbell. He answered, and I hugged him immediately.

"I'm so sorry, Aaron."

"No," he said. "I'm to blame."

"Could I come in and explain?" I asked.

He stood aside and said, "No judgments on the cleanliness. I've been in surgery all day."

It wasn't bad…just not as spotless as mine. "No judgment here." I crossed my heart with an X.

We sat at opposite ends of his couch. "This isn't easy for me to talk about, but you deserve the truth."

"Okay." He took a deep breath.

"I freaked out the other night…" I stopped. This was harder than I thought. Telling Hannah was easy. Telling an adult…one I may have feelings for was torture. "You treated me so kindly and made me feel so special…"

"You deserve…"

I put my hand up for him to stop. "Please, let me get it all out at once, or I won't be able to get through this." He nodded for me to continue. "You were great. But in the elevator…" He started to speak but stopped when I pleaded with my eyes. "When you grabbed me and kissed me…" I stopped and shook the numb feeling from my fingers. I could feel my heart pounding in my chest. I could sense my breathing speeding up. Just say it. "I was raped when I was fourteen." I blurted it out. I got up and headed for the door. "I'm sorry, Aaron. I'm just not ready."

"Please, don't go." I stood there with one hand on the door. "I'll give you as much space and as much time as you need," he said. "Just don't shut me out…please. I've never met anyone like you." A strange sensation filled me. The panic began to subside. "You take the lead," he said. "I want to get to know you…whenever you're ready to share with me." I didn't move. I didn't run. "I'm here when you're ready. I won't push. I promise. I didn't know."

I turned to face him. I wiped the tears from my face. "Thank you. I'd like to try." I opened the door to leave. "I am finally getting help to deal with it."

"I'll be as patient as I need to be. Take your time."

I closed the door and went home. I changed clothes, put my ear buds in, and listened to country music. All the while, I stared at the heart balloon.

Chapter Fifty

T he moment Sam walked into the office, I pounced, updating him on the entire conversation with Skylar. "I need your help getting past red tape with the school system and getting a copy of Skylar's attendance record. I'm supposed to call Jonathan's boss back at eight-fifteen to get his absences."

"You think they're going to match?" Sam asked.

"If her story has any truth to it, like Siamese twins." I kicked myself mentally. "I should have stuck with my gut and kept at his story from the start."

"We took him off the list because his alibi checked out." Sam tried to console me, but I kept repeating how stupid I was to give up on him.

"I should have known when he first threw us onto Alvaro's trail. That video was just too convenient. He had it ready. It wasn't an afterthought." I was livid. "Think about it, Sam. He was up there taking advantage of that little girl and got caught. That's why he killed Mark Ripley! And he had the audacity to look us in the face and act as if he loved the guy."

"Okay, Abbey. Calm down. We still have some holes to fill." Sam pulled out the timeline we made. "How'd he get in without being seen?"

"The bike. Remember the helmet?"

"Go on."

"We've already assumed Jonathan beat him and drowned him,

238

while Skylar tossed the club for him in the creek." I put my face in my hands. Sam let me vent. He'd felt this way a few times along the way, like the answer was right in front of you, and you missed every clue. And he'd also dealt with the frustration of facing the personification of evil. I couldn't bring myself to mention the death of the baby. My past slapped me in the face again. *Why God? Why would you let this happen?*

"Let's gather facts and close this case like a coffin on Jonathan Williams. No hearsay. No assumptions. No loose ends." Sam called down for the Admin to get someone from Davidson County School System on the phone who could get him Skylar Watson's school absences. He wanted an official printout from the school of all the days she's missed so far.

At 8:15, I called Jonathan's boss. He had neither seen nor heard from Jonathan since the afternoon he left the hospital. His boss agreed to email a list of all of Jonathan's absences for the past year.

I looked up, and Sam was at his phone, "This is a murder investigation! No, her father can't approve the request. He's in jail." After a long period of silence, the person said she could read the dates to him.

He held the printed absences from Jonathan's employer in his free hand and listened. "Thank you." He hung up and wiped the sweat from his face. "Abbey, They're identical, just as you thought."

Still circumstantial.

Chapter Fifty-one

After an hour-and-a-half meeting with the weekday homicide team and Sergeant McNally, Sam and I headed off to our cubicle. I was not only feeling more like a part of the team, but they were also beginning to look to me for input. Whether it was dumb luck or a keen sense of being in the right place at the right time, I was making my presence known. I'd managed to catch the attention of the Captain and the Chief.

"You know it's sad," I said.

"What is?" Sam asked, looking at the files on his desk.

"Mark Ripley accomplished so much. The church turned around and began to grow. Despite all that, he's killed while trying to make things better."

"I'm surprised his family is still here," Sam said.

"Me too, but I'm glad they are." I made a mental list of all the people we suspected during this case, everyone who had a reason to get rid of him. But each person we investigated had a better reason for Mark to stay...to live. Alvaro Garcia was suspected of killing the pastor out of anger, only to come for a meeting to make amends. The two old leaders tenaciously loved the church, even if they disagreed with the pastor's vision and methods. Quentin Green and Brandon Cook both had reasons to despise the man, but they too respected him. The only one with genuine hate and opportunity was cleared by the fingerprints. I really believed it would be Jamison Watson in the end.

As if Skylar didn't have enough problems with her overbearing, abusive father. Then to have the minister you've come to for help,

the one from whom you expect solace and comfort, take advantage of your innocence and vulnerability. All of this at a small Baptist church in East Nashville. None of this helped my feelings about church…or God, for that matter. But I had to admit, interspersed in it all there were so many who seemed to genuinely care. I was more confused than ever.

Was Susan right that God was not to blame for men's choices? Or was it like my father always taught me; that God was in control of everything, the good and the bad, and we were merely puppets in His grand scheme? And if he truly believed that, why did he blame me for being raped? I liked Susan's version of God better. I liked the thought of a God who let you make your own choices, but who never abandoned you…who walked through the fire, holding your hand the whole way. If that was really the picture of God, something good had to come of all this. Didn't it?

"How are we coming on that search warrant?" Sam asked. "Okay, thanks." He turned to me. "It's signed and ready to go."

"Let's go check out Jonathan's place," I said, "and get his fingerprints."

Chapter Fifty-two

10:37—Jonathan Williams' apartment

Sam knocked on the door. We could hear movement within the apartment, so he drew his Glock. I followed, pulling my Sig from its holster. "Detectives Tidwell and Rhodes, Homicide," Sam shouted. "Answer the door, or I'll kick it in." He could hear someone running to the front door. The locks turned and the door swung open. We pointed our guns at the strange face.

"Don't shoot!" he cried. "Please."

"Took your sweet time," Detective Tidwell said. He held up his badge and the warrant. "We have a warrant to search the premises."

"Why? I didn't do anything," he said.

"Maybe not," I said, "but your roommate has."

"Which one?" he asked.

"Really?" Detective Tidwell pushed past the young man in boxers. "Step aside."

He and I began searching while the man protested. "I have rights, you know. You can't just barge in here and turn the place upside down."

I looked at the mess around me. "Looks like somebody did that for us."

"Ha, ha. Very funny. We had a party last night and haven't had time to pick things up yet."

"Which room belongs to Jonathan Williams?" Sam asked, securing the Mylar gloves on his hands.

The man pointed to his left. "All the way back on the right."

I put my gloves on before tipping a kitchen chair, allowing the party debris to fall to the ground. "Sit here while we look around. Don't touch anything, or I'll book you for obstruction and tampering with evidence."

"You can't do that," he said. He looked to Detective Tidwell, "Can she?"

"That piece of paper in your hand says she can. Sit down and shut up."

We made our way back to Jonathan's room. The first thing we noticed were empty dresser drawers hanging out. "Looks like someone's been here packing," I said.

"Good. His fingerprints will be fresh." Sam grabbed a tall glass of milk. He smelled it. "Still fresh."

"We just missed him then," I said. I stood beside his desk and smiled. "Hey, Sam, check this out." He walked to the desk, and I showed him a framed baseball card with both the front and back displayed. "Louisville Cardinals," I said. "Look at the top of the back."

Sam read it aloud. "Jonathan 'JJ' Williams, first baseman. Throws right…bats left. Bag it."

I was becoming more secure in my theory. "Could he be more guilty?" I asked. We grabbed several items from his room. We could tell by the dust on the desk that a laptop had been sitting there recently. "I think we need to have a little chat with his roomy."

"Didn't both of his roommates say Jonathan was sick that Monday?" Sam asked. I nodded.

"Good cop, bad cop?" I asked.

"Only if I can be the bad one this time."

We walked back into the kitchen and noticed it had been cleaned since we walked in. "All right, hands behind your back." Sam pulled out his cuffs and secured both hands behind the man's back. He began spouting off his Miranda rights. "You have the right to remain silent…"

"Whoa, whoa, whoa! I didn't do anything wrong," he said.

"Well, let's start with falsifying your testimony, lying to the officer who established Jonathan's alibi. Then we'll add aiding and abetting a fugitive, allowing him to return and get clothing and his computer."

"Okay, okay, I lied. I'm sorry. He wasn't sick that Monday. He wasn't even here. Said he had a hot date and needed us to cover for him."

"That hot date," I said, "is fifteen years old."

"What? I didn't know that."

I gritted my teeth. Sam asked, "Where is he now?"

"I don't know."

Sam continued the Miranda rights. "Anything you say can and will be…"

"Okay, okay, I'll tell, but take these off first," he said, turning to show the handcuffs.

"No deal," Sam said. "Talk and I'll think about it." The man didn't say anything. "…used against you in a court of law."

"He's hiding out at the church…staying in the youth room."

"Turn your phone off." Sam unlocked the cuffs. "If I find out you tipped him off…if he's not there, we're coming back for you."

Once we got to the car, I couldn't help but smile. "You're pretty good as the bad cop." I paused. "Did you see what I did there? Good as the bad."

He shook his head. "That's the worst one yet." We left for the church and called for backup.

Chapter Fifty-three

12:15 pm—Living Water Church

Sam and I pulled up next to the three police cars. I explained the plan and the location of the youth room. We split up in pairs, taking each of the entrances to the church. We chose the side door nearest the parking lot. I used the key from the evidence box to unlock the side door of Living Water Church. Fitting…it would be Mark's key that allowed us to surprise his killer. I handed the key to the officer who unlocked the other two doors. At exactly twelve-thirty, we all entered the church.

Sam quietly scanned the main hallway. We waited for the team from the sanctuary to enter the hall and keep an eye on each exit. The church was eerily quiet. From room to room, area to area, we cleared the bottom level of the church. Back in the hallway where they could view the two other exits, T signaled to me.

Sam nodded to the far team, and they gave him a thumbs up. Each group began its ascent of the stairs, planning to converge on the youth room upstairs. I moved silently, my SIG firmly gripped in my right hand.

I held that team in position as Sam and I cleared the closets and classrooms on our side of the youth room. I eased each door open and glanced inside the room. I slipped through the doorway and closed it gently. I was hyper-vigilant, my SIG pointed wherever my eyes darted. I cleared the nursery, the toddler room, all the children's rooms and the HVAC closets across the hall.

Sam covered me as I made my way systematically to the

youth room, leaving it last. As I opened one of the two doors to the youth suite, I glanced over the room. Someone was lying on the couch by the far wall, but the pool table partially blocked my line of sight. I signaled for the other team to join us. Each team entered, closing their respective doors slowly, keeping their eyes locked on the couch.

I moved in and yanked the blanket from his body. He didn't move a muscle.

"There's something in his hand," Sam said.

I pulled it free and unfolded it. "It's addressed to me," I said. I handed it to Sam and checked Jonathan's vitals. "You read it. Wait! He's still alive." I rolled him over. An empty bottle fell to the floor. "Trazadone. Call for an ambulance."

T moved me aside and began monitoring his vitals. "Trazadone won't kill him. I got a heartbeat. It's faint."

Once he saw Jonathan was in good hands, Sam scanned the contents of the note and read, "Detective Rhodes, You just couldn't leave it alone!" He stopped. "I can't do this."

"Go on, Sam."

He turned to me. "Please, Abbey. We don't need to hear it." He eyed the other officers in the room. "Not here."

"Go on, Sam. We all need to hear it."

Sam reluctantly continued.

I gift-wrapped Alvaro for you…handed him over on a silver platter, but no…no…you just had to keep digging! And if that wasn't enough, you had to meddle with Skylar. She threw herself at me, and I just couldn't help myself. I don't know what she's said about me, but she's not innocent. She's a dark soul. I only kept up the relationship because she made me.

I'm not going to jail, and I'm not going through another witch trial. Yes, I killed Pastor Mark, but you probably figured that out by now. I swear, it was an accident. He wasn't supposed to be here. No one was.

Chapter Fifty-four

"**I** thought I'd feel better once this case was over," I said with melancholy in my heart. "I just feel sick to my stomach."

"Try not to let it get to you, girl. He did this to himself."

"Easier said than done." I keyed in the last comment and hit, Send. I sighed. "Well, that's that."

"I don't know about you," Sam said, "but I'm going to get a cold one after this case."

"I just can't help but feel sorry for Skylar," I said. "She's lost everything: her parents, her 'boyfriend,' her baby, and her home. Do you know what they're going to do with her?"

"No. DCS will find her a good home."

I thought of Danny and Hannah. They thought they were going to a good home too, only to be terrorized by the foster parents. "Susan keeps spouting off Romans eight twenty-eight to me over and over."

"There you go with those Bible references again," Sam said.

"This one I *have* memorized. I've heard it enough in the last twenty-four hours." I put on a fake smile, held my hands together as if in prayer, and said, "And we know that in all things God works for the good of those who love him, who have been called according to His purpose."

"Oooh. Now I know why you don't like church people."

"I like Susan. I just wish she'd keep those things to herself."
Hey God, how is this working out for good?

247

"The thing that gets me," Sam began, "is why a fourteen-year-old? A man with his looks and charm could get any woman he desired."

"I guess in the long run, he desired Skylar. He always gave off the vibe of a little boy, now that I think of it."

Spence leaned over the wall between our cubicles and said, "That was the lab. The fingerprints are a perfect match."

"The fingerprints?" I asked.

"Yes. Jonathan Williams's prints are on the murder weapon," Spence said, clarifying the comment.

"He was the proverbial wolf in sheep's clothing." I turned to Sam and said, "I take it you understand that metaphor."

"I don't have to know the Bible to get that one, Abbey."

"So that's it?" I asked.

"It is for us." He put a piece of paper on my desk and said, "Sign here, and I'll have it all sent over to the D.A."

"Then I'm calling it a day," I said. "I think I'm going to go see Skylar before she's discharged. See if she wants a ride."

"I'm going home," Sam said. "I advise you to do the same."

"I will," I said. "After I see Skylar." My phone rang. "It's Susan Ripley." I listened. "Really? You'd be willing to do that? What do the kids think about it?" I smiled. "I'll ask her. I'm heading that way now."

"What did she say?" Sam asked.

"She wants to open her home to Skylar."

"Bad idea!"

"I think it's sweet."

"The girl is responsible for her husband's death," Sam said. "That's just wrong."

"Skylar is the victim here. Everyone took advantage of the poor girl," I said. "I think it's great that Susan is willing to take care of her."

"Mark my words. It's a mistake. You'll see," Sam said.

I snatched up my coat and left. "I understand Skylar, and I know Susan."

Chapter Fifty-five

I reached for the door handle but stopped. I listened. Skylar was talking to someone. I looked through the glass in the door and scanned the room. Skylar was looking into the mirror over the sink talking to herself. She was nervous again.

I knocked. "Come in." I entered and Skylar smiled. "Oh, hi, Detective Rhodes. I'm glad it's you."

"I wasn't sure you'd want to see me after my last visit."

Skylar smiled again. "I don't know what you're talking about."

"Good. In that case, just call me Abbey." Skylar smiled. "I thought I heard talking," I said, wishing to see what Skylar would say.

Skylar blushed. "You heard that?" I nodded, and Skylar lowered her head. "I was just trying to encourage myself," Skylar said. She did something with her wrist.

"All packed up?" I asked, trying to change the subject.

"Yes. Can I go by the house and get more clothes?" Skylar asked.

"I'm afraid not," I said. "It's still a crime scene unfortunately. But I hear they got you a few outfits that should fit."

"I'm nervous," Skylar said, popping a rubber band on her wrist. "I've never been in a foster home before. What's it like?"

"They seem like a nice family," I said. "I told them I wanted to bring you over myself. It's the least I can do."

"Thanks." Skylar sat on the side of the bed. "The nurse said I could go as soon as an adult was here to sign my release papers."

249

"I already took care of it," I said. "We can leave any time." I reached my hand out to Skylar's free hand. "Did they say how long you'd be in the cast?"

"They called it a compound break, but at least I didn't need screws. So, a month, I guess." Skylar took my hand and smiled. "You're nothing like I imagined at first. I think we could be friends."

"Oh, really?" I said, taking Skylar's bag and putting the strap over my shoulder. "What did you think at first?"

"Well, when I saw you at the funeral, I thought you were trying to steal Jonathan from me. I thought we might be in competition with each other. Now, I know we are just alike."

"Oh." I stopped and stared at Skylar. I was speechless. What was she saying?

"I was sad at first." Did someone tell her? "It's okay. I know better now." She leaned in and hugged me. "I can trust you both."

"So, just for clarification," I began. "When I was talking to Jonathan, you thought I was flirting with him?" I asked.

"Yeah, but I understand. He's so hot, and so are you. It's understandable." She let out a heavy sigh. "Well, you know what I mean." I didn't say anything. Skylar let go of me and fixed a strand of hair behind her right ear. "Everyone was always looking at him and wanting him, but he was mine. We loved each other."

"Are you speaking in the past tense on purpose?" I asked.

"Of course," Skylar said. "I'm done with him."

I took a deep breath and let it out slowly. "Why is that?" I asked.

"Let's get going. I'm sure they're waiting on us."

Skylar was unusually chatty all the way to the foster home. I just listened. I was seeing a side of Skylar I never dreamed existed. After being freed from the tyranny of her father, Skylar was free, and her mouth was free as well.

Skylar finally took a breath, and I jumped in. "I need to tell you something before we get there." Skylar turned. "If you're interested, Susan Ripley would like to open her home to you."

"Really?" A strange smile played across her face. "Why would she do that?"

"Susan has a good heart, and she knows you're all alone right now." I turned the corner. "She said, if you were interested, she would like to talk to DCS about becoming your foster home… maybe even adopting you."

Skylar looked out the side window of the car. She became strangely quiet and popped the rubber band on her wrist again.

"This is the street." I noticed the police car and DCS vehicle in front of the house as I turned. "Everyone is here."

Skylar and I walked up the concrete steps of the two-story house. "So, I might not have to stay here?" Skylar asked. "That's if I'm willing to live with the Ripleys?"

Willing? She didn't mean it that way. She's just nervous. "We hope not. We'll talk to the director first thing Monday." I patted Skylar's shoulder and rang the doorbell. The DCS officer opened the door and made the introductions. They chatted for a while, and I slipped out. I felt so guilty for leaving Skylar there, but I couldn't take it anymore. I was just another adult clogging up the tiny foyer.

I pulled away and looked back in my rear-view mirror. Something was off, but I couldn't place it. A horn blared. I slammed on my brakes. I inadvertently drove through the stop sign. Thankfully, the other driver saw me in time. He honked a couple more times and gave me the finger. I mouthed my apology and waited for my heart to descend from my throat.

I glanced down at the passenger floorboard. *What's that?* I pulled through the intersection and parked on the side of the street. I unbuckled and leaned as far as I could, grabbing the little notebook. I opened it. Katy Watson's diary? Must have fallen out of the evidence bag. I put it in the seat and drove home.

Chapter Fifty-six

Saturday, December 2, 8:45 am—Harmony Apartments

I finished my bagel and juice and put my plate and glass in the sink. I glanced over at the small table set next to the door and spied the burgundy notebook. I stared at it. What harm could it do?

I flopped onto the couch and opened the journal. The first twenty or so pages were Katy's thoughts on her family. They seemed happy. Then, about page twenty-eight, everything changed. The diary suddenly shifted in its tone and nature. Katy turned her focus to her ten-year-old daughter Skylar.

Jamison and I are getting worried. Skylar is talking to herself in the mirror. I know that doesn't seem unusual, but she answers too. It's like there's another person in the reflection.

Ten pages further and a year later, Katy wrote, *She's getting meaner and meaner. Not just to other kids, but to us. Last night I caught her with a knife. I could swear she was going to stab Jamison, but when I confronted her, she smiled and said she just wanted to scare us.*

Five pages later, Katy wrote, *Skylar's counselor says she sees nothing wrong with our daughter. She's polite and compliant. But when we get home, Skylar screams at us. She hit her face with a book and threatened to tell her teacher we hit her. We don't know what to do.*

I put my hand over my mouth and gasped. *Today, Skylar found her birth certificate and learned Jamison was not her birth father. When she confronted me, I had to tell Skylar that her birth father was in jail. She threatened to tell Jamison if I didn't buy her a PlayStation 5 and some fantasy games. I didn't know what else to do. I think I'll have to buy it. I don't know what Jamison would do if he found out.*

Another page. *I bought the gaming system, but now she wants a laptop. I can't do this. I need to think. It's such a pretty day, I think I'll go outside and work in my garden. That always calms my nerves.*

The next page was stained…with Katy's tears.

Skylar told Jamison. She's turned him against me. I don't know if our neighbor saw, but he came out to the garden and hit me! I'm afraid to sleep now. Jamison doesn't trust either of us now. Skylar has something wrong with her. She used Jamison's card and had a freezer delivered to our house. I don't know what she's up to, but I'm terrified. Last night, when I opened my eyes after my prayer, she was standing over me with a wicked smile. I told Jamison, but he's shut me out now. I'm alone. God help us.

It was Katy's last entry.

I shuddered with a chill. Instinctively, I looked over my shoulder. I got my phone and called Sam. I summarized the entries in Katy's journal. "I'll warn the foster parents. You call your Lieutenant friend. Skylar needs mental help and someone to watch her."

I called Lieutenant Daniels and gave him the heads up. My phone flashed an incoming call. "Hey, that's Sam. I'll call you back." I hung up and switched calls. "Hey, Sam, what's…"

"Meet me at the foster house. It's on fire!"

"Accident or…"

"They don't know, but it started in Skylar's room. She's missing."

"On my way." I called Lt. Daniels and asked him to help us find Skylar before she did anyone harm.

Chapter Fifty-seven

Saturday, December 2, 10:27 am—Skylar's Foster Home

We questioned the foster parents, asking what happened since I dropped Skylar off yesterday. They said she was pleasant and seemed to make friends with the other children quickly. "She thanked us for dinner and the pajamas and went straight to her room to go to sleep. The only thing strange was when Penny, a little girl that lives here too, screamed in the middle of the night."

The father jumped in on the conversation, saying, "By the time I got to her room, Skylar was sitting on her bed, with her arm around Penny. I think she was trying to comfort her." He looked at his wife. "When I asked Penny if she was okay, she looked at Skylar and said yes."

I swallowed at the lump in my throat and snuck a glance at Sam. "When did the fire break out?"

"This morning, right after breakfast," the father said. "The smoke alarms went off, and we rushed to get the smaller children out of the house. It wasn't until later that we realized Skylar was missing and the fire began in her room."

I could tell they suspected Skylar of arson. I immediately thought of Susan and the kids. What if she'd been at their house? "Oh no!"

"What is it?" Sam asked.

"We need to get to Susan Ripley's house…right now!"

Sam drove as fast as he could to the Ripley's house, but Skylar was nowhere to be found. "Where else would she go?" Sam asked.

"Home!"

I rushed Sam back to the car and took off for Skylar's home. When we pulled up, we could see the living room window was broken. I got on the phone and asked for backup. We both drew our weapons and signaled our respective positions for approaching the house. "Shouldn't we wait for backup?" I asked.

"I can see her sitting in her father's chair," Sam said. "She's just watching television." Sam moved toward the door.

"Sam!" I tried to get him to stop, but he continued. I reluctantly followed him, keeping my gun trained on Skylar.

Sam checked the door. It was unlocked. He turned the knob and gently pushed the door open. "Skylar?"

"Do I know you?" she asked calmly. Then she saw me standing behind him. "Oh, hi, Abbey. I was hoping you'd come."

"You were expecting me?" I asked.

"Of course! I told you we had a connection."

Sam moved to the side. He kept his Glock pointed at Skylar. He nodded. I holstered my Sig. "Skylar, did you know the foster home was on fire?"

"Yes."

"Did you start the fire?" I asked.

"Of course, I did. I didn't like it there." She said it so matter-of-factly that I had to fight another chill.

"How did you get here?" I asked. "It's a long way from the other house."

"I took an Uber." She turned to Detective Tidwell. "Do you want a coke?" He shook his head. "My dad has alcohol if you'd rather." He shook his head again. He didn't know what to do. Skylar was acting so casually about everything.

"Skylar?" She turned her attention back to me. "How did you get money for an Uber?"

"I took it from Amanda's purse. I didn't want to stay there anymore." She popped the rubber band on her wrist. Once she realized we were watching her do it, she stuffed her hands in the sides of the seat. "It's not the only thing I took," she said.

255

"Abbey, stay where you are. I don't trust her," Sam said, looking down the sight of his Glock.

"That's rude!" Skylar's mood switched. Her eyes looked vacant.

"Skylar?" I started. "Skylar, look at me…just me." Skylar stared blankly at me. "Come on, Skylar, talk to me."

She blinked and smiled. "Oh, hi Abbey. I'm so glad you came. I think we can be best friends."

"Why is that?"

"Because you understand me…we're just alike."

"How's that?" I asked, inching forward.

"People look at us differently. We can't help being pretty…or smarter than everyone else."

"How do they look at you, Skylar?" I inched another step closer.

"Like an object." She turned to Sam. "Do you think I'm pretty?"

"What?"

"Your loss." She touched her breast and smiled. "Most men look at me like I'm something to possess, but that's how I get them to do what I want." I cocked my head to the side, hoping Skylar would continue. She obliged. "Pastor Mark refused to look at me that way. But I knew what he wanted…and when I saw what the Mexican man did, oh…I knew what I had to do."

"What did you do, Skylar?" I asked in the sweetest voice I could muster.

"It was easy to get Jonathan to the church. All he wanted was sex. But how could I get Pastor Mark to find us?" Skylar smiled. Her eyes lit up. "I emailed him to come meet the man, and I called the man to meet him."

"Uh-huh."

"Never attempt to win by force what can be won by deception." "*The Prince.*"

"What was that, Sam?"

"She's quoting *The Prince* by Niccolò Machiavelli."

Skylar directed her glance to Sam. "Very nice." She immediately turned back to me. "Once I knew Pastor Mark was there, I made lots of noise while me and Jonathan were…" She raised her left eyebrow and smiled at me. "But nothing happened. I moved to the pool table and knocked off a ball." She made quotation marks when she said, "accidentally." I could tell Skylar was so proud of herself. "Of course, Pastor Mark found us, and then…" Skylar stopped. She turned to Sam. "Let's try another one. 'There is no other way to guard yourself against flattery than by…'"

"'…making men understand that telling you the truth will not offend you.'"

"Oooh, you're good." Skylar put her finger to her lips. "'Everyone sees what you appear to be.'"

"'Few experience what you really are.'"

"Yeah, yeah. I'm tired of this game." Skylar looked back to me. "Anyway, I looked to Jonathan with embarrassment, but then… then I turned to Pastor Mark. That way they both thought I was speaking to them when I cried, 'Do something!'" Skylar clapped her hands and then put them back down the sides of the chair. "It worked out better than I imagined. Jonathan threw a pool ball and almost hit Pastor Mark. Pastor Mark ran downstairs to call the police. I didn't have to do anything." She touched herself again and then looked at my body. "I've seen the way others look at you too."

"Everyone sees what you appear to be, but few experience what you really are?" I asked.

Skylar nodded. "That's why it's okay if we use them to get what we want." Skylar looked into my eyes. "That's why I wanted you here. You understand me…accept me for who I really am. Because we're alike."

I paused. All this time, I never suspected Skylar, because I identified with her as the victim, the poor girl everyone else took advantage of. I just assumed the men were abusing her. It never dawned on me that Skylar could possibly be controlling them and abusing herself. That's why it took so long to realize Skylar wasn't what she appeared to be. She wasn't just the victim after all. She was the puppet master. She used them, killed them, and moved on without a thought. Nothing bothered her because she felt entitled…she had no empathy whatsoever, and that made her dangerous. She was a true female sociopath.

Watching Skylar's lack of empathy, I finally realized I didn't have to feel this way…I didn't have to be the victim anymore. "No, Skylar. We're not the same. I don't use other people."

"Of course, you do," Skylar said. "You just can't see it." Her eyes darkened again. She clenched her teeth. Her temples pulsed.

"Don't listen to her, Abbey."

"I'm okay, Sam. It all makes sense now."

Skylar tilted her head to the side. I could see the switch flip again. "You're really pretty."

I had to move her to another topic. "Thanks. Skylar, did you happen to see the yellow tape over the door?" Skylar continued to smile. "Skylar, we can't be here. It's a crime scene. Let's get in the car and go for a drive."

"I don't want to!" She turned back to the darker self.

"Okay, okay. What do you want to do, Skylar?"

Skylar sighed. "I don't want to be alone! I want you to stay here…to live with me."

"I can't, Skylar."

"Then let's go to Susan's house. I can live there."

I shook my head. "I can't let that happen either, Skylar. They're my friends, and I won't let you hurt them too."

"Then I want to see Jonathan."

I swallowed hard and took a deep breath. I could sense her escalation. "Skylar, you can't see Jonathan. Sweetheart, he's in the hospital, and then he's going to jail."

"I know." Her eyes lost their luster. Skylar had a wicked smile. She stood and put her right hand behind her back. She looked at me. "I don't think I like you after all."

"Abbey, be careful. She has something behind her back."

Skylar revealed the gun behind her back and pointed it at Sam. "You need to shut up. Men always mess things up. It's all your fault!"

Bang!

Bang!

With the second shot, Skylar's body lurched backward and fell back into the chair. Her gun fell to the floor.

Sam stood with his gun outstretched. His hands shook so hard, his gun fell from his hands. I looked at the wall where he stood and noticed the hole. She shot at him but missed. I looked back at Skylar. I shot her in the shoulder. Her eyes were wide open in shock. Convinced she was no longer a threat, I holstered my Sig.

"I couldn't do it," he said. "I couldn't shoot a young girl."

I collected Skylar's gun before calling for an ambulance. Then, I put an arm around Sam and said, "It's okay, Sam. I understand." Sam stared at Skylar. His body trembled. "Relax, Sam. I took care of everything. It's over."

Chapter Fifty-eight

Jonathan Williams opened his eyes and sighed. "You couldn't let me be, could you?"

"Well, it's my duty to serve and protect people, even from themselves," I said.

He looked to my left and noticed Sam sitting in a chair. "I don't suppose you're here to protect me from Skylar?"

Sam shook his head.

"You two don't know what she's like," he said.

"Oh, I think we have a pretty good idea," I said. "She's finally getting the help she needed—the help a minister should have gotten for her earlier."

"She's not so innocent," Jonathan said. "She threw herself at me and made me—"

"Nice try," I said. "You're still guilty."

"Of what?" he asked. "It's not my fault."

Sam stood and leaned over the side of the bed, putting his face inches from Jonathan's. "You've got a lot of nerve, JJ."

Jonathan's eyes widened.

"That's right. I figured it out before you're cop-out of a letter."

"That was a witch-hunt!"

"Well, this isn't. This is justice. You raped a fifteen-year-old girl repeatedly. You used…"

"She threw herself at me. What was I supposed to do?"

"What Mark Ripley did; kindly say no and try to get her help,"

I said. Couldn't believe I was using a preacher as a good example, but he was.

Jonathan tried to protest. Sam put his hand over Jonathan's mouth. "You have the right to remain silent, and I suggest you do just that." Jonathan tried to pull away, but Sam held him firm. I hadn't seen him this angry and firm before. "I'll give you the full version in a minute. You used your position of power and arranged for carnal meetings with a member of your youth group." Sam paused to look over at me. "You give Christian people a bad name, and you'll pay for it." He released his grip on Jonathan's mouth.

"I didn't…" Jonathan looked at me and then Sam. "I think I need a lawyer."

"We agree," I said. "Sam, read him his rights so I can get him out of my sight."

Sam began reading Jonathan's rights.

I walked down the hall on my way to the elevator, I spotted Aaron near the nurses' station. I raised my hand to wave. Just as I started to call his name, Aaron put his arm around a young nurse and kissed her passionately. She leaned into his embrace.

My heart broke. I ran to the elevator before anyone saw me and made my way to the car.

Chapter Fifty-nine

I looked through the peephole in my door and watched as Aaron walked from the elevator to his apartment. I waited for him to see the drawing of a broken heart I left on his door with a letter describing what I saw. It also let Aaron know, in no uncertain language, that we were done with whatever it was we were. As I predicted, he made a beeline to my apartment.

He knocked. I waited for him to knock again, pretending to be in the back of my apartment. He knocked again. I looked through the peephole. "What do you want, Aaron? I thought I made it clear to leave me alone."

"Abbey, I don't know what you think you saw."

I forced a laugh, even though my heart wasn't into it. "There's no 'think what you saw,' Aaron. I'm a trained detective."

He paused. I thought for a moment he was going to go back to his apartment. I was wrong. "Abbey, it didn't mean anything."

He waited for my response. What did he think I would say to that? Do men really think that is supposed to help the situation, saying, "I cheated on you, but it was meaningless"? How stupid.

"She was having a bad day and just needed someone to cheer her up."

Now, that was worse. I started to flashback to all of our encounters, to all of Aaron's comments. Everything was superficial. Come to think of it, I'd never seen him run, not once. And the only music I'd ever heard coming from his apartment was jazz or classical. No country. I'd been a fool, and he played me like a concert violinist. I was just another trophy in his case. "Go, home, Aaron."

"Fine." His voice was tight. Even through the closed door, I could sense his features tightening. "You'll regret this." Now, the volume of his voice rose. He was angry. I guess he'd never been told no before.

"I doubt it," I said in the calmest voice I could muster at the moment.

"Who'd want you anyway?" he shouted. "You're damaged goods." He stormed off and slammed the door, breaking what was left of my heart.

He was right. Who'd ever want me? I *was* damaged goods. I was rotten to the core. The pain, the self-loathing, the foul stench of my sin didn't stay behind in Guatemala. It followed me to Germany and here to Nashville. No matter where I ran, it would follow me because I was the problem. Nobody would ever love me, not in the way I truly needed to be loved. Not even God loved me anymore, that's if He ever loved me.

I forced myself to my feet and walked straight to the bathroom. I opened the drawer and grabbed my anxiety pills, but instead of putting one in my hand, I poured the whole bottle. I stared down at the pinkish, grey capsules. I filled a cup of water and lifted the pills to my mouth.

My phone rang, and I jumped, spilling the pills over the vanity and into the sink. Half of them slipped into the drain. It rang again. I glanced at the phone, half expecting it to be Aaron. *Susan? Something must be wrong with Hannah.* I answered, "Susan, is something wrong?"

"You tell me."

"What?" That didn't make sense. "I don't understand."

"God told me to call you."

I scoffed. *Yeah, God told you.* "What's His voice sound like?" I asked, not caring to hide my skepticism and anger.

"Abbey, please tell me. What's wrong? Are you about to do something you'll regret?"

I looked up in the mirror. How could she possibly know?

"What are you talking about?"

"Abbey, I've always been sensitive to the Holy Spirit, and I feel you need a friend right now. Can we just talk?"

I didn't say anything. Part of me wanted to hang up, grab the pills that didn't go down the drain, and swallow my life away. But the bulk of me wanted to spill my guts, to reach out and ask for help.

"Please Abbey? I need a friend right now, and I couldn't handle losing you too."

Me too? Was she comparing me to Mark? Did she say, 'a friend'? "Okay. I'll talk." I took a deep breath and let it out slowly. "When I was fourteen, a church group came to our mission in Guatemala." I could feel my pulse beginning to race. My muscles tensed.

"Abbey? Are you still there," Susan asked.

"Yes." My voice was barely a whisper. "You may not like me after I tell you."

"There isn't anything you could say to make us love you less."

"Okay." I steadied myself and chose my words carefully. "My dad was…is a missionary. We had a mission compound in Guatemala where we could host churches that would come to help us with our ministry." *So far so good.* "When I was fourteen, a group from Oklahoma came and spent a week helping us with a soccer outreach in a neighboring village." I took another deep breath and let it out. *You can do this.* Susan listened patiently, encouraging me to continue after long pauses.

"One of their youth ministers asked if I could help him in a small chapel. He said he couldn't read a message in Spanish. Not thinking anything of it, I followed him into the empty little church." I wanted desperately to stop talking. I wanted to hang up and finish what I'd started with the pills, but a strange calm came over me. "He gave me a little silver flask he had stowed in his back pocket and told me to take a drink. He said it might burn at first, but it would relax me. He said I looked nervous."

"Oh, Abbey."

"Well, one drink led to another. He was right. My body felt

strange, almost limp. Then he suddenly threw me down on one of the pews, tore my shirt and raped me." I stopped. I expected Susan to hang up or criticize me like my father had. She simply urged me on. I suppose she knew there was more to the story.

"I cried for what seemed like hours. My body hurt. My very soul hurt. I must have stayed there on that pew quite a while, because when I came to my senses and ran to my father, he'd already heard a different story." I felt a flutter in my chest. My stomach soured, but I'd come this far and she hadn't hung up yet.

"Abbey, go on. Get it all out."

"I didn't realize my shirt was hanging open and my bra was torn in half. I was exposed, and all my father could do was blame me for flaunting my body. He blamed me for trying to seduce the minister. He wouldn't even listen to my side."

"I'm so sorry," Susan said softly.

Was she crying? Well, I couldn't stop. I told her the story of my father kicking me out of the house. "I tried to run to my mother, but she turned her back on me, literally. Even my older sister Miriam shook her head and kept silent." I thought for a moment. I couldn't tell Susan everything. Not yet. "So, I had to survive on my own at fourteen." I let it end with that.

Realizing I wasn't adding anything else, Susan tried her best to comfort me, to soothe ten years of pain and heartache. "No wonder you're not comfortable in a church," she said. "Oh, Honey, what you must think about God."

Could she really understand? Was she different? "He left me alone."

There was a long pause before Susan said anything. "I know it may seem like He left you, but He didn't. You made it. You survived. And look at you now."

I did look at me now. Broken. A façade of control and success, but inside rotten to the core. "You don't know what I did to survive," I said in a whisper.

"No, but God does, and He loves you."

Before I could catch myself, I blurted, "If that's His love, I don't want it."

We talked for nearly an hour. Susan listened, and in her kind-hearted way, she continued to encourage me and tried to reassure me that I was loved. I certainly didn't feel lovable, especially after what Aaron had done. I told Susan about him, about seeing him with the nurse and his comments at my door. "He's right, you know. I am damaged goods."

"Aren't we all?" Susan asked. "But God loves us anyway."

I still wasn't ready to hear about His "perfect love." But I listened as Susan shared her story. She shared her pain and anger about Mark's death. Then, she returned to the Bible and shared verses that comforted her. The one that struck me as odd was, "'For I know the plans I have for you,' declares the LORD, 'plans to prosper you and not to harm you, plans to give you hope and a future. Then you will call on me and come and pray to me, and I will listen to you. You will seek me and find me when you seek me with all your heart. I will be found by you,' declares the LORD."

"That was on Mark's office wall," I said. "He didn't prosper, and he certainly was hurt." It was bold and rude, but the comment was true.

"I gave him that," Susan said. Her voice was shaky. "God didn't hurt Mark. Jonathan did."

"I was out of line." Even though I believed what I'd said, I knew Susan didn't deserve that. "Forgive me."

"To be honest, Abbey, I'd already thought the same thing." She sniffled. "But Mark reminded me that sin has consequences. Unfortunately, God loves us enough to give us free will." She took a breath. "Jonathan's choice took Mark's life. Although he stole my future with Mark, I know he is in a much better place."

I struggled with that. God promises hope and a future, but if someone takes that future away, God still wins because we get Heaven? "I don't know, Susan."

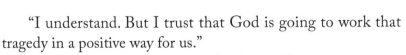

"I understand. But I trust that God is going to work that tragedy in a positive way for us."

"Can you tell Hannah that and believe it?"

"Yes, because God brought you into our lives."

It hit me like a bus. How could I be any kind of consolation for Mark? "How could a damaged person be God's way of replacing a Godly man who was doing so much good?"

"Because you've helped Hannah heal in a way Mark and I couldn't. God loves you, Abbey, and He's not through with you yet."

I listened quietly. I wasn't in a place to accept everything Susan said, but I did know she cared. It was nice to have a friend. It had been a long time since I had someone who knew my garbage but cared anyway. I told her about Miriam's letter, about the baby, and about the abortion.

Susan prayed for me. I just listened and hoped God would answer her.

Chapter Sixty

Saturday, December 16, 11:20 am

Nearly two weeks later, I drove to the intersection of Gallatin Road and Eastland Avenue and breathed a sigh. I looked in the front passenger seat, two pizzas and a box of cinnamon bread. Susan Ripley's voice came through the car speakers. "I'm glad you decided to come. They're going to love you."

"Are you sure about this, Susan?" I asked. "I don't want to invade your family time."

"Are you kidding? I arranged this whole thing just so they can meet you," she said. Susan had been instrumental in getting me through the heartbreak of seeing who Aaron really was. I had a big pity-party and started to tear myself apart. Susan helped me through my pain. I wasn't quite ready for the prayers, but the listening, nonjudgmental ear was perfect.

"You're sweet," I said. "I can't believe how kind you've been to me."

"I think God put us in each other's lives for a reason."

I rubbed the chill bumps from my arms. "Another sermon?" I asked, trying to slough it off.

"Not that you would listen." She laughed. "How far away are you?"

"Five minutes." A horn blared, and I realized I was still at the stop sign. Cars were gathering behind me. I hit the accelerator and headed for her house.

Susan, Hannah, and Danny walked arm in arm to the car.

They opened the passenger door and grabbed the food. A couple in their middle fifties followed them to the car but walked to my side. "Hello, Detective Rhodes," Susan's father said. "We've heard so much about you."

"Wonderful."

"My dear, it was all good." He opened my car door and extended his hand. "Hope you don't mind, but I'm a hugger."

"Thanks for the warning." He hugged me tightly. His wife joined in. I smiled. Hugs weren't so bad after all.

"You saved our daughter's life. Thank you."

"No sir," I said. "She saved mine." She did. If Susan hadn't called when she did that night, I might have done something really stupid.

"It's like I always tell him," her mother said. "Romans eight twenty-eight."

I shook my head. "Not you, too?"

Hannah pushed herself between her grandparents and said, "I know it's cold, but could we play a little soccer?"

"Why not?" I gave her a side hug. "If you think this is cold, you should see Germany in the wintertime." We walked hand in hand to the house.

Susan smiled. "Mark would have loved you."

"I'm pretty sure I would have liked him too."

Points to Ponder

1. I've always said, "If you don't own the truth, the truth will own you." How is this evident in the novel?
2. Would you agree that Susan Ripley and Abbey Rhodes serve as channels of God's blessings to each other? Explain.
3. The Bible tells us God "was reconciling the world to himself in Christ…and has committed to us the message of reconciliation" (2 Corinthians 5:18–19). Discuss ways Mark Ripley committed his life to that truth.
4. Throughout the novel, we hear the reference, "Romans 8:28," which says, "We know that in all things God works for the good of those who love Him, who have been called according to His purpose." Do you believe that statement? How is it shown in any character's life?
5. How are Abbey's and Sam's story arcs similar?
6. Do you believe the promise Pastor Mark had hanging on his office wall: *"For I know the plans I have for you" declares the LORD, "plans to prosper you and not to harm you, plans to give you hope and a future." (Jeremiah 29:11)*? Why? Why not?
7. How did Abbey and Skylar differ?
8. With which character do you most identify? Why?
9. God put Susan in Abbey's life to counteract the negative impressions she had of Christians and God. Who has God put in your life to show His love?
10. In what way is God using you to help others see His love?

About the Author

Mitchell S. Karnes is a husband, father of seven, and grandfather of nine. Mitchell uses his experience and insights as a minister, counselor, and educator to write and speak on challenging issues and concerns with an ever-growing audience. He has published five novels, three short stories, a one-act play, and numerous Bible study lessons.

Through two separate battles against Non-Hodgkin's Lymphoma, God has given Mitchell a new perspective on life that challenges him to create stories not only to entertain audiences but call them to action. Mitchell's mission is to reach and reconcile those who have been disillusioned with God and His church and inspire the church to live out the love of Christ Jesus in a broken and hurting world.

Connect with Mitchell online at:

mitchellskarnesauthor.com

Also available from

WordCrafts Press

Dreamreader
by Cathy Fiorello

Idiot Farm
by Susie Maddox

The Filbert Ridge Miracle
by Tamelia Aday

The Mirror Lies
by Sandy Brownlee

Wolfheart
by Hallie Lee

www.WordCrafts.net